DARK
TURNS

DARK
TURNS

Cate Holahan

NEW YORK

Published in the United States by Crooked Lane Books, an imprint of The Quick Brown Fox & Company LLC.

Crooked Lane Books and its logo are trademarks of The Quick Brown Fox & Company LLC.

The Library of Congress Cataloging-in-Publication Data is available upon request.

ISBN (hardcover): 978-1-62953-193-9
e-ISBN: 978-1-62953-206-6

Cover design by Tricia McGoey
Book design by Jennifer Canzone

Printed in the United States.

www.crookedlanebooks.com

Crooked Lane Books
2 Park Avenue, 10th Floor
New York, NY 10016

First Edition: November 2015

10 9 8 7 6 5 4 3 2 1

For Elleanor and Olivia

1

Fondu [*fawn-DEW*]

Sinking down. A term used to describe a lowering of
the body made by bending the knee of the supporting leg.

The lawn glittered in the late summer sun, a shining
emerald slate as uniform as Astroturf. The grass smelled
real, though. Realer than real. Each inhale filled Nia's
nose with a spritz of green, more pungent than mall per-
fume and far sweeter than the oniony weeds back home.
The lawn smelled like money.

Nia stared at the clock on the tower at the far end of
the courtyard. Its short hand pointed to the Roman numeral
seven. The long hand crept toward the X. He would arrive
soon.

A cramp pulled at the meat between her metatarsals.
She steadied herself on her good leg and folded in half to
grab the throbbing joint that had spurred the contraction.
Her thumbs slid beneath the clinging hem of her spandex

capris. She pressed into her heel until it grew hot. The pain's drumming slowed. Only a doctor could silence it. Until she got some real medical attention, she'd keep having bearable days and bad ones.

Today was a bad day. She blamed herself. The tendonitis always flared when she didn't stretch. She should have risen earlier to warm up. What if the director asked to see pointe work? Could he rescind the offer if he didn't like her performance?

An iron bench sat just to the right of the registration building. She limped to it. The metal was cool on her palms. She placed her feet in a line, heels together, toes pointed in opposite directions. She dipped into a demi-plié. Tightness trickled from her thighs. The familiarity of the move did as much good as the stretch. It was her morning coffee, a ritual that woke her body and prepared her for the day.

A breeze stirred the lawn, reassuring visitors that a school of Wallace Academy's caliber would not accept anything as gauche as faux grass. Nia didn't see any visitors to impress. School offices were closed. The academic buildings that flanked the courtyard remained locked. Classes didn't start until tomorrow.

The students had arrived, though. Parents had flooded onto campus over the weekend, pouring from imported SUVs with trunks and suitcases, filling the dorms with preppy debris while their teenagers flowed between buildings in search of lost friends. She'd watched the move-in from the bay window of her new studio, which overlooked the entire courtyard. Such views were rare, reserved for so-called resident advisors, a college title intended to trick high school students into befriending the teaching assistant down the hall. But she was more of a spy than a schoolmate. The dean had been clear: she existed to keep boys out and report anyone attempting to sneak in the opposite sex during the week. She was also expected to sniff around for pot and cigarettes.

She didn't know why the dean worried. So far, the dorm had gone quiet by eleven o'clock each night. These students weren't nymphos or druggies. How could they be and sneak past the admissions officer? Wallace prided itself on an acceptance rate that rivaled the Ivy League schools to which it funneled graduates.

Birds trilled somewhere above her. Nia listened to their music and dropped into a grand plié, thighs and calves apart, spine straight. Her back released more tension. The throbbing in her heel subsided. She arched her arms over her head. Endorphins chased the nerves from her system. She felt loose. Confident. She rose to her toes.

Pain crackled through her leg like a string of firecrackers. Her ankle wobbled with each small explosion. Her heel crashed to the floor. A smile parted her lips. Dancers didn't show discomfort. Fifteen years of training let her beam through cramps like the Virgin Mary in labor.

She shook her right leg. Stretching alone couldn't soothe this pain. She needed the shot. Once the health insurance took effect, she would head straight to the orthopedist.

Footsteps tapped somewhere to her right. A svelte man, clad in black, glided toward her. The bright morning highlighted a shock of silver in his black hair. The streak was Ted Battle's trademark and the single sign of his forty years.

An embarrassed flush heated Nia's neck. The dance director had seen her stumble. Nerves pinched the edges of her false smile. She forced a brighter grin.

"Mr. Battle."

He nodded in her direction but didn't pick up pace. She pushed back her shoulders, pulled in her abs, and angled her right foot in front of her left, a relaxed fourth position stance. She hoped her posture obscured her injury.

Battle stood before her and extended his palm, as if asking her to dance. He flashed a smile that illuminated his angular face.

She shook. "It's a pleasure to meet you, Mr. Battle."

"Glad we could talk before classes start."

His voice sounded higher than she'd imagined. In lieu of a commanding baritone, a musical tenor emerged from the director's lips. She detected a touch of femininity in the way his pitch climbed at the end of the sentence. Was he gay? About half of the male dancers she knew were homosexual, and Battle wasn't married.

She admonished herself for the train of thought. Her boss's sexual preference didn't matter. As for herself, it had been so long that she might as well have been asexual.

Images from the last time fluttered into her mind. The seam between Dimitri's pectorals. His shapely mouth, curled in a smile. She blinked to blur the memories. This job came with health care. She couldn't let heartache distract her.

"I regret that I didn't interview you personally," Battle said. "Our last assistant left so abruptly that we had to fill the position while I was still in Queensland."

Nia regained her focus. "I understand she had a baby."

Battle rolled his eyes. The expression seemed to compare maternity leave to claiming the dog had eaten your homework.

"Yes. Took us all by surprise. She wasn't married. Hid the pregnancy with baggy clothes and didn't let anyone know she wouldn't return until June."

He patted the breast of his dark T-shirt, an odd gesture, as if he were feeling for glasses in a nonexistent pocket. His eyes rolled over Nia's body, lingering for a fraction of a second on her flat stomach. The stare tempted her to blurt, *Don't worry about me. I haven't had sex in a year since my ex and I broke up.* She swallowed the overshare, aware it was motivated by awed attraction to her handsome, successful, and likely gay boss.

"I have of course seen your résumé," Battle said. "I was impressed with your training. The School of American Ballet since age ten. They don't accept many girls, and, I expect, they take even fewer on financial aid."

The comment stung. She knew he'd meant it as a compliment—evidence that she possessed a certain skill beyond her peers—but it reminded her of things she would rather forget: used toe shoes, slapping pickles on foot-long sandwiches to afford costumes, the dubious charity from anorexic rivals—*"Here's a leotard. I'm too small for it now."*

Battle's light-brown eyes flitted from her waist to her face. "They feed many girls to major companies . . ."

He trailed off, providing an opportunity for Nia to explain herself. Why was a woman her age not with an esteemed company or attending college? If not pregnant, then what, exactly, was her flaw?

Where should she start? She didn't have a classical dancer's ectomorph frame. Her hands could not circumvent her thighs. She possessed a stereotypical "black ass" that refused to disappear, even at a scant hundred and ten pounds. Puberty had somehow swelled her chest into a full C cup that appeared silicone enhanced on her petite frame, a problem she hid with sports bras and unnecessary layers. But her biggest problem of late was literally her Achilles' heel. Years of pointe work had strained the tendon. Over-the-counter anti-inflammatories no longer relieved the pain. She needed a cortisone shot, a flexible doctor, and rest.

"I performed with the Andrea Brooks troupe in Brooklyn for a couple years. They're more contemporary. I don't know if you would have heard of them."

The director smiled. He hadn't heard of them. A blush threatened to crawl from Nia's neck to her cheeks.

"And then this past year, I traveled with the Janet Ruban Dance Ensemble. I hope that, after this opportunity, I can audition for a larger company."

"Why not audition now?"

The director didn't need to add *while you're young and employable*. She couldn't confess to the injury. He might think it would compromise her teaching ability.

"My mother lives in Queens. My father's not around and I needed to stay close."

Battle's mouth tightened in apparent sympathy for her family's hardship. Nia thanked God that her nutmeg coloring masked any guilty blush.

She pumped earnestness into her voice. "I plan to audition next year."

Battle's thin smile relaxed. "Well, I hope you do. You're young. Now is the time. And it is difficult to get a job above assistant teacher, even in a public high school, without a few years of choreography experience and an MFA." He clasped his hands. "Okay. We're happy to have you this year. Let me take you on the tour."

He led the way down a red brick path. She followed a step behind, hiding the limp that would not disappear until she had soaked her leg. They passed a mix of gothic revival and neoclassical buildings, homages to the architecture associated with top universities. Battle pointed out those he found of interest—this is the library, that's the foreign language department, there's the English building—all the while dropping names of esteemed graduates.

He stopped before a gothic specimen capped by a massive dome. "This is the music hall. In addition to a recital auditorium, it houses practice spaces that are available to the students around the clock and an extensive music library."

The structure recalled the U.S. Capitol. It featured the same rows of white columns leading to an ice cream scoop hat. Instead of vanilla, the building's top shone pistachio.

"The verdigris really connects it to the landscape," he said.

Nia traced Battle's gaze to confirm he referenced the mottled green dome. She would have to Google *verdigris* later.

"Richard French became Richard French here."

Nia knew of the famous music professor. Dancers read his critiques to better understand the emotion of a piece. "I studied his writings on Idomeneo."

"Yes. I assign our students the same critique. Glad you know it, Antonia."

"My friends call me Nia."

"Oh, Nia. Well, in front of the students, you will, of course, be Ms. Washington. We don't want the kids becoming too comfortable, especially given your age."

The formal title surprised her. Ms. Washington was her mother. It hadn't occurred to her that the students would address her differently than anyone else.

Battle maintained eye contact. His lips pulled into a line. "You're just a few years older than our seniors, and in all honesty, you could easily pass for a student. We can't have them taking you for a peer. It might seem silly, but mistakes happen when distinctions become blurred."

"Of course," she blurted. "When I watched the parents moving the kids in, all I could think was that all the students were *so* young."

Battle rolled his eyes. "Well, they certainly don't think so." He pointed down a gradual hill. A silent expanse of crystal blue stretched beyond it. "The lake is over there and, as you know, the dance facility is just above it."

She followed Battle down the sloping path to the water. The lake was small, perhaps the size of four football fields. A dense forest surrounded two-thirds of it, obscuring the narrow road that defined the shoreline to her right. The path led to a clearing where the trees had been removed to make room for a boathouse and beach. Long racing shells with the school logo—a monogrammed W—lay stacked upside down in a wooden structure. A couple of rowboats floated atop the water, tethered to posts.

Sunlight painted the lake a pale gold. Nia stepped to the water's edge, careful to maintain her dancer's posture despite her sore ankle. She loved the water.

"Beautiful, isn't it?" Battle said. "The view always gets my creative juices flowing."

"Yes. It's so calming." Healing, almost.

"It started as a small canal. Wallace's founder, Gregory Andrew Wallace, had the idea to create the reservoir and the little beach you're standing on."

Battle continued the history lesson. Nia listened to the inflections in his voice, nodding at what sounded like the appropriate time. She didn't care who carved the lake. She watched the breeze stir the ripples into meringues. Water lapped at her feet.

A strange darkness blurred the surface just beyond her toes. Brown, seaweed-like strands crawled toward the sand. Did lakes have seaweed? She crouched to get a better look.

It was hair.

Her mouth opened in a silent scream. Instinct pushed her feet backward. She stumbled during the retreat. Her butt hit the beach. Sand scraped against her leggings.

Battle splashed into the shallows and pulled the figure onto the shore. Wet hair clung to the face like a tangled net. He peeled the mop back, exposing the mouth and nose, preparing for CPR.

Nia regained her composure. It was a girl, a teenager judging from the lithe figure and curved face. Her white skin had turned sallow and translucent. Blue veins puckered from her arms. A deep purple colored her lips. Battle positioned his head above the girl's mouth and pinched her nose. Before he exhaled, he released the face and sank back onto his calves. Nia followed his frozen stare to the girl's neck. A pattern of interlocking purple bruises cut above the body's clavicle like an ornate choker.

Nia's hand dove into her sweatshirt pocket for her cell phone. She dialed the police.

"Nine-one-one. What's your emergency?"

"Hi. I'm . . . I am at Wallace Academy. My boss just pulled a girl from the lake."

"Is she breathing?"

"No."

"Do you know CPR?"

"There are marks around her neck."

"Do you know CPR?"

"It won't help." Nia's voice trembled. "She's dead."

2

Coryphée [*kaw-ree-FAY*]

Leader. A leading member of corps de ballet.

A campus officer arrived first. The young man exited a white golf cart stamped with Wallace's elaborate monogram. He wore a black jacket with "POLICE" in blinding white lettering, but it was the only thing that conveyed authority. The whistle hanging around his neck dangled on a blue school lanyard. Instead of a gun holster, a clip-on cell phone case hung from the side of his black belt. Less a cop than a costumed college student.

The man approached the edge of the beach where Nia sat, waiting for the cavalry to arrive. She stood, careful not to put too much pressure on her still-throbbing foot, and pointed to where Battle's figure was still crouched beside the body.

"She's over there."

The cop scratched at nonexistent stubble. He peered over Nia's shoulder. "Do you know her?"

Battle rose from his haunches. "I've seen her on campus. She was one of the students that read in last year's poetry jam. Unfortunately, I don't remember her name."

"You found the body?"

Battle's cell rang. He put up a finger before digging into his pants pocket. "This must be the dean."

The cop stared at Battle, as though willing him to hang up. Nia doubted he had the authority to demand it. Police on private campuses were akin to security guards. They observed and reported, not enforced.

"I saw the girl's hair in the water and then my boss ran to pull her out."

The officer shuddered. He looked over his shoulder, up the hill.

"Aren't you going to check on her?"

"I'm just here to secure the scene. Make sure that you don't leave. The police will want—"

A siren interrupted. Blue-and-red lights flashed atop two gray cruisers with "State Police" emblazoned on the side. Another blue sedan, without the lettering, followed the police vehicles down the road leading to the boathouse. The cars each rolled to a stop beside the campus officer's golf cart. The big guns had arrived.

A pair of male officers exited the first car. Badges adorned their hats, sleeves, and even belt buckles. Guns pressed against blue button-downs. More cops stepped out of the other cars. Their uniforms didn't match. Two men sported cargo pants and hard plastic briefcases. Notepads, larger than the guns hitting their hips, protruded from side pockets. The other two men wore straight-legged pants and ties.

The campus cop moved to the side, a small kid giving the football team free reign of the lunchroom.

"Where is the body?" one of the men in cargo pants asked. Nia and the campus cop simultaneously pointed toward Battle.

Officers brushed past them to the water. A man in a suit brandished a badge and waved Battle over. Battle slipped the cell into his pocket. "Dean Stirk is on her way."

The officers didn't seem to care. They surrounded him, blocking Nia's view of her boss.

The other plainclothes officer stood in front of her. Gray hair sat atop a rugby player face, complete with the broad forehead and crooked nose. A large chest filled out the baggy material of his shirt. He spoke with a Massachusetts accent.

"Hi. Detective James Kelly. You placed the call?"

"Yes. My boss and I were walking—"

He put up his hand like a stop sign. "Let's start with a name."

"Oh. Sorry. Antonia Washington. I'm a new dance teacher here and a resident advisor. My boss, Ted Battle, was taking me on a tour of the campus. He stopped to show me the lake. I saw the hair floating in the water. He ran in to get the girl's body."

"And you immediately called nine-one-one?"

"Yes."

"You said she wasn't breathing."

"It seemed like she'd been in the water awhile. And there are these marks on her throat, about the size of thumbs—"

"Did anyone try CPR?"

"There wouldn't have been a point. I think she's been strangled—"

"Officer! Officer!" A middle-aged woman slipped down the embankment. She wore low heels, a pencil skirt, and a sunny tweed jacket, fit more for high tea than a murder scene. Nia recognized Dean Martha Stirk from the high school brochures. The woman reminded her of someone's proper English grandmother, the kind of older lady who wouldn't leave the house in sneakers and jeans—even in an emergency.

"I'm the dean here and I would like to know what's going on." Stirk strode toward Nia. One of the officers in a more elaborate uniform stepped in front of her.

"Ma'am, could you step back, please? We are assessing the situation."

"Ted," Stirk called over the officer's shoulder. "Is it one of our students?"

"Ma'am, again, could you step back?"

The policemen made a tighter circle around Battle.

"I am the dean." Stirk folded her arms across her chest. "I demand to know what is going on."

"There's a girl's body," the campus cop piped up. He pointed to Nia. "This girl says she was strangled."

Stirk's hand flew to her mouth, as though trying to keep something from escaping. She shook her head. "No. An accident? She must have fallen. Maybe it was dark and she was on the dock by herself. It gets slippery." Stirk turned her attention to Nia. "Who are you to speculate?"

The words, or rather their scolding delivery, snapped Nia to attention. "I'm the new dance teacher. The girl has marks—"

"We don't know yet how the girl died or if she is a student," Detective Kelly said. "And no one will start any rumors."

"I should hope not." The dean gestured toward the officers on the lake's bank. The motion implicated the group rather than indicated the crime scene. "We can't have anyone making this tragedy worse—"

"Ma'am, please follow me." The officer with the wide-brimmed hat brought Stirk and her accusing stare up the hill.

Nia watched them walk out of earshot, toward the dance building. The ballet studio overlooked the lake. How would she teach tomorrow?

"Did you have any contact with the body?"

The question returned her attention to the detective standing in front of her. A small spiral notebook lay in his left hand. A pen was pinched between his right thumb and forefinger.

"No. My boss pulled her from the water. I didn't touch her."

"So you could tell she was dead?"

Nia's eyes fell to her feet. The girl could have been alive, and she hadn't tried to help. She'd been too busy recoiling from the body. "Not until I saw the bruises. The hair frightened me. I fell backward."

Kelly scrawled notes onto his pad. "And did you know the deceased?"

"No. I just started a few days ago. I don't really know any of the students yet."

Kelly continued writing. He looked at her sideways, keeping his chin pointed toward the paper. "So you've never seen her before?"

"No. Never."

Nerves tightened her muscles, sharpening the pain in her heel. She shifted her weight onto her good foot. Detective Kelly seemed to note her uncomfortable body language. He scratched his cheek.

Nia read the gesture as skeptical. She mentally cursed her heel. The pain had made her seem shifty.

"When did you arrive on campus?"

"Saturday morning."

"Where were you before that?"

"My mom's apartment in Queens."

"After arriving on campus, you were here the whole time?"

"Yes. In the dorms, mostly."

"Did anyone see you?"

The barrage of questions felt like an interrogation. Did she need a lawyer? She dismissed the idea. Cops didn't offer condolences and coffee to people at crime scenes. The detective's lack of warmth didn't mean that he thought she had anything to do with the girl's death.

"A few kids stopped in to say hello."

"Names?"

"Um, I don't know full names. Natalie and Jennifer, I think. They're roommates. And another girl with reddish-brown hair. Sara, maybe? It definitely started with an S. Suzie. Sally. Something like that."

The corner of Kelly's mouth turned down. His expression seemed to admonish her.

"I would remember her face," she added.

Detective Kelly withdrew a business card from his wallet. He held it out to her. "Call us if you think of anything else. And, please, use discretion until the family is notified."

Nia slipped the card into her pocket. The detective then asked for a number where she could be reached, in case any more questions occurred to him.

"And, just to be clear, you're living in the dorms?"

His eyebrows slanted toward his nose as though he found something offensive about her living arrangements. She tried to stand up straight, but her injury forced her to adopt the leaned-back posture of a teenager.

"It's part of my job."

"Right." He scribbled something on his pad. "We will be in touch. You're free to go."

Nia glanced back toward Battle. The police still surrounded her boss. They wouldn't want her to wait for him.

She limped up the hill, wishing she could run—away from the crime scene, away from Stirk, maybe all the way back to New York.

3

Leçon [*luh-SAWN*]

Lesson. The daily class taken by dancers throughout their career to continue learning and maintain
technical proficiency.

The students flitted into the room, more starlings than
swans in the school's navy leotards and white tights.
They chittered to one another, oblivious to the new
assistant teacher waiting to greet them. Perhaps they thought
her a classmate who didn't have the uniform. Unlike the
students, Nia wore dance pants snipped at the most unat-
tractive part of the leg, just below the knee. A loose cardigan covered her tank. Battle had urged against the typical
leotard in order to avoid "distracting the young men in
the room."

Only two male students stretched in front of her.
Both sported navy spandex pants with fitted white tanks,
hemmed at the navel. Their dress emphasized large-limbed
bodies, pulled like taffy by teenage hormones. One boy

smacked his heel against his butt and grabbed it, stretching out his hamstrings. The move belonged on a soccer field, not in a studio.

The girls possessed better proportions. Nia examined the young women, determined not to think about what lay beyond the wall of windows behind her. The idea of the lake made her nauseous. She couldn't risk a glance outside.

She stacked each student's body against the ideal type, the way so many teachers had unfavorably compared her own frame. Dance companies required a certain "look." Ballerinas that didn't fit the willowy Balanchine aesthetic had a hard time getting into major companies, no matter how talented. She knew all too well how the wrong silhouette could sink a career.

The girl seated on the floor, clasping her toes, was the antithesis of the Balanchine body. She looked more rower than dancer, with broad shoulders and bulky arms that boasted strength but not grace. If the kid wanted to go pro, she would have to trade weight lifting for Pilates. A pear-shaped student at the barre needed to shave fat from her thighs to achieve the sought-after appearance. Additional leg lifts would do the trick.

One girl needed to lose significant weight—as much as twenty pounds. The young woman's leotard fought against her belly as she bent in an off-balance plié and stared out the picture windows. As she rose, she put her hand on her lower back, perhaps aware that her spine had curved to hide the weight of her stomach.

An Asian student lowered into a split. She possessed the preferred petite body but lacked sufficient muscle. Matchstick legs jutted from her leotard. How would she jump? Nia would encourage strength-building exercises and protein shakes. Two more girls joined the waif, falling into splits that seemed to stretch from wall to wall. Each topped five foot nine at least, too tall for most—if not all—companies.

Shame forced Nia to look away. She knew her criticism was unfair. There were some things you just couldn't change.

A blue glimmer outside the window sneaked into her vision. Stringy dark hair came back to her. She shuddered and rubbed her eyes, erasing the mirage with the pressure of her fingertips, forcing herself to focus on the tall girls.

So what if the girls would tower over any partner once on their toes? Skill could trump body type, occasionally. Nia's nonwaif appearance had pluses. When her Achilles wasn't inflamed, she could jump higher, spin longer, and leap farther than most dancers. She also looked pretty good when the leotard came off—not that anyone had noticed lately.

Only one young woman fit the Balanchine mold: delicate frame, sloping shoulders, small torso and head, long limbs, flat chest, and little body fat. The ideal type tipped onto her toes, rising four inches to about five foot eight, the perfect partner for the average male dancer. She placed a curved leg onto the barre. Her arms rose above her and bowed outward, as though she held a glass ball above her head. Her hands fell to her hair. She twirled her long mane into a dark cyclone, which she gathered at the nape of her slender neck. She slipped a black rubber band over the bun. The smoothness of her movements made the simple act seem choreographed.

A shiver shook Nia's shoulders. She could feel a presence behind her, intense and focused. She turned to see a latecomer standing in the doorframe. The young woman resembled a life-sized doll with a pixyish face and porcelain complexion. A blond bun coiled atop her head like a golden rope. The teen's eyes reinforced the doll impression with their saucer size and surreal, electric-blue color.

The girl was staring at something as though willing it to catch fire. Nia followed her eyeline to the prima-in-training. She welcomed the young woman into the room with a broad smile. "Come on in. We're just about to get started."

The stare transferred to Nia.

"I'm the new assistant teacher, Nia—um, Ms. Washington."

"Aubrey Byrne."

"Why don't you warm up with your classmates? The teacher will get things started in a moment."

Aubrey strode toward the barre. A faint scent of seawater trailed her, as though she'd mixed salt water with her soap. She lifted a gazelle leg to her chin and then placed it atop the wooden pole. She arched her back, dropping her head to waist level. Ribs jutted from her leotard. She reached behind her toward one of the boys in the class, hand bent like a beckoning lover. The young man stopped stretching to stare. Aubrey closed her eyes, as if too lost in her own movements to notice the attention from both the boy and her new teacher.

The teen's combination of flexibility and appearance impressed Nia. Aubrey's body nearly matched the ideal. She was a touch tall, a hair over five foot seven if Nia hazarded a guess. With luck, the teen had finished growing. Most girls leveled off at sixteen.

A bell sounded. The students lined up at the barre and stood in first position—all except one. The dark-haired ideal surveyed her classmates and then dropped her leg from the barre and copied their stance.

Ms. Vishnevaskya stepped into the studio from an adjoining office. A fist-sized golden bell dangled from her fingertips. She glided over the hardwood, settling in the center of the room. Her lithe body belied her sixty years, but her movements possessed a control that could only have come from decades of study. She walked like a whisper one moment and a shriek the next, all sharp turns and stabbing elbows.

"Welcome back, class." The teacher spoke in a Russian accent that tried for French. "I trust summer has treated you all well. Some of you have clearly kept up with your studies." She gazed at Aubrey. "Others . . ." Her coal eyes shifted to the overweight girl and rested there. "Others need to get back into shape. Quickly."

The instructor curved her arms in front of her as if cradling a beach ball. The students imitated her stance. "As you all know, this class is for preprofessionals, dancers who aspire to join companies after graduation or, at least, to dance as though they belong in one." Her attention fell on the dark-haired ideal. "I am happy to welcome a new student. Miss Lydia Carreño. Lydia trained at the Miami Ballet Conservatory. She is transferring here as a junior. She—"

"I'm looking forward to dancing with you all."

Ms. Vishnevaskya tilted her head, a gesture Nia couldn't quite decipher. Annoyance at the interruption? Acknowledgment of her new student? Aside from the reintroductions before class that morning, she had met the instructor only once before, at the interview. Nia had butchered the teacher's last name. She still wasn't sure she could pronounce it. In her head, she referred to her as Ms. V.

"MBC is run by graduates of the School of American Ballet," Ms. V continued. "I am pleased to say we have a new assistant teacher this year who hails from the School of American Ballet, Ms. Antonia Washington. Ms. Washington studied at SAB for nearly a decade. Since you were ten?"

Nia nodded, unwilling to voice agreement and risk the same head tilt.

"She is taking time off from performing to be close to family. I suggest you make as much use of her while you can. Her experience in today's dance world will be invaluable."

Nia refrained from her usual wide smile, bestowing a reserved one instead that she hoped fit a woman with an illness in her immediate family. Her real reasons for needing some time off were far less sympathetic: damaged foot, broken heart—both her own fault.

Ms. V clapped her hands. "Okay. Let's begin."

Nia had hoped the instructor would introduce all the students. Apparently, Ms. V felt no need. She'd have to learn the roster another time.

Nia stepped to the laptop on a small side table tucked behind the door. She turned on the music. It slipped through speakers embedded in the walls, surrounding the students with a lazy waltz.

"Adagio." Ms. V commanded. "And plié."

The students bent in painstaking precision, holding each pose in time with the protracted tempo. They extended and retracted their arms, slow motion swans struggling for flight. Mrs. V marked the beats by counting. She alternated between English and French: *One, two, three. Un, deux, trois.*

Nia inspected the line of young women like a drill sergeant. For the most part, their form looked good. The heavyset student was off-center, as if unaccustomed to the weight of her belly. Nia touched her back.

"Straighten up a tad," she said, smiling to soften the criticism. The girl flushed and adjusted her posture.

Demi-pliés turned into grand pliés, which morphed into arabesques. The students extended their legs behind them as Nia corrected angles. She refrained from telling the overweight girl that her leg fell too low. The teen's grimace showed that she recognized her problem.

By the song's end, Nia had critiqued every girl except Aubrey and Lydia. They looked practically perfect, though different. Lydia's motions displayed a softness that Aubrey's lacked. The blond ballerina attacked positions. Nia preferred Lydia's gentleness, but there was value in a more technical, intense style.

Ms. V clapped her hands for a music change. Nia switched to a faster waltz.

"Aujourd'hui nous étudions fouettés," Ms. V said. "Today, we learn fouetté turns. Ms. Washington, if you would demonstrate."

Stares heated Nia's face as she walked to the center of the room. These teens knew enough ballet to recognize proper technique, even if they couldn't pull it off. They would judge her. If her movements lacked precision or wanted for grace, the teens wouldn't trust her corrections.

Nia tipped onto her toes and held herself en pointe, testing her Achilles strength. Her feet bore her weight without a shudder. The confirmation relaxed her muscles. She performed a series of chaine turns to reach the center of the room, spinning off her nerves like water in a dryer cycle. She assumed the required fifth position, right foot in front of the left, facing opposite directions. She pliéd and then extended her leg in the air while rising onto the toes of her supporting foot. She whipped the airborne leg around her side to touch the knee of her standing leg. Her arms mimicked the motion. Open, snap close, spin.

Ms. V nodded approval. "See how she keeps her hip down? Everything arrives at once. Arms and legs retract together." The instructor gestured toward her with the expanse of her arm. "Class, watch again."

Fouettés were typically performed in groups of four. Nia rotated on her toes again and again. Confidence surged through her muscles. For a moment, she forgot the class and the teacher's ongoing commentary. Everything faded except for the music. She imagined herself the Black Swan, but her triumph was over her Achilles rather than a white rival.

The lake whirled by as she spun, a shimmering blue that faded into the studio's peach walls. A female voice whispered, "Twelve." The lake flashed by again, and an image of the girl's dead body assailed her. Nia forced herself to keep spinning. Sixteen. Thirty-two and she would perform the coda of the Black Swan's pas de deux.

Ms. V continued to point out proper form, allowing her assistant to twirl in front of the class while the students attempted the turn at the barre. Twenty. The lake swam in Nia's vision. She pictured a net of hair falling back to reveal a bloated face. Her stomach churned. Something tugged at her heel. She stopped midset and landed back in her starting position. Until she got her mind and feet back in shape, she was no Black Swan.

Nia touched her hairline, ensuring that the strands remained swept back in a tight bun. She scanned the students' faces. The Asian girl beckoned with her eyes for instruction. The tall girls nodded approval. Lydia beamed before spinning herself, approximating Nia's own form but with less surety. The girl's hip raised, betraying that she had not snapped her legs and arms together fast enough. The heavyset student stared ahead of her, lips pressed together as she tried to maintain balance on one foot. Ms. V instructed the pear-shaped girl.

Aubrey did not acknowledge Nia. The girl stepped from the barre and spun on her toes. Technically, she reproduced everything the assistant teacher had just done. But her movements missed beats, as if she were concentrating

24

so hard on imitating Nia's performance that she could no longer hear the music.

Nia gave the Asian student a correction on toe position. She watched the girl try to spin with her pointed foot pressed against her knee, tongue protruding from her lips, brow furrowed. Next time, she would caution about expression. She moved to Aubrey. She snapped the rhythm as she approached. "Beautiful. Just remember the time. And turn."

Aubrey stopped. Her bow mouth turned down. Nia didn't know whether the frown stemmed from the mistake or the criticism.

"Really beautiful movement, though," Nia said.

"But not perfect." Aubrey returned to fifth position and began the turns again. Her face betrayed no more emotion. Determination punctuated her movements, now in sync with the downbeat.

The students practiced the turns until nearly the end of class. Ms. V retreated to her office for the last ten minutes, leaving the cool-down under Nia's supervision. Nia helped the students relax their legs. She asked names as she pushed and pulled limbs. The Asian student was June. The tall girls were Tatiana and Talia. Nia knew she would forever associate them together: the T twins, though they weren't sisters. The heavyset girl was Marta, the broad-shouldered one Kimberly, and the other girl who had largely blended into the background was Suzanne. The boys were Alexei and Joseph, though she found herself thinking of them as the Russian boy and the one Aubrey liked.

With Ms. V gone, the atmosphere relaxed. The class split into conversations as students swapped pointe shoes for slippers, stuffing the former into cubbies beside Ms. V's office. Lydia introduced herself to Marta, Kim, and Suzanne.

Alexei joined the T twins and June by the windows in hushed gossip.

Joseph gravitated toward Aubrey at the barre. He announced that he had missed her over the summer. Aubrey didn't respond. Instead, she slid to the ground in a split before leaning forward until her chest touched the floor. She pulled her legs together in a push-up stance and flipped onto her back.

"Stretch me."

Joseph dropped to both knees and lowered his head, a boy begging mercy from a queen. He placed both hands on her foot. The pink ballet slipper disappeared in his palms. He pushed Aubrey's long leg to a ninety-degree angle.

"You can do better than that." Aubrey said.

Joseph's hands moved to her calf. Aubrey's leg ticked a few more degrees. Her lips parted.

"Harder."

His hands slid to her thigh. He pushed the leg to her chest, splitting the girl like a scissor.

Nia clapped her hands. "Okay. That's enough. Let's all sit up and massage our feet. Come on, everyone. Sit up."

Joseph's hand recoiled from Aubrey's thigh, as though burned. His eyes looked glazed.

"You don't want those tendons to tighten up," Nia continued, moving closer to the other groups of students. "That's how injuries happen."

June, Alexei, and the T twins sat in a circle. They obediently rubbed their arches and ankles without breaking conversation. When Nia neared, their voices dropped to whispers. But their words still pierced the air: *Dead. Drowned. Devastated.*

Nia sat a few feet from them, massaging her own ankle as she eavesdropped.

"My little sister, Darya, hung with her," Tati said. "Lauren's dad just shows up outside Dar's room last night, fucking furious. Ready to kill someone, you know? Totally freaked her out. He wanted to know if Lauren had problems with anyone."

"She seemed so sweet . . . I just can't believe it." June's tiny face fell into a cartoonish sad expression. Eyebrows slanted. Mouth turned down. She hugged her arms to her chest and rubbed her forearms.

"Did you guys know the girl that died?" The question slipped out before Nia had thought it through. The police had cautioned against talking about the murder. But she couldn't stop thinking about what had happened. These kids had information, and knowing why the girl died might erase the horrific images in her head.

Alexei's eyebrows raised at the interruption.

June reddened. "Um, yeah. I kind of knew her. We took Mandarin together. Did you know her?"

Eyes turned on her like spotlights. She had to say something. "Director Battle and I found the body." She offered June a penitent smile. "I'm sorry for your loss."

"Oh, you don't have to be." June waved off the condolences. "I mean, I didn't really know her." She turned back to Alexei. Her hands fell into her lap. "Poor Theo. He must be beside himself."

"Maybe," Tati mumbled at the floor.

"So you found the body?" Alexei's wide-eyed expression lacked real concern. "Did it look like she'd been murdered or like she'd jumped into the lake?"

The necklace of red welts flooded Nia's vision. Whatever had happened to that girl, she hadn't just drowned.

Alexei continued to stare at Nia, willing a juicy detail to fall from her parted lips. Nia closed her mouth. The dean wouldn't want her "speculating."

"I wouldn't know." She shrugged. "I didn't get a good look."

Alexei frowned. His brown eyes continued to beg for more information.

Nia shifted her view to Lydia. The little prima stood in the center of the room, folded like a pocketknife. Her hands lay flat on the floor, elbows bent. Her head rested by her shins. Lydia was certainly limber. A few feet away, just in front of Ms. V's door, Aubrey sat in a Russian split. She pointed and flexed her toes as Joseph talked to her—or tried to. It was impossible to tell from Aubrey's expression whether she was listening.

"You must have seen something," Alexei said.

Nia returned her attention to the boy. "Why do you think it wasn't an accident?"

"The girl you found, Lauren, had problems with an ex." Alexei glanced sideways at June. "Everyone knows about it."

"No, she didn't." June shook her head. "They always seemed so happy."

Alexei chuckled. "Come on."

"They were totally into each other, always kissing and holding hands, giggling." June turned to the T twins for support. "Totally in love, right? Romeo and Juliet style."

Tati and Talia each fidgeted with their feet, stroking their arches without really working them.

"You're kidding, right?" Alexei said. "You didn't see it? I thought everyone did."

"See what?"

Alexei laughed. Talia glanced over her shoulder toward Ms. V's shut door.

"What?" June asked again. She wasn't even pretending to stretch anymore. "I was in China for the summer, sans Facebook."

Talia spoke like she wanted the whole room to hear. "China, really? What were you doing?"

"Um, oh, improving my Mandarin. My parents think I have an American accent."

Alexei touched June's arm in mock flirtation. "Oh my God. You have to see it."

The gossipy tone of the conversation made Nia uncomfortable. She cleared her throat, and Alexei's voice dropped to a whisper.

"Over the summer, Theo met up with a certain someone I won't name right now. He made a video of him and this person being . . . amorous." Alexei wagged his eyebrows. "He then texted said video to his buddy, which of course got forwarded to the whole crew team. Then the school. Then the world." Alexei stifled a giggle. He elbowed June. "You can probably even search that shit in China."

Nia frowned at the boy. A girl was dead and he joked as though he'd seen an embarrassing celebrity story on TMZ.

Talia rolled her eyes. "Some people can't shut up about it, even when they should."

"A sex tape?" June more mouthed the words than said them. "Theo's not *that* type."

"Add alcohol and every guy is that type," Alexei said. "I always thought he was a jerk."

"He's always been nice to me."

"Because you're a pretty girl. He was never so nice to me."

"I would have been, like, utterly devastated if I was Lauren," Talia said. She dragged her lower lip beneath her top teeth. Sad eyes looked up at Nia. "Some people think she committed suicide after she found out that he cheated."

"People jump off bridges for less," Alexei said.

"Who was the tape with?" June whispered.

Alexei trapped his left tricep in a bent elbow and turned behind him, as if stretching his shoulder. Nia traced his gaze. He stared straight at Aubrey.

"Little Miss Perfect," he chuckled. "In the flesh."

4

Ligne [*LEEN-yuh*]

Line. The outline presented by a dancer while executing steps and poses. A dancer is said to have a good or bad sense of line according to the arrangement of head, body, legs and arms in a pose or movement. A good line is absolutely indispensable to the classical dancer.

Nia limped down the hall toward her apartment. The pain that had nibbled at her heel during her demonstration of fouetté turns was now chomping on her swollen tendon. She shouldn't have taken the long way home, but she'd wanted to avoid the lake.

Her fixation on the drowned girl was aggravating her injury. She felt anxious. Jittery. Tight. And the conversation in class had only made things worse. Rather than soften yesterday's images, knowing the girl's name had sharpened her mental pictures. The bluish face hiding behind her eyelids no longer seemed an out-of-focus photo from the nightly news that had flickered into her real life. The face belonged to Lauren.

Nia hoped a long soak would soothe both her mind and body. She thought of the box of Epsom salt in her vanity while feeling for the key in her sweater pocket. As the metal jangled in the lock, she noticed a letter tacked to her door with a yellow pushpin. She examined the note. Wallace's script monogram was stamped in the left-hand corner of the cream-colored card stock. She flipped over the paper to see words scrawled in blue ink:

Please meet in my office during first period to
discuss a matter of utmost importance.
–Dean Martha Stirk

Pain relief would have to wait. First period started at nine, following morning electives, which only some kids opted to take. There was a twenty-minute window between the end of dance class and the first academic lecture, enabling her students to change into their uniforms and head to the main campus. But the time had already expired thanks to Nia's lumbering walk back to the dorms. She was late.

Nia hustled back down the stairs as fast as she could. Dean Stirk's office sat above the registration building, across the courtyard surrounding the girls' dorms and back up the hill to the main campus. She had never been inside, but she'd seen signs during move-in weekend when she'd collected her orientation packet.

The sun beat down on her bare neck like a broiler. She was baking in her sweater. Still, she didn't remove her cotton pullover. The microfiber tank beneath hugged her body, and while form-fitting attire was appropriate for the studio, it wasn't for a sit-down with the big boss.

By the time she reached the registration office, sweat beaded beneath the tight bun affixed, like a button, to the top of her head. It dripped behind her ear and on her forehead. Her underarms felt damp.

She dabbed at the perspiration on her face with her sweater sleeve. Nia regretted not bathing for the umpteenth time. An hour of dance instruction followed by a half hour of dragging a bum foot across campus in eighty-degree weather would make anyone sweat. Still, she doubted Stirk would give her appearance a pass. The woman took pains to look proper.

Nia entered the building and ascended a wide staircase that led to an open second floor. The architecture reminded her of a television courthouse. Greek columns framed a waist-high bronze banister, enabling visitors to look over the railing at the checkered tile below.

She scanned navy walls and white wainscoting for an office. Bright white double doors marked the center of the room. A bronze plaque mounted above them read Stirk's full name and title: Martha Elayne Stirk, Dean of Students and Faculty, Principal of Academics.

A secretary's desk stood outside the dean's office. The accompanying chair sat empty, as did the blue upholstered seats pressed against the banister. Nia hesitated before knocking and then went ahead, rapping firmly on the door. She didn't need to sit outside. She'd been summoned.

The knock reverberated in the high ceilings. A voice came from behind the closed doors. "It's open."

Nia stepped inside like a mouse peeking from a hole in the wall, unsure of what she'd find. The office looked like a formal living room. French blue walls. More wainscoting. A pair of linen chesterfield sofas flanked a dark blue Persian rug with a white-and-pink starburst pattern at its center. At the far end of the room, Dean Stirk sat behind a masculine, mahogany desk.

The dean looked over the top of her frameless glasses. Her gray-and-blond bob shook around her cheekbones. "Ms. Washington. Good. My secretary delivered my note." The dean put down a pen atop an open book in front of her and gestured to one of two slipper chairs facing her desk. "Please shut the door behind you."

With the door closed, Nia realized how cold Stirk kept her office. Air conditioning blasted from vents in the floor and the ceiling. Her sweat turned icy against her skin. She pulled her sweater tighter around her chest and sat on the edge of the indicated chair.

The dean folded her hands atop her book. "You're a new teacher here. So I wanted to make you aware of the school policies relevant to yesterday's incident."

Incident. Was that what the dean was calling a student's death?

"We here at Wallace have a duty, not only to individual students, but also to the well-being of the school community as a whole. As such, we must handle any issue involving law enforcement with the utmost caution and care."

The dean paused, waiting for some kind of agreement. Nia nodded. "Of course."

"Tragically, the young woman whom you discovered yesterday was a returning student. Lauren Turek was fifteen and would have been a sophomore this year. Her parents have been notified."

"I'm so sorry."

Stirk cleared her throat. "Yes. We all are very sorry for her loss and our sympathies are with her family."

The dean removed her glasses and folded them on top of her desk. She leaned forward until her shoulders hovered above the book. Her body language said the time for pleasantries had ended.

"The police have not yet determined the cause of Lauren's death. We must take care not to speculate and unnecessarily alarm the student body or parents."

Nia shifted uncomfortably, glad she'd kept quiet when Alexei had asked about Lauren's body.

The dean cast another grave look across the desk. "Unfortunately, I am aware that Mr. Turek's grief-stricken actions have spurred discussion of his daughter's death as a homicide or a possible suicide. But police may yet determine that what occurred was a terrible, freak accident."

The dean's brow wrinkled. Her chin lowered. The expression indicated that the most serious part of the conversation was yet to come. Nia braced for a scolding.

"I understand that you saw marks on Lauren's neck and that you believe they indicate she was strangled. However, we do not yet know if the body was damaged in the lake or if the marks were from some other, unrelated injury."

The dean took a breath, allowing her words to sink in. "We have, of course, increased campus security and tightened all exit and entry points onto school grounds as a precaution. But we cannot have faculty, students, or their parents jumping to false conclusions. The assumption that Lauren was murdered would be, in all likelihood, incorrect and could lead to mass panic."

Stirk eyed her. Nia picked up on her cue. "I understand."

"We will notify the student body as soon as the police release a cause of death. Waiting prevents undue alarm, should Lauren's death prove accidental or," Stirk cleared her throat, "self-inflicted."

The dean rubbed her forehead as though the whole speech had given her a massive headache. For a moment,

Nia thought that the woman might become emotional. But when Stirk held up her head again, her gray eyes looked just as dry as before. "To be clear, we do not want to discuss anything that we saw or didn't see. I am in communication with law enforcement, and the school will release statements when appropriate. Do you understand?"

The question sounded patronizing. Of course she understood. She had to shut up lest the school be unnecessarily held liable or suffer damage to its reputation for what might yet prove to be an accident.

Nia doubted Lauren's death would be ruled anything but homicide. Though she didn't know whether she'd seen thumbprints or rope burns on Lauren's body, the placement of the marks right above the girl's clavicle couldn't have been caused by random abrasion. Stirk had to suspect as much as well.

The dean cleared her throat for the third time. The sound demanded a response.

"Yes. I won't say anything."

"Good. We appreciate your discretion. More information is not always better." The dean gave a weak smile. She put her glasses back on the bridge of her nose. "The students will, naturally, wish to discuss a classmate's death as the news circulates, particularly in the cafeteria, where they have the opportunity to socialize without teacher oversight. I am asking all four resident advisors to take shifts in the student dining hall during meal times today and tomorrow. We need to monitor conversation and make sure rumors don't get out of hand."

Stirk opened a drawer in her desk, withdrew a sheet of paper, and passed it to Nia. It featured a long grid, constructed in Microsoft Excel or some similar data analysis program. In the first column were four names including her own: two female, two male. Time slots topped the subsequent columns.

"I took the liberty of blocking out the cafeteria schedule and assigning monitoring duties that did not interfere with teaching or extracurricular obligations."

The kids ate three times a day. Breakfast was three hours long to accommodate the students' varied morning schedules. Lunch was one hour. Dinner was two. The row with Nia's name had the first hour of breakfast and the first half of lunch highlighted.

Nia didn't like trading her morning stretching time for cafeteria duty. She needed to loosen up her heel before class to avoid damaging it during demonstrations. But she doubted it would be easy to switch shifts. Most faculty taught or coached at least one extracurricular.

"This is how the RAs earn that free housing." The dean sighed. "You and your colleagues are our eyes and ears and, often, the first adults that students turn to for guidance. Breakfast is already over for today. Your shift can start at lunch."

"Okay. I'll be there."

Stirk's expression darkened, as though concerned by Nia's response. "Remember, it's our job to protect both the student body and this institution."

The dean again waited for some kind of affirmation. Nia managed a nod. The gesture seemed to satisfy. Stirk reclaimed her pen and resumed reading the book on her desk. Conversation over.

Nia picked up her new schedule, rose from her seat, and exited. The implication of Stirk's parting words was not lost on her. All the teachers and students were responsible for student safety. They had all failed at their collective job.

They would all need to help cover the school's butt.

5

Bras bas [*brah bah*]

Arms low or down. This is the dancer's "attention."
The arms form a circle with the palms facing each
other and the back edge of the hands resting on the
thighs.

N ia exited the registration building into the late morning sunshine. The brief rest and the cold air had taken
some of the sting out of her foot, allowing her to focus
on a new pain in her stomach. Hunger roiled her insides.
She needed food.

Black coffee had served as breakfast, and that was three
hours ago. If she remembered correctly from the orientation
map, a pay cafeteria for faculty lay somewhere on the west-
ern edge of campus, just beyond the boys' residences. She
could cut through the boys' quadrangle to shorten the walk.

Trees rustled overhead. The sound was one of the few
noises on the quiet campus. Second period had started. All
students would be in class, lest they risk Saturday morning

detention. She would be one of the few people traipsing around outside—if not the only person.

Nia increased her speed. As she walked across the boys' quad, she lectured herself about odds. Wallace hid in cow country Connecticut, nestled between a lake and a forest. The nearest real town lay beyond acres of farmland, at least thirty miles down the highway. The closest city was an hour by car or bus. Regardless of who had murdered Lauren, the school was far more secure than any of her old neighborhoods—especially now with officers combing the campus for strangers.

The sight of a police cruiser snapped Nia's attention back to her surroundings. It was parked on the courtyard lawn beside a wall of gothic buildings, looking every bit as futuristic as a hovercraft. The two detectives from the prior day stood beside it. They wore khaki dress pants and navy blazers. Blue-striped ties. Their clothing mimicked the Wallace uniform, but their graying hair ruined the camouflage.

Nia walked toward the car, eager to ask for—or overhear— news about Lauren. The cops had seen the neck bruises. Surely they didn't believe the girl had fallen, or jumped, into the lake.

The police faced a young man. Unlike the boys in ballet class, this teen had filled out his six-foot frame. His broad shoulders propped up his navy jacket, making it appear tailored rather than borrowed from Dad's closet. Well-defined forearms flexed beyond rolled-up sleeves. His chin punctuated a firm jawline, underlining a handsome face.

"There's no need to get defensive. We just want to ask you some questions." Detective Kelly addressed the boy. Nia recognized his gravelly New England accent.

"No. You can't." The student's tone didn't share the confidence of his words. His voice rose at the end, like a question. "Not without my parents."

"You don't need your parents to talk to us." Detective Kelly rubbed the back of his neck. He shrugged like everything was no big deal. "We're just trying to figure out what happened to your girlfriend."

"Lauren wasn't my girlfriend." The boy's voice rose in pitch and volume. He sounded panicked. "And you can't be here."

Kelly stepped toward the boy. "Well, even if you two weren't together, you were friends, right? Her friends say she went to meet you."

The boy shook his head. "No." His voice grew louder. "I hadn't talked to her since last summer. I'm calling my father. He's an attorney."

"There's no need to worry your dad. We're all just trying to figure out why Lauren went to the dock that night."

Detective Kelly walked toward the boy. Just as he hit the bottom step, another man appeared in the doorway. He moved the teenager to the side, blocking the entrance with his taller figure.

"Excuse me. What seems to be the problem?"

A badge flashed in Kelly's hand. "Detectives James Kelly and Ed Frank. And who are you?" The question shot out like an accusation.

The man appeared too old to be a student but not old enough to be the parent of one. A dust of dark blond hair lined his angular jaw and upper-lip. Maybe an older brother still helping with the move? He wore a white undershirt and jeans. Fine blond hair hung around his cheekbones, giving him a rumpled, crashed-on-the-couch appearance.

He didn't resemble the kid. The student had a Greek look about him, with thick dark hair that was cropped on the sides, large olive eyes, and tan skin. The man looked plucked from one of those Scandinavian countries that produce towheads with deep-set sea eyes and fair skin.

The man reached behind him and pulled the door shut. "I'm Peter Andersen, the resident advisor in this building. Now, what seems to be the problem?"

"A student's dead body was found on campus yesterday. We're trying to talk to friends of the girl to figure out what may have happened."

The boy turned to his new ally. "I told them I hadn't seen Lauren since June." He pulled a cell phone from his pants pocket. "I'm calling my father. He's a lawyer."

Detective Frank pointed like he wanted to jab a finger into the boy's chest. "I don't care who your father is, kid."

Peter stepped from the entryway. He placed himself between the boy and the policemen. "Okay. How about I call the dean and she can help us sort this out?"

"We're just trying to talk to people that knew her." Detective Kelly sounded less sure of himself. "You want to help us solve this, don't you?"

Peter held one hand up in surrender. He dipped the other into his pocket, withdrawing a cell phone. "Look. I'm no lawyer, so I'm not arguing with you or trying to keep you from doing your jobs. But it's my job to call the dean whenever there's a problem." He turned to the boy. "Why don't you go back inside and wait for Dean Stirk?"

The teenager pulled a keycard from his pocket. He kept his eyes on the officers as he flashed it at the door. A beep, like a microwave timer, sounded.

Detective Frank threw up his hands. "Why don't you want to talk to us, Theo? Usually folks want to help the police. Seems suspicious."

The boy spun back around to face the group. His attention darted from the officers to the resident advisor and then zeroed in on Nia. His face reddened.

"I didn't do anything," he yelled, announcing his innocence to her and anyone else in the vicinity. "Everybody's looking at me like I had something to do with it but we hadn't even spoken since before school let out." He extended his arms, imploring the officers. "It's not fair. If people see us talking, everyone will think it's my fault."

Detective Frank put his hands on his belt. "No one is here except us and a teacher."

The boy pointed to the courtyard. Detective Kelly looked over his shoulder to where Nia stood. He had to recognize her from the lake, and it would seem strange, her turning up again near a suspect. She needed to explain.

Nia strode toward the group, compensating for her embarrassment with overconfidence. "Hello, detectives." She turned to the student and the young teacher. "I'm Nia Washington, a new resident advisor in the girls' dorm. I saw there was a problem and thought I might be needed. Can I help here?"

The detectives' annoyance coated her skin, but she held her head high as she walked past their glares. Her phone vibrated in her pocket. She didn't dare answer it. This was a serious situation and police made her anxious.

Peter tucked blond strands behind his ear before gesturing with the phone. "Just sit with Theo while I call Dean Stirk." He descended the steps and then motioned to the policemen, inviting them into the telephone conversation while diverting their attention from the trembling student.

Nia sat beside the young man. The sun-baked stone burned through her thin dance pants. She crossed her legs and uncrossed them, giving her thighs momentary reprieve from the heat. Instinct prompted her to place an arm around the boy's shoulders, but Battle's voice cautioned against it. *No blurring lines.* Instead she patted the step.

"Your RA is calling the dean. And your dad will come. He'll help get this all sorted out."

Theo rubbed his eyes as if trying to wipe them from his face. "People break up. Not everyone kills themselves afterward."

Everyone wanted to blame the dead girl. Again, she thought of the bruises around Lauren's neck.

Nia pursed her lips, trapping the words on her tongue: she didn't kill herself.

6

Attitude [*a-tee-TEWD*]

A pose on one leg with the other lifted in the back,
the knee bent at an angle of 90 degrees and well
turned out so that the knee is higher than the foot.

The police huffed back to their cruiser like men ready for a fight. Noses flared. Heads lowered like charging bulls.

Dean Stirk had arrived with the school's expensive-looking attorney, who had insisted that Theo couldn't be questioned because he had requested a lawyer. In reality, Theo had only asked for his father, who happened to be a lawyer. But the boy quickly corrected his mistake and demanded to speak to his father and his attorney.

Dean Stirk ushered Theo back to the dorm with instruction to reach his parents. As soon as the door shut behind him, she and the lawyer took off, spouting a mix of bureaucratic slang and lawyerese: *accelerated communication timetables, appropriate language, security enhancements.* Nia guessed an e-mail would go out later in the day.

Peter watched his superiors until they disappeared behind a stone building. He looked down at Nia, still seated on the steps. She returned his gaze, waiting for instruction or permission to leave, something along the lines of "Thanks for your help. I got it."

"Well, that was stupid," he said.

"The cops are only trying to do their job."

"Not the cops. Stirk bumbling around like that. She should have sounded the alarm as soon as they found that girl. Now when all these parents descend on campus wanting someone to blame, they're going to look straight at us." He shook his head and brushed back the hair that fell from behind his ear into his face. "Watch. The press will say we care more about spinning the story and the school's reputation than student safety."

Nia met Peter's eyes straight on, thanks to the extra few inches given by the steps. Stirk's earlier speech had made her feel culpable for the school's actions. Peter's criticism put her on the defensive.

"The dean doesn't want to alarm anyone until the police announce the cause of death And she has to give Lauren's parents time to notify the rest of the family. Imagine if the girl's grandmother found out from a news report. The press will understand."

"They won't."

How could he know? She didn't like Peter's cocky attitude.

"A student's death needs to have all the adults running around like chickens with their heads cut off," Peter said. "Even if she committed suicide—"

"She didn't commit suicide."

His brow furrowed. He scratched behind his ear as if the hair he kept tucking there irritated it. The nervous tick pleased Nia. Her words had knocked some of the sheen off his self-righteousness.

He exhaled loudly. "Look. Don't assume the kids know anything. I know the students are all abuzz about their bad relationship, but they just don't want to blame a dead girl. I doubt Theo would have hurt Lauren." His ice-blue eyes captured her gaze. "I was his RA last year. People think he's one of those beer-sneaking jocks because he's on the crew team. But he's a sensitive kid."

She could almost believe him. The crying student on the steps didn't seem like the kind of testosterone-pumped teen that would make and broadcast a sex tape. She'd pictured a handsome bad boy with unkempt hair, half-unbuttoned shirt, and a permanent smirk on his face—a younger version, perhaps, of the man standing in front of her. But, for all she knew, Theo was that guy. She'd seen him confronted by two bullying detectives. Fear could make even the worst men vulnerable.

Peter still stared, waiting for acknowledgement of his character defense.

"I wasn't implying anything about Theo."

"I'm not saying he's not a teenage boy who does stupid things. But all teenagers do stupid shit, you know?" Peter's mouth cracked into a smile. The expression wasn't a genuine grin as much as a guilty one. It invited complicity.

"Even so, she didn't kill herself."

"Why? You think rich girls don't kill themselves? Kids here think high school romance is everything. My bet is she got worked up about the breakup and jumped into the lake, intending to make a big show of attempting suicide, and then had trouble getting back out. The bottom of that lake is pretty muddy."

"Everyone wants to accuse this girl."

"Because she probably made a mistake."

Nia stood up to face him head on. "I found her body. She had marks around her neck, like thumbprints or a rope."

Peter's mouth dropped open. The pink drained from his face, exposing a yellow undertone. His Adam's apple bobbed. "Strangled?" His chin retreated into his neck. "No. That . . ." He trailed off, shaking his head.

The severity of his reaction erased Nia's satisfaction at pushing him off the blame-the-victim bandwagon. She felt bad for him. It was one thing to think a teenager had done something dramatic and gotten herself killed and another to think she'd been murdered—maybe even by a student.

"Did you know her?"

"What?" Peter dragged his fingers through his hair again, pinning the strands behind his ears. "No. I mean, not really. I'd seen her with Theo. I mostly teach upperclassmen."

"Could he have done something?"

Peter rubbed his palms over his face, as if trying to erase his shocked expression. "Well, I don't know then." A hand retreated into his jeans pocket. He retrieved his phone and began rotating it in his palm like he was itching to call someone. Probably the dean.

"No." He shoved the phone back into his pocket. "Theo's a good kid. It's not fair for him to be accused just because he dated her."

Peter pointed at Nia's chest. The action seemed as aggressive as the cop's behavior toward Theo moments before. She stepped back.

"Even if she was strangled—like you say, I didn't see the body—some sicko probably sneaked onto campus and found her by herself. She drowned during move-in weekend, right? There are a thousand people on campus then.

Security probably wouldn't notice a weird adult. Someone could pretend to be a student's sibling or uncle."

Nia's stomach growled like an irritated dog. Hunger, coupled with the heat and the stress of the conversation, had made her light-headed. She couldn't keep debating a stranger's innocence or guilt.

"I guess . . ." She descended the steps, planning to give Peter some version of a sign-off: *See you around. Good luck with everything. Nice meeting you.*

He towered over her as she stepped onto the walkway. His hands hit his hips. His chin jutted out.

"You know, you really shouldn't be telling people about any marks on Lauren's body. You can't know what caused them. It's bad enough that the cops are questioning Theo in broad daylight. You start spreading rumors about strangulation and people will crucify the poor kid."

Nia copied Peter's haughty stance. "I wasn't spreading anything around. I was telling you what I saw because you're a teacher, and the police were here, and I thought you should know the facts before trying to convince people that this girl killed herself."

"She still might have. Maybe she jumped in and got tangled up in a rope."

Nia shrugged. "Well, I'm sure the police will have something to say soon. Nice meeting you."

Though she'd said the polite thing, her tone conveyed their meeting hadn't been a pleasure. His lips parted. Before he could retort, she marched past him. As she exited the courtyard, she swore she could still feel his eyes burning into her back.

7

Cavalier [*ka-val-je*]

The male partner of the ballerina.

The cafeteria hummed with high-pitched teenage voices. Occasionally, the clatter of silverware pierced the din, like shrapnel hitting a fan blade. Nia chewed a bland bite of chicken salad and struggled to pick out individual conversations from the crowd noise. How could the dean expect her to keep rumors in check when she couldn't hear anything?

She glanced at the group of girls sitting to her left at the long, rectangular dining table. A teen with curly brown hair made eye contact and then turned inward toward her friends. The girls' voices, already unintelligible, lowered another notch.

Nia ran her tongue beneath her back teeth, dislodging a bit of mayonnaise-glued chicken. She tasted the tangy flavor of the sandwich again. The cook must have put lemon in it to make it seem fresher. The thought made her long for Listerine.

She still had another fifteen minutes of dining hall duty. Nia scanned the room for her students. She spotted Alexei and June with a throng of upperclassmen. The group's seniority was evident by the loud sounds coming from their table. No need for them to keep their voices down. They owned the place. Nia thought she recognized the T twins and Joseph at the same table. She had seen Suzanne earlier on the arm of a guy with gelled boy-band bangs. Kim had joined them. She'd also briefly spotted Lydia eating at the edge of a long table, mostly with younger-looking students. The girl had seemed unattached to the group, as though she were eating alone rather than with her classmates. She hadn't stayed long.

Aubrey was nowhere to be seen. Neither, for that matter, was Marta.

"Looking for your relief?"

The voice came from behind her. Nia turned to see Peter standing in the aisle on her right side. He'd changed into khaki slacks and a pale-blue button-down shirt that highlighted his eyes. He'd slicked his hair back into a style that reminded her of the 1920s. The man cleaned up good. He looked appropriate, handsome, stylish. *Still a jerk*, she reminded herself.

Instead of a dining tray, he held two books in his left hand. He held them out to her. "Stirk sent me with a present. Take one."

She pulled the top book from his hands. The cover depicted a black-and-white picture of a stork standing beside the water on an empty beach. The image was lonely yet peaceful, befitting a condolence card.

"An e-mail is going out. You'll see it in your inbox when you get back to your room."

Peter slid into the empty seat across from her as he spoke. There was plenty of room for him. No one, apparently, had wanted to sit near the new RA.

"We are expected to provide twenty-four-seven counseling about Lauren's death," Peter continued. He waved his own copy of the book. "This is supposed to give us guidance on how to help the students deal with their loss. Stirk wants us to read it."

"Oh. Thanks."

Nia's flat tone didn't convey any appreciation. Grief counselor would have been her last chosen occupation. She wasn't good with tears or providing solace. She preferred her emotions—and everyone else's—kept on the inside.

Peter offered a sheepish smile. "Look, I'm sorry."

Nia shrugged. "No, I get it." She recalled her conversation with the dean before. "It's how we earn our free housing, right?"

He rubbed the back of his neck. "Yeah. But I didn't mean about bringing you more work. I know we got off to a bad start."

He glanced at the girls at the other end of the table and lowered his voice. "It's just that I feel protective of Theo. Rumors are swirling about him. I guess the girl's dad asked a few classmates questions, which started a whole 'It's Theo's fault' thread on Facebook. Last night, I found him throwing up in the bathroom. The kid is sick about Lauren. He thinks she killed herself because of him."

"I wasn't accusing him of anything."

"I know. But I talked to him until four in the morning, and then, when I finally get him off the ledge, the police show up and intimidate him. If the school doesn't handle this better, that kid's going to jump out a window."

Nia tapped the book on the table in front of her. "Well, guess that's why we have these."

Her pocket buzzed. She recognized the vibration as her cell's silent ring. She reached into her sweater. Her mother had called before to ask how she was settling in. She hadn't had a chance to phone back.

Peter's hand grazed her forearm. A familiar tingle tickled her spine as his fingertips brushed her skin. She didn't want a man, but her body missed the touch of one: the thickness of a man's fingers, the breadth of a male palm. The way a man's hand could engulf a shoulder or a thigh or a breast.

"Shit. That wasn't an apology as much as it was an excuse." He again rubbed the back of his neck. The gesture made him appear shy, almost humble. "I was in attack mode this morning and I lashed out at you unfairly. I'm sorry."

Her phone continued buzzing. Nia stopped trying to find it. "It's okay. I'd be edgy too under the same circumstances."

He smiled and extended his hand above the table. "I never introduced myself properly. Peter Andersen. I teach tenth- and eleventh-grade European literature. I also advise the student poetry magazine: *Wallace Words*."

His boyish grin invited an answering smile. She clasped his hand.

"Nia Washington. I'm the new teaching assistant in the dance department."

"Very nice to meet you."

Her phone beeped a loud response, announcing a missed call. "Sorry about that."

"No, don't be. Feel free to get it. I have the next shift and I'm already here. No reason for you to stay too."

"Really? Thanks." This time she meant it. Her foot throbbed. With any luck, she'd be able to soak it while scanning her *homework*.

She slid out from the table and stood in the aisle. "It's really nice of you to take over early."

"No problem. Hope to see you around."

"Likewise."

Nia exited the cafeteria into bright sunshine. A wall of sticky heat greeted her. She swapped her new book from one hand to the other as she pulled off her sweater. Once free, she grabbed the phone from the pocket. Time to tell Mom about her strange first day.

A text dominated the home screen.

Missed call: Dimitri Bovt.

She froze, feeling vaguely nauseous. Was that what love became when it ended? Blind fear? Sickness?

He hadn't left a voicemail. Why would he call after a year? What could he possibly want?

She stared at his name on the screen.

The night he'd ended things, all the lights had been on in the apartment. They were constantly penny pinching, turning off every bulb in order to save on the electricity bill. But that evening, she'd walked in to the equivalent of a theater with the house lights turned all the way up. Closing time. She should have gotten the hint.

The apartment had smelled of whisky. The physical demands of their jobs kept them from drinking much, but there'd been a brand-new bottle of Johnny Walker on the coffee table, a third gone, and a glass half-filled with amber liquid. No ice.

The liquor had tipped her off to trouble—just not what kind. She'd immediately dropped the groceries on the kitchen counter and joined Dimitri on the living room couch. She'd expected him to spill a story about his disapproving father or maybe share unwelcome news about his grandparents.

Dimitri had leaned into her and then abruptly scooted away on their Ikea sofa.

"What's wrong?" she'd asked.

"We need to talk."

The infamous phrase. Still, she hadn't realized what was happening. At worst, she'd thought he would ask her to pay a larger share of the rent. The discussion had lasted hours, even though only a few points were made. Dimitri's family thought that they had become too serious for a pair of twenty-one-year-olds. They were living together prematurely, and at his age, he shouldn't be subsidizing her rent. Most importantly, they had too little life experience to know whether or not they really wanted each other.

Shock had turned Nia into a lawyer. She'd protested each point without emotion: they weren't like other young people; their careers had made them grow up faster; they saved money by splitting a studio apartment, even if they didn't divide the rent fifty-fifty. After an hour of arguing, though, her adrenaline had faded. She'd grown quiet while he justified "their" need to "have experiences outside of each other."

She'd held the tears at bay during the whole cab ride to her mother's house. It wasn't until her mom had handed her a box of Epsom salt that the faucet started flowing. Her mom had directed her to the bathroom with two well-worn mantras in the Washington household: "Tears aren't a social drink" and "A soak does more for the soul than wasted salt water."

Her tears could have filled the tub. She'd cried until she was dehydrated. The following morning, she'd collected her things from Dimitri's apartment while he was at practice. Three days later, she'd auditioned for the traveling group and gotten a soloist position. He'd called her twenty times before she left. She hadn't returned one message.

Deep down, Nia knew he didn't deserve the silent treatment. She understood his argument. How could anyone know what they wanted at twenty-one? It was a question she had asked herself.

But she hated him for answering it.

She wouldn't call him back.

8

En Croix [*ahn krwah*]

In the shape of a cross. Indicates that an exercise is to be executed to the fourth position front, to the second position and to the fourth position back, or vice versa.

"**S**udden death can bring up many feelings to deal with all at once."

Nia peeled back the page of the book propped against her knees, struggling to focus on the large print. It didn't help that the sun had long set, leaving the fluorescent bulb in the living room to fight, alone, against the darkness invading from the bay window. She adjusted her position on the bed. The comforter underneath her beckoned.

"It may seem incredibly unfair, especially if the person is young."

Nia snorted. She closed the book and glanced at the name under the big, bold title: *Understanding Grief and Grieving* by Harrison Lovett, MD, MSW. The degrees were unnecessary. A hundred pages in and Nia hadn't read one revelation on dealing with grief or helping others cope with loss. Common sense, drawn out into pointless paragraphs, littered each page.

An opportunity to apply the book's chestnuts had yet to present itself. Though Nia had sequestered herself in the room to wait for the students, no one had knocked. She wasn't surprised. Who would talk to a stranger when friends were next door, if not in the same room? Besides, her building housed juniors and seniors. Judging from June's comments in dance class, most of the upperclassmen didn't know Lauren well enough to grieve her loss. The few conversations Nia had overheard referred to the victim as *that girl Theo cheated on.*

The school's e-mail had upped the volume on the hallway chatter. Though it had encouraged students to discuss their feelings with faculty, the teens seemed to take the letter as a permission slip to publicly share theories. A bookmaker listening to the gossip would put the short odds on suicide. Nearly every teenage girl thought it natural that a smart, attractive sophomore would end her life after her older, popular boyfriend cheated. The assumption said something about the smallness of the students' world. Life and death revolved around high school romances and college acceptance letters.

Then again, her world wasn't much bigger. All she'd cared about two years ago were ballet companies and her boyfriend. Now, though, she had to focus on her health and rebuilding her career.

Dimitri had not called again. Maybe he'd never meant to phone in the first place. He'd probably pocket dialed her. Soon, he would realize and delete her number so it wouldn't happen a second time. Her chest tightened at the thought.

She squeezed her eyes shut, an attempt to blind herself from the memory of his face. She couldn't speculate on Dimitri's call anymore. It was almost eleven o'clock, and she needed sleep. Round-the-clock counseling sounded good in a letter, but the school couldn't require such vigilance. She taught in the morning. Injuries happened to tired bodies.

Nia marked her place in the book and set it on her nightstand. She extended her legs until they dangled off the edge of the bed, pulling her weight toward the floor. Time to get ready for bed. Soap, shampoo, shave, stretch, and sleep—in that order.

She plodded over to the bathroom. A knock echoed in the room. Nia stopped, unsure the sound she'd heard came from her door. It sounded again: three staccato raps.

Nia ran through bullet points she knew without the book. Listen. Reassure the student of her own safety. Refrain from any mention of Jesus, God, Allah, or any other deity. The school was officially nondenominational, despite the massive Christian chapel lording over the main campus. Besides, most students wouldn't take comfort in the idea that a master plan somehow included a young girl's death.

She opened the door. The overweight girl from ballet class stood in the hallway. Marta wore a boy's Wallace sweatshirt that hid her belly. With it covered, she didn't seem heavy. Youth, not added pounds, rounded her face. The girl's big brown eyes shone like river stones. Red rimmed the bottom lids. "May I come in?"

"Of course."

Marta checked over her shoulder before stepping into the room. She shut the door behind her.

Nia gestured toward the gray-and-tan-striped sofa in the center of the room. It appeared pilfered from a retirement home. Even Wallace had to skimp on something. Clearly, the RAs' furniture budget was not a high priority.

Marta sat on the couch like it was upholstered with cement. Nia joined her on the opposite cushion. The girl's hands folded in her lap. She rubbed the back of her knuckles with her thumb. Her bottom lip trembled. "I, um, just didn't have anyone else to talk to . . ."

"I'm glad you came. Would you like some water?"

Fresh tears filled Marta's eyes. She shook her head.

"Let me grab you some tissues."

Nia realized she didn't have tissues as the words escaped her mouth. She left Marta on the couch to grab a roll of paper towels from the kitchen counter. Marta stared at her lap as Nia held out the poor substitute for Kleenex.

The girl accepted the roll without eye contact. She unwound a sheet and pressed it to her eyes before balling the rough paper into a giant worry bead.

"I'm sorry for your loss," Nia said.

The girl's head snapped upward. Her mouth dropped like she'd seen a ghost. Her eyes darted toward the door.

Nia didn't understand why the words bothered her. Didn't everyone say that when someone died?

"Were you and Lauren close?"

Marta's shoulders slumped. "I didn't know her. I'm not here about Lauren."

Then why are you crying? Nia folded her hands into her lap and, like a television shrink, said, "I'm here to listen."

Marta twisted the paper towel into a rope. "You can't tell anyone what I tell you, right?"

Can't? No. Attorneys and real psychiatrists had client–patient privileges. Nothing Marta said fell under protected speech. But she couldn't help if Marta didn't feel safe.

"As long as what you tell me isn't a crime, I promise I won't tell anyone."

Tears carved their way down Marta's cheeks. She tucked in her lips and looked at the ceiling. "It's not a crime. But maybe it should be."

The words fit everything together like a final puzzle piece. The girl's belly, her uncertain posture and off balance, the reason she sat here confessing to her RA rather than one of her friends: Marta was pregnant—or she had been.

"You can talk to me."

The girl met her eyes for a moment, as if agreeing to a pact. "I had an abortion three days ago. I went to a clinic in Claremont on Saturday, as soon as my parents dropped me here. I wanted to do it sooner, but I was home for the summer and there was no way to get to a doctor. My parents are Armenian Catholics—that's basically double Catholic. They think abortion is murdering a baby. It's, like, the worst kind of killing a person can do. They would think I'm worse than a terrorist."

"You are young. You didn't feel ready to have a baby."

Marta twisted the tissue back and forth. Bits of paper flaked into her palms. "You know what's messed up? I passed that clinic every Saturday when I was tutoring. There were always teenagers hurrying into the doors and I'd always think they were these horrible people, too weak to abstain, too stupid to use condoms, too selfish to save their babies for adoption. And then . . ."

Marta's face reddened. She balled up the paper in her fist. "I'd gained, like, a million pounds in just three months. I couldn't have hid it. I wouldn't have been able to dance. I'm banking on ballet to help get me into college, you know? But Ms. V is ready to sideline me in the fall show, like, tomorrow, because of all this disgusting fat."

The girl grabbed her skin through her sweatshirt and yanked it as if she wished she could tear the extra flesh from her frame. "Please, don't let her make me, like, the girl waving her arms in the background. My parents would ask questions. I promise, I'll lose this in a couple weeks. I'm a good dancer. That's really why I'm here. If you tell her that I'm working hard, maybe she'll cut me some slack."

Nia swallowed. She felt bad for Marta, but she wasn't sure she could help her with Ms. V. The teen's extra weight left her off balance, and the fall show was at the end of the month.

"Please tell her. I'm not a bad person. I just couldn't go four more months with everyone here looking at me, making jokes. And my mother would have totally *insisted* I raise the baby. Have you seen the reality shows? Teen moms are completely ruined. Their parents resent them. Their friends abandon them. No one dates them. They end up totally alone."

Nia understood her fear of being alone. The same one curled up with her every night since breaking up with Dimitri.

"Does the father know?" Nia asked, hoping to silence her own thoughts.

"He doesn't care." Marta examined the couch pattern. She found a loose thread and picked at it. "He was just this college guy I met during a summer Spanish intensive in Barcelona. He was, like, amazingly beautiful and smart and well traveled, and he'd probably done it hundreds of times. I didn't tell him that I hadn't, or that I was in high school, or that I wasn't on birth control.

"It kind of hurt the first few times. He blamed the condoms, something about the latex irritating my skin. The fourth time, he said we shouldn't use them and he would pull out."

She placed her palm on her belly as if feeling for the life no longer there. "I didn't realize I was pregnant until I got home. By then, he was totally over me." She made air quotes with her fingers. Bitterness hardened her voice. "'You need to be a big girl and take care of it.'" Fat tears tumbled down her cheeks. "You probably think I'm a murderer."

Nia winced at the word. Lauren's body waited behind her closed eyes. It floated into her vision, purple and blue skin like a stillborn. She forced her lids back open.

Marta sniffed loudly. She rubbed at her nose with her sweatshirt sleeve. "You have to swear you won't tell anyone. You're the only one who knows. I didn't even get a friend to take me home from the clinic. I took the bus. I looked like a homeless kid in big baggy clothes. I even walked to the far bus stop, like half a mile down the road, after I saw someone from school at the closest stop. I can't have anyone know. You have to promise."

Clear snot shimmered above Marta's trembling, puffy lips. She looked scared and beaten. Nia wondered whether the fear was justified. Maybe Marta's parents were the *spare the rod, spoil the child* variety. Nia didn't think wealthy people practiced corporal punishment, but maybe religious righteousness trumped riches.

Nia raised her right hand. She swore over an invisible Bible. "I won't tell anyone."

9

Chaînés [*sheh-NAY*]

Chains, links. A series of rapid turns on the toes or pads of feet.

Nia sat alone at the end of a long table in the students' dining hall, a sleepy sentry waiting for her shift to end. Dawn bathed the near-empty room in white light. She sipped a tepid black coffee and watched the molasses movements of the minute hand on the cafeteria clock. Another RA would relieve her at five minutes to seven.

Her head ached like a cheap vodka hangover. A steady alarm pulsed from her heel. Marta hadn't left her apartment until nearly two o'clock in the morning. Nia would try to sneak a nap sometime between dance class and her evening meeting.

A hefty black man in a white apron emerged from the staff-only kitchen, pushing a cart topped with pans and portable gas burners. He brought the cart to a tablecloth-covered counter at the far end of the room and then hoisted two baking trays atop a ministove. He peeled back the foil tops. The smell of bacon and eggs filled the room.

A group of boys at the other end of Nia's table rose to get their trays. Hot breakfast would start the morning rush. Though some kids with morning electives like crew or dance had already popped in for bagels and pastries, the early risers were in the minority. Most school activities took place after the end of the academic day. As a result, most kids ate between eight o'clock and the start of first period.

Long blond hair swished into the room. Nia recognized Aubrey from her straight, dancer's posture and the navy leotard stretching above her sweatpants. She'd probably thrown the bottoms on over her tights. Nia would have done the same if she hadn't been instructed to wear yoga pants and a top.

The group of boys snickered as Aubrey entered. One boy licked his lips like a dog salivating before a steak. "Bow chicka wow wow," he said, mimicking the soundtrack to seventies skin flicks. "I love the Internet."

His friend laughed and slapped him five.

Aubrey ignored them. She took a brown dining tray from a stack beside the hot breakfast counter and brought it away from the guys to the cold buffet. If she'd wanted eggs, she wasn't willing to stomach standing next to those boys in line to get them.

Aubrey poured herself a bowl of bran cereal and milk. She added a banana from one of several bowls of fruit before carrying her tray to an empty table.

Nia considered joining her. Perhaps her presence would keep the guys from talking about the tape.

Nia started to rise from her table. As she did, she saw Joseph enter the room. He grabbed a tray from the cold buffet and slid it in front of Aubrey, claiming his seat. The appearance of Aubrey's boyfriend made Nia return to her chair. Joseph would keep the chatter from becoming too loud.

Joseph squeezed Aubrey's shoulder and then headed to the hot breakfast line. The boys stopped laughing as he approached. He wasn't a broad guy, but he was tall and muscled. Moreover, he had a confident air that probably kept people from messing with him.

More kids filed into the dining hall. Nia recognized ballet students in the crowd: the T twins. Alexei. None acknowledged her. The room grew louder. Plates clattered on trays. Conversations tangled together, creating a web of human sound. Nia glanced at the clock again. Twenty to seven.

"Is this seat taken?"

For a moment, she mistook Peter for a student. He was dressed in khakis, a white button-down, and a blue blazer, akin to the school uniform. He held a tray topped with a whole-grain bagel and a mug of something steamy.

"Good morning." Nia gestured with an open hand to the chair across from her. "Are you here to take over for me again?"

"Sorry. No." He lowered his tray onto the table and took the seat. "I teach a poetry elective on Wednesdays. I'll keep you company for twenty minutes, though."

"I'd like that. Thank you." Nia yawned. She covered her mouth with her hand. "Excuse me."

"Not an early riser?"

"Usually I am. A student wanted some counseling last night."

Peter's eyebrows raised. "You actually got a taker?"

"Not really." She swished the cold, muddy water inside her coffee cup. "She wanted to discuss something else."

Peter put a tea bag into his mug. He moved it up and down in the hot water, a fisherman with a lure on the line.

Nia propped her elbow on the table. She let her head fall onto her half-closed hand. "So what do you teach in your poetry elective?"

"Emerson. Eliot. Some Eminem."

"The rapper?"

Peter chuckled. "I try to keep my quatrain analysis interesting."

A genuine smile stifled Nia's coming yawn. "Which songs do you use?"

"Just 'Stimulate.'" He grinned.

"They're arresting Theo!"

A boy shouted the news from the lunchroom doorway. Students fell out of their seats in an effort to be first out the door. Their rubber soles squeaked on the wooden floor like scurrying rats. Peter jumped up and ran to the exit, trying to beat the swarm of students.

Nia followed him, but too slowly to catch up. Boys' voices bounced off the walls. She hurried in the direction of the commotion.

A crowd clogged the vestibule outside the dining hall. Nia watched Peter push through it. She trailed after him, slipping through the clearing he'd created.

"What's going on?"

"Peter. Good that you're here."

Dean Stirk stood between Detective Frank and a campus cop. Theo stood behind her, flanked by Detective Kelly and another uniformed policeman.

"These officers are taking Theo in," Stirk said.

"And you're just going to let them?"

"A student is dead, Mr. Andersen." She raised her voice, ensuring that all the whispering kids could hear the exchange. "We here at Wallace must make every effort to help authorities learn what happened and to ensure our students' continued safety."

"But like this, Martha?" Peter lowered his voice. "Couldn't his parents have brought him in discretely?"

Detective Frank cleared his throat. "Both of Mr. Spanos's parents were notified. The boy's father has been less than helpful."

"Well, you can't question him without them."

Frank waved a piece of paper. "As this arrest warrant makes clear, we have every right. Theo is no longer a juvenile. He's eighteen as of August third."

Peter ran a hand over his hair. "You don't know that he's done anything wrong. Doing it this way—"

"He texted the victim right before her time of death, begging to meet at the boathouse."

The officers steered Theo toward the double doors leading outside. Theo wore the school's full uniform. He stared at his black leather shoes. Stirk followed behind the arresting officers, head held high, a fellow jailer.

Peter whirled to face the hovering students. "Everyone go to your rooms or return to the cafeteria. If you don't leave, I'm citing you for unbecoming conduct. Your parents will be notified."

The kids shuffled down the hall, looking over their shoulders at their classmate, sandwiched between two officers. Theo held his head down as though locked in stocks. Nia saw snickers among the shocked faces in the crowd. She could imagine the Facebook posts. The students would convict by morning.

10

Penchée [*pahn-shay*]

Leaning, inclining. An arabesque penchée is an arabesque in which the body leans well forward in an
oblique line, the forward arm and the head being
low and the foot of the raised leg the highest point.

A platinum sky shone outside the dance studio windows. Raindrops streaked the glass. Nia debated
whether she could make it home before the sky really
opened up. She'd forgotten to check the weather that morning and didn't have an umbrella.

She covered a yawn before returning her attention to the
students, now stretching their backs over the barre following an hour of Ms. V's instruction. Their bodies formed a
bridge of stomachs, flat enough to roll a quarter down.

She walked beside the line of upside-down faces. "Good
job. Really reach for your calves."

Marta avoided eye contact as she passed. Nia didn't blame
her. Confessing to a stranger was embarrassing enough without

having to see said stranger the following morning. Nia tried not to let her eyes rest on Marta's stomach, which already looked less bloated than yesterday. Water weight drained fast. She clapped her hands. "All right, let's loosen our hamstrings with some grand battements."

The students pulled up from the barre, a wave of rising bellies. They stood beside the beam and placed their right hands on the wood. Nia admired the collective precision.

"Brush your foot on the floor before you kick," she ordered. "Really massage your toes against the ground."

Legs lifted into the air at ninety-degree angles or more. Aubrey and Lydia's working legs shot up toward their ears. Tati rolled her eyes at the pair. What the T twin didn't realize was that Aubrey and Lydia weren't showing off so much as competing with one another. The rest of the class didn't matter. The girls watched their reflections in the mirror, each noting the angles of her rival.

A competitive germ itched Nia's insides. She could easily extend into 180 degrees en pointe. More if she wanted. She looked away from the class stars, suppressing the desire to show off.

"Okay. Let's try some arabesque penchées," Nia said. "Use the barre for support."

Kim's athletic thigh stuck out at a right angle behind her. The girl had muscle, but the flexibility wasn't there. Marta had it. Her leg lifted to an oblique angle. Unfortunately, her balance was still off. Her standing leg wobbled, begging to bend. With luck, she would regain her center of gravity once she lost the weight.

June was also considerably flexible, though she lacked technique. Nia cupped the girl's heel in her palm and pushed her spindle leg a few inches higher, nearing a standing split.

"You can do it," Nia said. "Really feel the length in your legs. Stretch as high as you can go."

June's jaw clenched. Her pale face reddened as she brought her tiny foot higher. She reminded Nia of a child's drawing of a person, all lines with a circle head. No shape.

"Hey, Lydia." Nia turned to see Aubrey sashay over to her only competition. The girl smiled as though she'd just had a fantastic idea. "Let's get a pic of us in penchée position. It will make a cool shot for the yearbook."

Lydia's face lit up. Nia understood her excitement. An older, relatively popular kid was taking an interest. It couldn't be easy to break in at a boarding school where most kids had lived together for a year or more. Dance class was particularly cliquey.

Aubrey grasped Lydia's hand and led her into the center of the room. She dipped forward until her working leg made a straight line in the air. Lydia faced Aubrey and copied the motion, letting her torso drop parallel to the ground. Her raised limb, however, didn't form a vertical line like Aubrey's own. Lydia was several degrees shy of a full split.

"Ms. Washington," Aubrey shouted, "will you take a picture?"

"Okay. Hold it." Nia pulled her phone from her sweater pocket and hit the camera application. She centered the frame on the two girls and clicked.

"You got it?" Aubrey asked.

"Yes."

Aubrey's leg whirled down like a propeller. She ran over to Nia, hand outstretched. "Let me send it to myself."

Nia handed over the device. Aubrey typed in a number and hit the send key. A muffled beep sounded from a bag in one of the cubbies.

"I got it." Aubrey turned the phone to Lydia. "Look at our lines. We're almost mirror images."

Nia detected a slight dig in Aubrey's statement. The girls were "almost" mirror images because Lydia couldn't match Aubrey's flexibility. Judging from the photo alone, anyone would believe Aubrey to be the superior dancer.

Lydia continued to smile as though her fellow ballerina was being friendly.

Nia clapped, breaking the class' attention away from the primas-in-training. "Okay. Let's free stretch. Work out whatever feels tight. Pay special attention to your feet."

Marta sat on the ground and reached toward her toes, lengthening her back muscles. Lydia dropped into a deep lunge and then twisted to grab her back leg, stretching her inner thigh. The T twins joined Kim and Suzanne at the barre. They took turns pushing each other's legs toward a standing split, apparently determined that the starlets would not be unchallenged when it came time to audition for the fall performance.

Alexei approached June at the far side of the room. He rotated his ankle as he whispered. The girl rubbed the back of her shoulder. Her expression tightened.

It was okay to socialize on Nia's watch, but they still had to stretch. She walked toward them. "Alexei, if your ankle feels tight, you have to do more than just rotate it or the ligaments could get damaged. Resistance bands really help." Nia pointed to one of the cubbies by Ms. V's office. "I can grab you one and show you some strengthening exercises."

Alexei dropped his foot on the floor. His mischievous smile turned embarrassed. "My ankle is fine. I was just telling June what she missed in the dining hall this morning."

June looked up at Nia. Her pained expression wasn't from any physical ailment. "You saw Lauren's body. You

71

don't think Theo really killed her, do you? It could have been an accident, or maybe she was upset . . ."

Stirk's warning bellowed in Nia's head. "I don't know." Disappointment drew down June's face. She looked near tears.

Nia thought of the grief-counseling book on her kitchen counter. "If you feel upset by Theo's arrest, you know I'm an RA and I'm always available to talk."

June nodded vacantly, and Alexei stepped between her and Nia, ending their conversation. Nia scanned the room for other students that needed help or reminders to stretch during warm-downs.

Aubrey stood at the wall of windows. She stared outside, her face blank, eyes unfocused, as if lost in her own head. Joseph came up behind her. He grasped her waist. She pivoted to face him and then bent backward, using his grip like a support beam.

Joseph's hands inched down to just below Aubrey's hipbone. The moves fit a modern dance class, not high school ballet practice.

Nia approached the pair. "You guys look ready to practice lifts."

Joseph's hands retreated back above the belt. As Aubrey rose, his gaze zeroed in on the girl's small bust.

"We'll work on partner combinations soon. You can prepare for lifts by strengthening your wrists." Nia blathered to dissipate the tension. "I find a nice stretch is rotating the wrists with weights. A ten-pound weight in each hand is a good start."

The boy released Aubrey. Her cherry-painted lip protruded in an exaggerated pout. Joseph kept his eyes on Nia. "I'll try that," he said.

"Thanks, Nia." A Mona Lisa smile curled the edge of Aubrey's mouth. She batted her eyes at Joseph. "I have some ideas for exercises, too. Things that can really open up the pelvis."

The boy's hand grazed Aubrey's waist. "Really?"

Nia frowned. Making veiled sexual comments to your boyfriend in class was inappropriate, especially in front of a teacher.

"Aubrey, I'd appreciate—"

A bell rang. Ms. V stepped from her office. "Okay, class," she said, drawing out the *s* as if employing the French word. "See you tomorrow."

Aubrey's doll eyes fluttered at Nia, waiting for her to finish her interrupted statement.

Nia reconsidered making a big deal of Aubrey's innuendo. Ms. V would monitor their conversation. It would be difficult to explain what had happened to someone who hadn't seen the body language.

"I'd appreciate it if you would call me Ms. Washington."

Aubrey looked down her nose at her as if to ask, *Are you serious?*

"Mr. Battle was pretty adamant that I shouldn't let students use my first name."

Aubrey smirked. "Oh. Okay. I wouldn't want you getting in trouble."

The kids put on street shoes. Aubrey walked toward the door first, Joseph following at her heels. Before she exited, Aubrey looked over her shoulder at Nia. She flashed a triumphant smile. "Thanks for the picture, Ms. Washington."

Ms. V closed the door behind the last student. Her heels clacked against the floor like tap shoes as she returned to the center of the room. Taut cheeks wrinkled into a smile. "You are doing well with them. I believe yesterday's fouettés even impressed Aubrey."

"She's a polished dancer."

Pride lit Ms. V's face. "She came to me with considerable training, but I think we really brought out the shine in her."

Nia was tempted to say something about Aubrey's borderline inappropriate behavior with Joseph. But Ms. V's admiration for the girl made her rethink it. "She's not just a beautiful dancer. She's brilliant." Ms. V continued. "Top of the senior class and graduating a year early." The instructor leaned in and lowered her voice. "Her accomplishments are all the more impressive given her history. Aubrey's father died in a tragic accident when she was just seven. Her mother grew so depressed that she became something of a shut-in. The woman works and cares for Aubrey's younger brother, but that must be all she can handle. She never visits her daughter, hasn't seen one performance."

Ms. V touched Nia's arm. "Aubrey seems to have trouble really relating to the other students because of it all. Battle and I try to extend ourselves when we can."

Nia swallowed her anger. Flirting in class wasn't *that* big a deal. Hadn't she and Dimitri had inside jokes at SAB? There was no need to hassle the girl.

"She is a great dancer," Nia said.

11

Poisson [*pwa-SAWN*]

Fish. A position of the body in which the legs are crossed in fifth position and held tightly together with the back arched. This pose is taken while jumping into the air or in double work when the ballerina is supported in poisson position by her partner.

The rain waited behind an ashen curtain. Nia considered escape options. The path beside the lake was quickest, but she would have to pass Lauren's deathbed in the near dark. The lake would look like a black mirror, reflecting the blue girl in her nightmares.

She reassured herself that the long way made more sense. If it started to pour, she could take shelter in the boys' dormitory or the school store.

Nia hurried down the path. Droplets smacked the base of her neck. She increased her speed to a jog, but her soft-soled shoes couldn't keep pace. They slipped on the wet brick path. Her Achilles shivered. Her ankle wobbled. She slowed to a walk.

Just as the boys' quadrangle emerged beyond the hill, thunder cracked open the sky. Curtains of rain unrolled onto her. Water poured from her forehead and stuck on her eyelashes, clouding her vision. Her heels skidded on the walk. She yanked off her soggy leather shoes and ran. The boys' residences loomed like a mirage. She scanned the gothic structure for an archway or a balcony, some overhang capable of shielding the worst of the rain. A wall of blurred gray stone stood in front of her. She fumbled toward the entrance. The rain couldn't keep up like this for long. She needed someplace dry to stand for a few minutes, lest she slip and do more damage to her injured tendon.

Nia stumbled up the steps and dug her free hand into her sweater pocket for her photo keycard. Wet fabric clung to her fingers as she pulled the slick plastic tag into the open. She pressed it against the black keypad and slammed her weight against the entrance. The door didn't even jostle in the frame. No click or beep sounded. She pressed her key to the pad again. Still nothing.

Water overwhelmed the fabric band holding her hair in place. The bun tumbled loose. Strands stuck to the side of her face. Why wasn't her keycard working? Was it too wet?

She shoved her shoes beneath her armpit to free both hands. She rubbed the plastic on the inside of her soaked sweater and pressed it to the keypad again. No beep. She wiped the back of her hand against her eyes to better see the magnetic strip. It was just like the one in the girls' dorm: tap to unlock. Why wasn't it working?

The door clicked open. Peter stood in the frame. His muscled arms swelled from a fitted white T-shirt. He pulled her inside.

"Wow. You really got caught in it."

Water dripped from her clothing onto the stone floor. "I didn't check the forecast this morning. I thought I could make it to the school store before it really came down. Then I tried to get in here, but my keycard didn't work—"

"Yours won't open the boys' residences."

She peeled the sweater from her arms. "Why?"

"Safety precaution. Boys' cards don't open the girls' residences and vice versa. The school thinks it cuts down on inappropriate fraternizing." He chuckled. "It doesn't do much, but I guess it makes the parents feel better."

Nia draped the sopping sweater over her slick forearm. The rain had soaked through to the tank top underneath. Peter's eyes fell upon her chest. The wet tank clung to her breasts. She folded her arms over her top, hiding the nipples that the cold rain had called to attention.

His gaze fled to her bare feet. "I'll get you a towel. Follow me."

She walked down the dim hallway. Her wet toes squeaked on the cold stone floor. "But I'm a teacher. Shouldn't my card work?"

"The rule extends to teachers. My card won't open the girls' residences."

He pushed a door open. Light poured from the room into the dim hallway. "It's in case any perverts make it through the interview process. There was that case at Granger a couple years back. A gym teacher—volleyball coach, I think—got caught with a sixteen-year-old girl. Kids got pulled. The girl's parents sued. That school still hasn't recovered."

He held the door open. She stepped onto a mat just inside the doorway. The rough fabric scratched the soles of her exposed feet. More droplets ran down her legs onto the burlap.

The door shut behind her. Peter crossed the dark wood floor to another door. He'd changed out of the business casual outfit he'd worn at breakfast into basketball shorts and a Wallace T-shirt. He ducked into the other room and then emerged with a folded white towel in his palm. Nia dropped her shoes on the welcome mat and extended her forearms, careful to keep her dripping body centered on the two-foot square beneath her bare feet.

"Thank you." She pressed the terrycloth to her face, rubbing her eyes. Her cheeks dry, she shook open the towel to wipe down her arms and legs. Finally, she squeezed the damp rag around the hair clinging to her exposed shoulders.

"You came from the gym?" she asked.

"I was thinking of heading there before it started to pour." He looked out his window as he spoke, perhaps unwilling to watch her drag the towel across the slick cleavage spilling from her tank. His politeness pleased and embarrassed her. She wrapped the damp towel around her like a tube dress, covering her breasts.

"I teach that poetry elective I mentioned on Monday, Wednesday, and Friday, and I don't teach again until third period." Peter's eyes returned to her face as he spoke. "I find it's easier to go work out when I'm already up."

The weight of the wetness pulled the towel down her torso. She fought it up. "I only teach during the morning elective period and on Sundays, but I have choreography meetings every other evening this week. When we start rehearsing for the fall performance, I'll get some more after-school hours."

"I think that towel's had it. Let me grab you another one." He dipped back into the bathroom.

Peter's studio had the same layout as her dorm, but the décor was far richer. A tufted-leather sectional separated the living area from the rest of the apartment. A long, wood coffee table sat in front of it. Several books lay on the surface. She caught the title of the top one: *Portrait of the Artist as a Young Man*. To the right of the couch, a pair of matching bookcases reached toward the ceiling. Volumes filled each shelf. She could just see the bed to the left. It was at least double the size of the extralong twin that came with her room.

He strode from the bathroom with a thick white towel. "I found this. Not just washed, but not just used." He handed it to her. "I haven't gotten around to the laundry yet."

She shed the damp cloth and wrapped the new one around her torso. The dry, fluffy fabric drew the chill from her skin.

"Sorry to wash up on your doorstep like a drowned rat."

She regretted the adjective as soon as it slipped out of her mouth. She couldn't get Lauren out of her head.

"Don't mention it." He collected the used towel and tossed it over the back of the couch, apparently unconcerned about staining the leather.

"Do you want some tea? Warm up your insides?"

The scene outside Peter's window appeared dark and dashed, like a fuzzy television picture. She didn't want to go back out there, especially not when an attractive, apparently educated man was offering her tea in a comfortable, dry apartment. But the wet hair sticking to her face and her towel dress made her want to hide.

"I've put you out enough already."

"Not at all. I was just going to make some tea for myself." He walked into the kitchen. "The rain won't let up for a bit. Why don't you sit?"

Nia stepped onto the hardwood. "Thanks a lot. I'm sorry for showing up like this."

"Stop apologizing. Really."

Water clinked into a metal kettle. He pulled two mugs from the cabinet. Etched crystal glasses lined the shelf above the school-issue coffee cups.

She perched on the edge of the couch, folding her knees at a ninety-degree angle to minimize contact between her wet pants and the leather.

"Your place is really nice."

"Well, it's not exactly my place. But it's my furniture—whatever I could fit."

"You have good taste."

"Yeah, well . . ." He placed the mugs on the counter and joined her on the sectional, several cushions away. He crossed his foot over his knee. His exposed calf muscles looked long and bowed. Swimmer's legs. Nia traced the curve of his leg to the firm thigh, visible through the wide shorts.

Peter brushed the hair from beside his eyes. The gray weather had turned them an oceanic blue. He sipped his tea.

The silence unnerved her. Nia struggled to come up with some other compliment to pay for the hospitality. "Well, your apartment looks torn from a design magazine."

His foot jiggled against his knee. "My wife bought this stuff. She has expensive taste and she had an expensive decorator."

Of course he was married. Her luck with men demanded that he be somehow unavailable. Everyone that sparked her interest was either married, gay, or too young to get serious.

"Oh. Well, your wife has good taste, then."

Peter's nose wrinkled as if blasted by an offensive odor. "I meant ex-wife. Ex. Ex. Ex. We divorced over a year ago."

"I'm sorry."

Peter tucked away the blond strands that had fallen into his face. "We weren't right for each other. I met her when I still worked on Wall Street."

The kettle whistled, a soft hiss like a distant train. It grew louder as Peter walked into the kitchen. "She came from money." He yelled to be heard above the spitting kettle. "Her dad owned a hedge fund. I think she thought I would follow in his footsteps."

"You didn't want to?"

"No way." He transferred the kettle to a cool burner and then opened a cabinet. "I've got lemon, chamomile, Earl Gray." He smiled over his shoulder. "And plenty more."

"Lemon would be wonderful. Thank you."

He opened a yellow box and dropped a tea bag in each mug. Steam rose from the cups as he poured. He returned to the couch, a school mug in each hand. He put one on the coffee table in front of her before resuming his seat. She claimed it by the handle and blew away the wisps of white curling above the cup.

"What did you do on Wall Street?"

"Waste my best years." He sipped the drink.

Nia wanted more detail. But her questions had imposed enough. Guests—particularly uninvited, drippy ones—weren't supposed to give their hosts the third degree. She dipped her chin into the steam rising from the mug.

Peter sighed. "I always wanted to be a writer. I even got an MFA. But that's worth zilch in New York, and grad school wasn't cheap. So I took a job as an entry-level analyst, with the idea of paying the college loans off in a couple years and returning to writing. Flash forward nearly a decade and I'm married to a socialite, making a ton of money, and completely miserable."

Peter leaned back into the couch. His foot dangled lazily from his knee. He seemed completely relaxed, as if he'd explained many times how he ended up thirtysomething and bunking in high school dorms.

Nia felt uncomfortable enough for the both of them. She hated that her presence in his room made him feel the need to explain his choices. She wasn't anyone to judge.

"So, long story short, I quit four years ago, took a job here as an English teacher, and finished up a novel that I had started in grad school."

"Good for you. And I understand all about chasing dreams." She raised her mug in a show of camaraderie. "I've spent my whole life chasing a career that usually ends by forty."

"I wish my wife had understood that. At first, I think she thought it was romantic. She had this idea of me becoming famous. We got a house in the country, which she furnished to fit Hemingway. But, a couple years later, as the rejections flowed in and the savings dwindled, she realized she didn't want to be the wife of a high school English teacher, and she went back to her family."

He gestured with his mug. "We sold the house at a loss, and I got the furniture as a consolation prize."

Nia took a long sip. What could she say to that story? *Sorry? You're better off without her? Thanks for the tea?*

Peter rubbed the back of his neck. "I'm not bitter. I get it. I changed the game on her. And I'm happy here. I like teaching English and living on a campus and dreaming up imaginary people."

"Sounds like a nice life."

"So how about you? What brings a big-city ballerina here?"

Nia shrugged. "A downpour."

He raised his eyebrows. His hospitality and honesty demanded a real answer. But she didn't want to delve into the two-pronged reason that chased her to Wallace.

"I danced with a traveling company all last year. I over-exerted myself a bit and my foot needs some rest and rehabilitation. The company offered health insurance that I couldn't afford. Wallace has a pretty reasonable policy, even for me."

He raised his mug as if offering cheers for the school's medical plan. "Plus, I thought it might be nice to get a feel for teaching. Good dancers end up teaching at prominent schools, if they're lucky."

Peter reached his cup out toward her. She brought it down from her mouth. Ceramic clinked against ceramic. Peter flashed a naughty grin. "Here's to getting lucky."

12

Adagio [*ah-DAZJ-eh-o*]

At ease or leisure. A series of exercises following the centre practice, consisting of slow, graceful movements, which may be simple or of the most complex character, performed with fluidity and apparent ease.

D ry ringlets framed Nia's face. Her mug rested on the coffee table, long emptied of its contents. Peter had refilled it twice. When he last handed her the tea, he had settled closer than before, choosing the neighboring cushion rather than the bottom stroke of the L-shaped sectional.

Conversation had turned to classes and students. Peter discussed the work of several budding writers, beaming like a father. When you loved teaching, pride must stem from nurturing others.

He rolled his mug between his palms as he spoke. His hands were always in motion: pouring, patting, picking up, passing. His hairstyle provided a constant excuse for fussing with the long, slicked-back strands that continually broke free from his crown. She liked that his hands fluttered about. It allowed her eyes to follow them to different body parts: high cheekbones, broad shoulders, defined forearms.

"Theo had a poem accepted to a literary magazine just last month. I sent it in for him."

The arrest had been the elephant in the room during the conversation. Nia had avoided any mention of the morning, not wanting to upset her host. But now that Peter had brought Theo up, it seemed callous *not* to discuss the case.

"Have you spoken to him since . . ."

"Stirk doesn't want me reaching out." He bit his bottom lip and shrugged. "But his father says he's alright. All they have on him is some text message and a trumped-up motive about losing it because Lauren didn't want him back. I guess he was by himself on Saturday for a few hours too, so the police are claiming he doesn't have an alibi."

Would a lovesick poet kill his ex-girlfriend for refusing him? It didn't seem likely. But it did seem possible that Peter was romanticizing a favorite pupil. Everyone wanted to think the best of those they'd spent time with, if for no other reason than to excuse their own lack of observation. Every serial killer had some neighbor willing to volunteer as a character witness. *Nicest guy. Loved barbequing. Sports. A little quiet but in a pleasant way. No one could ever have believed he kidnapped young women and held them in his basement.*

Nia never bought that nobody actually suspected. People sensed evil. Most were simply too hell-bent on politeness to dig it out.

"If you ask me," Peter continued, "the police need to be looking for some weirdo in the area that might have sneaked onto campus during move-in madness."

Peter seemed so sure Theo wasn't guilty. But if rumors of the sex tape were true, then Theo couldn't just be the nice, sensitive student that Peter knew. The kid had sent around an intimate video, presumably without his partner's permission. That didn't show much respect for women—or, at least, for Aubrey.

"Did you see him with Lauren much?"

Peter seemed to withdraw, as though her question had created a wall between them. Nia wanted to bring him back with some compliment or comment about the weather, but she also wanted to know what happened to the girl she had discovered.

He cleared his throat. "They were together all the time last year. I would see them outside on the quad holding hands and talking."

Nia looked out Peter's window. The sky had spent its fury, and sunlight was breaking through. Droplets still tapped the walk, but there were too few to tell whether they shook from the trees. She imagined Lauren alive, sitting on an iron bench beneath the sagging willow at the end of the courtyard, cuddling with the boy Nia had sat next to just the day before. Theo was a big kid with large rowing arms. Lauren had looked slight and young, every bit fifteen. Physically, he could have killed her. But mentally?

"I think he really liked her," Peter continued. "But I don't think that he loved her intensely in any crime-of-passion way. Theo told me that she was really religious. I think that was basically code for she wouldn't sleep with him."

"She was fifteen."

He threw up his hands like a yielding soldier. "I'm not saying she should have done anything. But Theo's a popular kid, and I guess other girls offered. It sounded like some of the older rowers had ribbed him pretty hard last year about being a virgin."

Nia sighed. "High school. I wouldn't repeat it."

Relief spread across Peter's face. "I thought it would've been easy for a beautiful dancer. It's the shy guys that get the worst of it."

"Girls are worse than boys with bullying. They're just subtle about it. They make pointed comments about weight or clothes. They don't invite you to birthday parties or they tease you about your parents."

"You were bullied?"

Nia shrugged. The truth was yes, but she'd had bigger problems, like trying to afford toe shoes. The snide comments from fellow ballerinas had never been more than petty annoyances.

"I'm surprised a big kid like Theo would be bullied."

Peter picked up his mug and walked into the kitchen. "Bullied isn't the right word. Just teased, I guess." He placed the mug into the sink. "Nothing that would have made him angry enough to hurt Lauren. I think he was just done waiting for her and broke it off. He said he'd been seeing another girl."

Aubrey? The girl was a teenager's fantasy: classically beautiful, smart, and confident, with a contortionist's abilities and an aggressive sexual presence. Any horny high school kid would have traded in the good girl for a chance with the badass ballerina.

"Was the other girl a student?"

Peter pushed out his hands as though directing a car to stop. "I don't ask names. It was uncomfortable that he got into so much detail in the first place."

He filled his mug beneath the faucet and then dumped it back into the sink. Doing the dishes was a clear sign that the party was over. She unwrapped the towel. "Thank you for helping me warm up and dry off."

Peter's eyes darted to her cleavage, then to her face. "Anytime. Are you dry? Do you need a shirt or anything?"

She held out the towel to him. "If I leave in your shirt, the boys' quad will have something new to talk about."

Peter crossed the room to take the towel from her. "I can handle teasing."

"I'll change when I get back."

"I've enjoyed talking with you. Maybe we can do it again? Trade the tea mugs for some food and drink?"

Nerves tingled through her body. Peter was attractive and interesting. Leaving Wall Street for a greater passion was admirable. But should she date a coworker? What if it ended badly?

"We can go to Siwanoy. It's an Indian reservation just fifteen minutes outside of campus." A charming grin crinkled his blue eyes. "They have a casino with a nice restaurant. No one will see us."

Her body began to answer for her, nodding along to his words.

"Great," he said. "How about tomorrow, around seven?"

"Sounds good."

"I'll pick you up at your place."

13

Passé [pa-SAY]

Passed. An auxiliary movement in which the foot of the working leg passes the knee of the supporting leg from one position to another (as, for example, in développé passé en avant) or one leg passes the other in the air (as in jeté passé en avant) or one foot is picked up and passes in back or in front.

The cell alarm buzzed beside Nia's head. She slapped at the phone, face still pressed to her pillow. After a minute, she rolled up to a sitting position and glanced outside the window. A blue sky sparkled outside. The late morning sun had chased away the rain clouds.

She felt more tired than before. The taste of the sleep had made her hunger for a full eight hours. That was the problem with naps. Sometimes they refreshed, but if you were really exhausted, they just wiped you out.

She rose from the bed, body cracking like popping bubble wrap. The time on her phone indicated that it was 11:40 a.m. She had to get to the lunchroom.

She splashed water on her face and slipped into leggings and a tunic. The outfit worked outside of dance class and would be fine for later when Ms. V and Battle wanted her to demonstrate choreography suggestions. Her toe shoes were still in the studio.

Her ballet flats sat beside her door, as sad and soggy as a wet newspaper. Sneakers would have to do. She pushed her feet into a pair of tennis shoes and stepped out of the room.

"Hey, Nia."

Aubrey smiled as she locked her door. With all the running around, Nia hadn't realized that her own student lived next door. She made a mental note to introduce herself to the girls on her floor.

"Hi, Aubrey. I didn't know we were neighbors."

"Yeah. I'm always next to the RA." She snorted. "Guess my mom likes people keeping their eye on me."

The mom that never came to see her? Nia listened for any bitterness or sarcasm in Aubrey's tone. The girl sounded nonchalant, but that didn't mean she didn't care. Teenagers made it their business to sound as though everything was no big deal.

"You have a minute?" Aubrey asked.

In truth, no. She had to get to the cafeteria, all the way on the main campus, before lunch started at noon. But Aubrey was her student.

"Were you heading to lunch? I have to be at the student cafeteria but would love company on the walk."

"We all have to eat."

Aubrey led the way down the steps and out into the courtyard. In her uniform, the schoolmarm skirt shortened a few inches to show off ballet-sculpted legs, the girl was a walking advertisement for prep school. Aubrey continued to walk a few steps in front of Nia as they crossed the crowded quadrangle. Whatever she wanted to discuss, she didn't want to do it during the walk. Maybe she figured they would talk over lunch.

Nia guessed that Aubrey wanted to ask questions about auditions. She'd have to decide this year whether to sign up with a major company or go to college. Maybe she wanted to know why Nia hadn't been accepted into the New York City Ballet. What better way to learn than from others' mistakes?

Aubrey veered suddenly off the cobblestone path and onto the grass. She called over her shoulder. "I know a shortcut."

Nia followed her into a narrow area behind the girls' residence. She smelled garbage. A large dumpster sat beneath a square hole in the building, its contents broiling in the sun. This was where the trash chute let out.

Aubrey turned to face her. "So you found Lauren's body?"

The girl had brought her here, away from other students, to ask about Lauren's murder. Stirk's warning replayed in Nia's mind. But she couldn't pretend not to have seen the body. She'd already confessed to half the class.

"The dean doesn't want me to talk about it."

"The cops arrested Theo, though. So they think he did it. Do you know why? Did the police find anything near the body—hair or skin—to tie to the murderer?"

"You mean, did they find DNA?"

"Or anything else."

The intensity of Aubrey's stare bothered Nia. She tried to guess what was fueling it. Had Aubrey known Lauren? She had, apparently, been with Theo. Did she think he was innocent?

Aubrey's mouth twisted. She covered her eyes with her hand and sobbed, suddenly. "I'm sorry to have to ask." Her hand fell to her mouth before reaching out to Nia. "I was, um, kind of involved with Theo over the summer. Things didn't end well. It's frightening to think he might have hurt Lauren and that maybe, if I'd stayed with him, he would have hurt me instead."

Aubrey bit her bottom lip. She looked up and scrunched her brow, as though struggling to hold back tears.

"I'm sorry, Aubrey. I wish I could help. I don't know whether or not Theo did it."

"So you didn't see the police gather any evidence to indicate Theo did it? They didn't collect anything?" The girl blinked rapidly. "It's just, I need to know. I can't sleep thinking I might have come so close . . ."

Nia tried to put herself in her student's shoes. How would she feel if police had accused Dimitri of murder? Of course she'd want as much information as possible. Stirk had said the RAs should help the students. Aubrey didn't need platitudes. She needed answers.

"I heard that the cops think he did it because he sent a text message asking to meet Lauren at the boathouse and that he doesn't have a good alibi for his whereabouts Saturday. I didn't see anything by Lauren's body that they could tie to anyone, but I didn't stay that long."

Aubrey sniffed. Nia didn't see any tears, but if Aubrey were anything like her, she wouldn't cry in front of a stranger.

"Even if he did do it, he can't hurt you. The police have him."

The girl exhaled. "Thanks. I better let you go. Lunch already started. The cafeteria is up that way." She pointed to the road. "I'm going to wait for Joey. I just feel better when he's around."

Nia recalled the boys' lewd remarks from breakfast that morning. The poor girl probably didn't want to eat alone.

Aubrey hurried back toward the quadrangle. Nia watched her go, wondering whether she'd helped her student or just hurt herself by spilling her guts. She turned in the opposite direction and headed up the road.

*

Nia pushed the pasta on her plate with her fork. The acidity of the marinara sauce reminded her of the garbage. Nerves had squelched her appetite. She'd disobeyed Stirk's multiple warnings to keep quiet. The dean could fire her for insubordination if word got out.

She needed the health insurance to fix her foot. If she didn't get the shot, she wouldn't be able to get back in shape in time to audition in January. Even worse, her condition could deteriorate further. She was already walking, running, and dancing on an injured foot. What if the tendon burst? Her career would never recover.

The prospect made her physically ill, and the cacophony in the cafeteria wasn't helping to calm her nerves. She withdrew her phone, looking for something to distract her.

She hit the search application. A blank, rectangle box appeared beneath Google's multicolored icon. What could she search for? She answered the question with another. Would Aubrey tell the dean? She knew a little about the girl. The search engine would know more.

She typed in "Aubrey Burn, Wallace." The all-knowing Internet giant refined her query: "Did you mean Aubrey Byrne, Wallace?" She selected the corrected spelling.

A row of pictures topped the page. In each, Aubrey held a different plaque of some kind. A dozen links followed. Nearly all appeared to be press releases about awards and accolades. Aubrey had won a national science competition. She'd been accepted into Mensa for an IQ of 152. And she'd been admitted to American Ballet Theatre's summer intensive for the second year in a row.

One link read, "Dancers do IT best." What was *it*? Nia could guess, but she clicked on the link anyway. She wouldn't watch the video. But she did want to see if it was still up. Maybe she could help Aubrey get it removed.

A site opened with a large media player. Instead of a still image in the box, a message sat stamped in the center. "This video has been removed due to violation of the site's policy on nudity and sexual content." Beneath the video was a counter. It had 25,000 views.

For a noncelebrity, the number was massive. The school only had about a thousand students.

Nia hit the back button, returning to the page of Aubrey links. More awards, pictures of beaming teachers with arms draped around the sloped shoulders of their prized pupil. Aubrey's parents were not pictured or, judging from her scans of the articles, even mentioned. Wasn't Aubrey's mother alive?

Nia clicked the "next page" button. One link stood out from the list of academic societies, a *New York Times* article from nearly nine years earlier titled "Lifesaving Surgeon Dies in Crash." Nia clicked.

Philip Byrne, a prominent cancer surgeon whose pioneering methods of tumor removal saved thousands, died in a car accident this week. He was 53.

Police said Byrne was driving south on US Route 9W Tuesday night, during moderate snowfall, with his 7-year-old daughter in the front seat. They were returning from the girl's school in upstate New York. According to a statement by the child, a northbound tractor-trailer drifted across the yellow line. Byrne swerved sharply in an apparent attempt to keep the

*car from impacting with the passenger side. The
vehicle skidded on the icy road and slammed into
a tree. A branch pierced the driver's side window,
killing Byrne. His daughter suffered a concussion.
No other injuries were reported. Police are searching
for the truck driver.*

Nia stopped reading. Many teenagers lost parents, but
Aubrey's father had died in a particularly sudden, horrible
way, right in front of her. Nia scanned the article for survivors. His daughter, Aubrey, and a two-year-old son were
listed along with his wife, Nicole Withers, an attorney with
Bingham, Meyers, and Young in Manhattan. No uncles. No
aunts. No grandparents.

Nia typed in Aubrey's mother's name into the search box.
A headshot of a striking blond woman topped several pages
of links. Most were related to Philip Byrne's death. Several,
from before the father's accident, linked to precedent-setting
bankruptcy cases. Aubrey's mother either hadn't done anything notable since her husband's death or had ceased working altogether.

Nia tried to imagine the woman in the photo: privileged,
successful, unaccustomed to tragedy. What would a woman
like Aubrey's mother do after losing her husband? Would
she become drunk and depressed, barely able to care for
her young children, forcing her genius daughter to mature
early? Or would she remarry and ship her eldest to boarding
school, starting a new life free from painful memories?

Nia put her phone on the lunch table. Poor Aubrey. Her
father dies in front of her. Her mom abandons her. And,
after all that, her ex-boyfriend is arrested for murdering his
last girlfriend. No wonder teachers tried to look out for her.

Tragedy stalked Aubrey Byrne.

14

En Arrière [*ah na-RYEHR*]

Backward. Used to indicate that a step is executed moving away from the audience.

Nia shoved half a protein bar into her mouth as she walked across the girls' quad to her apartment. Her lips could barely close over the volume of food, but she already wanted another one. Why hadn't she bought more bars at the faculty cafeteria? She needed the calories.

Grueling didn't begin to describe the choreography session with Ms. V and Battle. The pair consistently disagreed on the moves the students would be capable of performing. They'd demanded she run through variations on dozens of combinations, arguing all the while.

Ms. V championed less intense choreography. The instructor envisioned a stage filled with pretty ballerinas performing facile positions that, when in sync, looked impressive. Battle wanted to push it. He imagined each girl showcasing a mastery of intermediate and advanced techniques. The parents, he'd maintained, donated to the dance program when they saw their kids performing like professional soloists, not members of the corps. In the end, the pair had struck a compromise. The majority of the students would execute pretty, synchronized steps; two female students would perform challenging pas de deuxs with Alexei and Joseph; and one star pupil would command the stage for five minutes with a dance filled with bravura: pointe work, fouetté turns, petite allegros, grand jetés, and an arabesque penchée.

Her sneakers squeaked up the stone steps leading to her building. It had rained again sometime that evening, painting every surface with a slick of water barely visible beneath the dorm's outdoor lights. She slowed. One bad slip could do in her Achilles for good. A dancer's feet were her prized possession. She'd sooner lose a hand than a toe.

Her pocket buzzed. She'd forgotten to call her mother back. Her thumb swiped the screen as she pulled it from her pocket. She'd inadvertently answered.

"Hello? Nia?"

Dimitri's voice slipped from the speakers. The sound of it stopped her breath. She wasn't ready to talk to him. But what could she do? Hang up?

"Nia?"

Her stomach felt hollow. She put the phone to her ear. "Hello?"

"It's Dimitri."

"Hi. Um, it's been awhile." She forced air into her voice. She needed to sound light and preoccupied, not sad and shocked.

"Yeah. Too long."

She couldn't murmur agreement. She wouldn't show any sign that she'd pined for him for the past year. She needed to continue climbing the steps. The motion would make the conversation more casual.

"How are you?" he asked.

"Good. Good." She added more conviction to the second word.

"I saw that the Janet Ruban troupe would be in New York City. Your mom had said that you were performing with them. I thought, maybe, we could get dinner while you're in town and talk."

Nia bit her lip. So he'd called to catch up because he'd seen that her small, former dance company would be in his neighborhood. He'd probably wanted to boast about his great life working with the New York City Ballet.

"I'm not with Janet's troupe anymore."

"Oh. Where are you?"

She surveyed her surroundings. Moonlight reflected off of the magnolia trees lining the courtyard, making their broad, wet leaves shine like crystals. The girls' dormitories resembled a sprawling, gothic castle. She was teaching at a beautiful, prestigious school. But she was still teaching. At her age, not dancing was failure.

"I'm actually an instructor at Wallace Academy. You know, the boarding school in Connecticut? They—"

"Are you okay?"

The concern sounded genuine. She didn't care. She didn't want his sympathy. Above all, she didn't want him to feel sorry for her. Pity was worse than rejection.

"Yeah. Of course. They just offered me a really great deal to teach for a year. Anyway, I was a bit tired of all the traveling with Janet's troupe, so I thought, why not? The students are very impressive. Most of them will go on to major companies, and I'm really involved in the choreography of the biannual shows, so I'll be able to add that to my résumé. Plus

I'm getting to work with Ted Battle. It's been great, like having a master class on grand jetés every day. When I go back to audition next year, I think all this experience will really put me in a better position." She spat out the sales pitch in one breath, afraid that a pause might sap her courage to go through with it.

"You should be here. You're better than these girls."

The compliment needled her. If she'd been better, then she would have gotten picked for NYCB's company.

"I'm sure they're just fine."

"Yeah, well . . . I thought you were still traveling. I miss you."

The three words sounded stale. She'd waited to hear them for months after their breakup. She'd imagined him surprising her at a show with roses and a teary-eyed apology for caving to his parents' lectures about the perils of settling down young.

"I could drive up to Connecticut. Saturday, maybe?"

"They keep me pretty busy."

"I want to . . . We should talk."

"We are talking."

"In person. I want to see you."

No. He would have the advantage in person. The sight of him would weaken her. She would let her attraction to him blur the only fact that mattered: he'd wanted to see other people. He'd said he wanted her, only her, forever. Then he'd changed his mind.

"What do you want to talk about?"

"I don't want to do this over the phone."

"Do what?"

"How about I come up Saturday? We can go to brunch. I'll take you—"

"I don't think I'll have time. There's so much choreography to—"

"So you don't ever want to see me again? Is that it?"

Panic gripped her chest. They'd never said anything that final. "No. It's just they keep me busy. And—"

"I'll come up Saturday. Say, ten o'clock?"

Dimitri wouldn't give up. When he wanted something, he kept after it. She'd admired his persistence in dance school. Now it overwhelmed her. "Okay. I guess it will be good to catch up."

"Yes. I'll see you Saturday. I love you, Nia."

The dial tone rang in her ear. He'd hung up before she could reply. She was glad that he had. She was afraid of what she might say.

15

Brisé [*bree-ZAY*]

Broken, breaking. A small beating step in which the
movement is broken.

Nia removed her pointe shoes, revealing a large bunion
where the phalange bone in her big toe connected to
the longer metatarsal. The bunion wasn't the cause of
the pain shooting from her foot up her calf. Neither was the
fresh blister that had formed during the morning's extended
demonstration of échappés sur les points, which were like
ballerina jumping jacks. It was her heel again, throbbing
from constantly rolling her foot onto her toes.

She shoved the pointe shoes into her cubby and then dug
her knuckles beneath her ankle. She rubbed her foot as the
class filed out of the door. The health insurance couldn't
come soon enough.

Marta exited the studio first. The T twins and Kim followed behind, walking slowly so as to overhear Alexei and
June's competing opinions about the school e-mail concerning

"a student's arrest." Alexei insisted that the school should have revealed Theo's name. After all, he said, everyone knew he did it.

Lydia and Suzanne brought up the rear. They, too, were in the midst of conversation, but classical technique, rather than school gossip, was the subject. As the new girl, Lydia couldn't lend any insights into Theo's guilt or innocence. Aubrey and Joseph were last out of the room. He draped his arm around her shoulders, a possessive and comforting gesture. Aubrey leaned into his side. Nia wondered whether she'd told him about being with Theo and about her concerns that he would have hurt her too. Joseph had probably heard about the tape.

Nia's foot still ached as she took the long way back to her dorm. Not wanting to pass the lake was the primary reason for taking the roundabout way. But there were also other benefits. The path passed the boys' quad, where she might run into Peter. *Best way to forget about an old flame is to stoke a new fire.* That was also one of her mother's sayings, though not one that Nia had taken to heart—at least, not yet.

She was still hung up on Dimitri. His parting words from their brief phone conversation replayed in her head. He'd said he'd loved her. Loved her! Had he realized that they were meant for each other, or was he between girlfriends and suffering a momentary pang of nostalgia?

Nia tried to extinguish her excitement. Even if he did love her, so what? His love wasn't lasting. She couldn't open herself up to getting hurt again. She'd just started to consider moving on. Of course he would show up now, reminding her of the past, trying to make sure she still waited on the sidelines for him while he played the field.

An SUV parked on the lawn outside the boys' dormitory. This one didn't have police badges or lettering. Nia doubted that it belonged to the detectives. The words "Range Rover" glimmered in the sunshine. Surely, Connecticut police departments didn't pay for detectives to cruise around in a car that expensive.

The SUV's trunk arched in the air like a mechanical claw. The dormitory door swung open. Peter carried a box out to the trunk. Theo followed behind, rolling a suitcase.

Nia stepped toward them and then stopped. She didn't want to appear nosey. But she did want to know why Theo, who'd only been arrested yesterday, was out of jail and leaving campus.

She waved to Peter. "Do you guys need any help?"

Peter turned to Theo and said something inaudible. The boy shrugged a response. Peter waved her over.

Her heel still throbbed as she hustled to the stairs. Carrying boxes was not recommended exercise for a foot injury. But curiosity beat out her better judgment.

"Theo is going to spend some time with his folks. His parents are in there packing. If you want to grab a box, that would be great." Peter leaned toward her. He lowered his voice so that Theo couldn't hear. "It probably would be good for them to see that the whole school hasn't abandoned him and that the faculty is being supportive."

Nia hadn't made up her mind about Theo's innocence. But she had already offered to help pack his bags. "Sure. Is the door open?"

"No, I'll—"

A crash interrupted him. Theo had thrown the suitcase into the interior. It had collided with a ceramic table lamp, exploding a hole in the lamp's belly. The missing piece sat on the trunk's carpeted floor, an unconcealed shiv glinting in the sunlight.

"It's so messed up." The boy shook his head. "It's just so messed up."

Peter squeezed his shoulder. "You'll be back. They don't have any evidence except some circumstantial nonsense about a phone call—"

"Not a phone call. A text message that they say came from my phone but that I didn't even send." Theo raked his fingers through his hair. "I wasn't even on campus when they think she was killed. It's like they're out to get me or something. I didn't do anything." He shook his head and rubbed beneath his nose. "It's totally messed up."

"I know." Peter again laid a hand on Theo's shoulder. The gesture would have seemed frigid if Nia hadn't known that any teacher-student contact was forbidden. Peter was risking reprimand for even such a small measure of support.

Teacher and favorite pupil shared a moment. Nia felt awkward witnessing it, but she couldn't slink away now. She spoke to remind them that she stood there. "What can I help pack?"

Theo eyed Nia like a poker player trying to determine if the other guy was bluffing. Brow lowered. Forehead wrinkled. He swatted at a tear on his cheek.

"Thanks, but my parents have it. They're not really up for talking."

"I understand," she said before Peter could press the issue. She didn't want to meet Theo's parents. They'd probably be crying. And what comfort could she offer?

She didn't know whether Theo was guilty of murder. But, given the rumors, he wasn't *that* innocent.

16

Divertissement [*dee-vehr-tees-MAHN*]

Diversion, enjoyment. A suite of numbers inserted into a classic ballet. These short dances are calculated to display the talents of individuals or a group of dancers.

Too sexy. Nia frowned at the little black dress as she examined her reflection in the bathroom mirror. The built-in bra squeezed her bust, propping it above the scoop neckline like a shelf. The dress didn't say come hither so much as *come 'n' get it*.

She didn't want Peter to get the wrong impression. Though she wasn't sure *come 'n' get it* was the wrong impression. Her body craved contact, and the call from Dimitri had made it worse, bringing back memories of the two of them together. She felt tight, anxious, uncomfortable beneath her skin. She needed a release.

Still, this LBD wasn't approved for first dates. Better to opt for a more casual look capable of blending in at an upscale place. Something pretty, feminine, and summery. Floral.

Nia shed the second-skin fabric and frowned at the scant contents of her closet. She didn't own anything sufficiently girly. Dance clothes, a skirt suit, and a few solid-color dresses hung in front of her. Nothing flirty. Nothing expensive. Peter's ex-wife would have worn pricey, designer clothes.

She pulled a Grecian-looking frock from a hanger and slipped it over her head. The cowl neckline cradled her cleavage. About the same amount showed as with the tank dress, but the draping and creamy color softened the impact. The cowl continued in the back, exposing the cappuccino expanse from her shoulder blades down to the v of her waist. Sexy, but not begging for attention. Better.

She swept her flat-ironed hair into a high ponytail that highlighted her defined back. If she didn't flaunt other assets, she could show off her jutting shoulder blades and narrow waist. She opened her makeup bag. Neutral eyes and red lips were the look of the moment. She swept a taupe shadow from eyelids to brows before lining her lashes with a deep brown pencil. She finished with a coat of black mascara and cherry-colored lip-gloss.

The clock on her nightstand showed ten minutes 'til. Better early than late. She dusted her fingertips against her forehead, pulling down some face-framing hairs from her ponytail. She glanced at her reflection one more time before locking her door for the night.

Nia descended the stairs and stepped out into the warm evening. Peter wasn't meeting her at the door for multiple reasons. First, students could see him. She didn't know if Wallace frowned upon workplace romance and didn't want to find out. Second, gossip circled the campus via an indelible digital network of smartphones and computers. A web search for her name and "dance" yielded three results: a winning video audition for SAB's summer intensive, a favorable review of her solo with Janet Ruban's troupe, and a blurb from one of SAB's calendars. She didn't want a fourth result to point to a message thread about the new dance teacher's dating life.

She rounded the building and entered the student/faculty parking lot behind it. Half a dozen cars were scattered across the asphalt: Volvos and Hondas, a few older luxury sedans, BMWs, Mercedes, Audis—all brands rich parents either purchased for the safety ratings or passed down when they traded up for the new model. A campus security car blocked several empty spaces. Its lights shone, prepared for the last of the daylight to slip behind the buildings.

Nia heard a door open. Peter stepped from the driver's side of a black BMW. The shiny black color and sleek lines hid the sedan's age. She guessed the vehicle was at least three years old, given Peter's history. Wall Streeters, not high school writing professors, bought status cars. He probably couldn't sell it for anything close to what he'd paid. Or maybe he didn't want to renounce all the comforts of his former life.

"Wow." He mouthed the compliment as she approached. His lips brushed her cheek. Warm breath caressed the nape of her neck. She wanted him to kiss her already.

Wow was good. Better than nice. Almost as good as beautiful.

"I can clean up?"

"You look amazing."

Amazing trumped wow. But it didn't necessarily mean she looked appropriate for their date. Nia examined Peter's clothes to gauge whether she had chosen wisely. He wore near-black pants and a matching button-down. The outfit was part suit alternative, part bus boy, fit for a fancy restaurant or a coffee shop. The dark navy color electrified his eyes, and the close fit displayed his lean body and defined arms.

Muscles tensed in her back where she wished he would touch her. She wanted to feel his hand rest right on her waist, to sense the warmth of his fingertips on the small of her back.

Nia pinched the light jersey fabric flowing around her thighs. "I thought this might be an improvement from terry cloth."

"That was a good look too." He offered his hand. "We're this way."

He opened her door. She slipped into the passenger seat and leaned over to release the driver's side. Her stomach grazed the gearshift as she stretched for the door handle. The awkwardness of the move didn't matter. The act helped level the playing field. It said, You open my door, I'll let you in. You pay for dinner, I'll get drinks or dessert. Sex will be a mutual decision, not a way of repaying an evening out. Her body wanted to sleep with him, but she hadn't made up her mind about whether she would. It was only their first real date.

Peter smiled "thanks" as he slipped into the leather seat. He turned the ignition. His hand reached toward her thigh, then landed on the shifter.

"It's manual," he said. "They're a dying breed. Even sports cars come automatic now. The computers switch faster than any human."

"Then why do manufacturers still make them?"

He palmed the shifter and jerked it into position. He grinned at her. "They're more fun."

He revved the engine. The car growled. The seat rumbled, vibrating her thighs like a massage chair. She eyed the gearshift, trying to anticipate his next move.

The security officer flashed his high beams, visually admonishing them to keep the noise down. Peter yanked the stick. The car leapt out of the lot onto the street and then zoomed down the hill to the guard stand.

They each flashed their IDs to a young campus security officer. The man pressed a flashlight against the cards, like a convenience store clerk looking for the magnetic strip on a hundred-dollar bill. Rather than hand her ID back to Peter, he emerged from the guard booth to deliver the card through the passenger window. He checked the card once more before passing it over.

The car sped through the school's gated entrance. Sunset washed Peter's face and hair in a golden hue. She cracked her window, unleashing the country smells outside: cut grass, flowers, the faint sweetness of manure mixed with asphalt and rubber. The wind whipped her ponytail around her face like a tassel and freed Peter's slicked back strands.

She liked his hair loose. It gave him a reformed grunge vibe. He looked like a cleaned-up Kerouac: educated and artistic but still a bad boy. Who didn't like a bad boy?

"What's the restaurant like?"

"Nervous?"

"No. Why?"

"I heard ballerinas are picky about food."

"Nope. When you dance for six hours a day, you can gobble up anything."

He smirked. "That so?"

"Steak, chicken nuggets, a Big Mac—I'm game. As long as it's not a Blimpie's."

"Got something against footlongs?"

She eyed him. Did he intend the sentence to have a sexual connotation or did he find the addition of "sandwich" unnecessary?

"I worked there in high school to pay for whatever the ballet scholarship didn't. We ate for free. Let's just say too much of a good thing."

They had the kind of conversation that didn't require eye contact, sharing generally favorable opinions about Wallace and life in the dorms. Mostly, Nia talked. Peter seemed comfortable enough in his own skin to listen to the air barreling through the windows without additional commentary. Nia couldn't relax into silence. Each quiet moment criticized her conversational skills. She admonished herself for failing to fill the space with some opinion certain to create a connection between them. She only knew of three things Peter liked: writing, his students, and driving. They had already discussed driving.

She yelled over the wind. "What's your novel about?"

Peter dragged his bottom teeth over his top lip like a bulldog. "Ah, the dreaded question."

"Oh. If you don't want to talk about it, I—"

"No. I do want to talk about it. It's just that's part of my problem—arguably *the* problem. I'm shit at condensing it for discussion."

"I understand." She didn't. Didn't storytellers tell stories? If he wrote it, why couldn't he talk about it?

"It's about class differences, I guess, and what American society values . . . How people are able to overlook poor qualities in pretty packages."

His explanation didn't sound like a story. Stories—even those in ballets—had a framework. Who was his hero? What was the plot? What happened to his characters?

"Who's telling the story?"

"A wannabe options trader." Peter laughed. "But it's not really about the narrator. It's like . . ." He smacked his lips together. "Imagine *American Psycho* told by *The Great Gatsby's* Nick Carraway."

She'd read the latter in high school. She didn't know the former. Stories about serial killers never interested her. Too violent. Too removed from her reality. In Nia's experience, the biggest threats were people you knew and your own limitations.

"Sounds interesting. I'd like to read it."

It wasn't a complete lie. If Peter's book proved brilliant, she could justify her attraction to him as about more than good looks and availability. If it was horrible, well . . . How could someone who landed a job at one of the most prestigious boarding schools in the country lack talent?

Peter smirked. "My ex read it and that didn't turn out so well. I'm not sure my book does me any favors in the romance department."

The highway suddenly widened into four lanes. A blue glass building pointed above the trees like a trapped glacier. The road curved. As the pavement straightened out, she could see the building in its full glory: a miniskyscraper in the middle of nowhere. Nia couldn't decide whether the monolith was a beautiful surprise or a blight on the bucolic landscape.

Peter pulled into a semicircle driveway. He killed the engine. Her door clicked open. Nia stepped onto a slate walkway as Peter handed his keys to a man about her age and color.

The man slid into the driver's seat. As they walked into the restaurant, Nia felt Peter's fingertips on her bare back. She pressed against him, coaxing his palm to stay without words. Body language worked so much better for her than banter.

*

Blimpie's couldn't hold a candle to the casino's restaurant. The Wapasha "Red Leaf" Trattoria was located on a separate floor from the casino, away from the smoky blackjack tables and dinging, whistling slot machines staffed by elderly ladies. A tinted glass exterior belied a cozy interior filled with old world Italian decorations and smells. The designers had retained intimacy by tucking tables beneath archways and in corners rather than putting them right against one another in order to fill the place with as many patrons as possible. The menu was expansive and reasonably priced, enabling Nia to order the branzino without fear of breaking Peter's bank.

He selected an $80 bottle of red wine to accompany the meal. Her palate wasn't sophisticated enough to parse the flavor difference between the pricey wine and the far cheaper bottles she'd sampled after opening night shows, but she could tell the texture seemed smoother and dangerously easy to swallow. The glass she sipped while they'd waited for dinner filled her head with warmth. It settled her down and allowed her to enjoy relaxed conversation. By the time they exited the restaurant, at least one more glass of wine had slipped down her throat, sneaking past her first-date defenses thanks to Peter's habit of topping off her drink each time he refilled his own.

She snuggled into his side as they approached the elevators. "Thank you for dinner. I've had a really nice time."

"The night's not over yet."

Was he assuming she would return to his place? She couldn't exactly blame him, given all the gazes and giggles that had bubbled from her during dinner. She blamed the wine and his good looks, not to mention a year of pent up sexual energy. Still, she didn't want him thinking her easy. It was just the first date.

"What do you have in mind?"

"I want to see you dance."

They took a glass elevator up to the top floor. A burly bouncer in a black suit stood outside an onyx wall beside a velvet rope. There wasn't a line. There wasn't even an indication that there would ever be one. The casino crowd Nia had glimpsed on her way to the restaurant hadn't seemed like clubbers, though maybe one or two had a grandchild that listened to house music.

The bouncer grasped the rope as they approached, as if debating whether to let them in immediately or make them wait as advertisements to passersby. He scanned the elevator bank. Apparently not seeing anyone to impress, he checked her ID and unhooked the rope.

Techno music battered her ears like a jackhammer. She gripped Peter's hand as they made their way through a near-black hallway into a dim open room. The club appeared about a third full, which was more than Nia had expected. Women gyrated in the center of a black floor. Men watched at a clear-glass bar, illuminated by blue LEDs and adorned with blown glass spikes to resemble something deep sea and threatening—part bar, part anglerfish.

Peter weaved through a group of men clustered near the exit, ensuring last licks at whoever caught their attention. Some of the dancing women watched as they approached, breaking the illusion that the music had entranced them past the point of noticing the men on the sidelines. The women checked her out. They ogled Peter.

He seemed not to notice. He pulled her to him as they reached a clearing. The beat consumed her body. She pressed her pelvis against his and dipped back until her ponytail grazed the ground. She popped up and rose to her toes. His arms wrapped around her waist. She slipped from his embrace, gyrating to the floor in a modified grand plié, more Beyoncé than ballet. She slinked back up toward him. His blue eyes shimmered, wide and wild. He pressed his lips to hers.

One techno song blended into another. Nia didn't like the second one: a clunky remix of a current pop star's hit with a sped-up country song. It never settled into a rhythm. After trying to gyrate to a few bars, she stopped in the middle of the floor and pulled Peter toward the bar. Water would help ward off any foot cramps.

Peter misread the tug. "You're right. Let's get out of here."

His hand cupped her side as they walked past the men watching them leave the floor. He strode with one arm propped out, as if ready for a fight. One of the men shouted.

"Wow, look at that."

The group's attention snapped toward the bar. Instinctively, Nia and Peter followed their head tilts, rubberneckers beside a car crash. A girl stood on top of the glass counter, her leg stretched out behind her in an arabesque. Long, blond hair hid her face, but it fell away as she tossed her head back to swallow the shot in her hand. Aubrey.

Men hollered for the kid to have another drink, unaware or unconcerned that the contortionist was only sixteen. Aubrey tossed her head like a teenager asking for daddy's wallet.

Peter turned away from the bar. His hand pressed against her side, urging her to keep walking.

"That's one of my students."

"No. Wallace kids can't get in here. They check ID."

"No, it is." She stepped toward the bar. Aubrey dipped into a grand plié that exposed whatever she wore beneath her mini dress to the crowd of guys sitting below her. The men howled.

Nia knew she had to do something. The girl didn't have involved parents, and she'd already had to deal with the fallout from a sex tape. Nia didn't want to stand by while Aubrey put her safety at risk.

Her student took another shot to loud applause. Nia slipped into the crowd. Peter followed.

They pushed through the cheering men. At first, the group parted to let them through. When it became clear they were headed toward Aubrey and not the bartender in the corner, elbows shot out. Openings filled with flesh. Peter bumped against her as some guy shoved him.

"Get back to the cheap seats, dude," the man snarled. Puffy, veined biceps protruded from the stranger's short-sleeved black shirt.

"That girl is a minor, dude." Peter mocked the man's Long Island accent. "You touch her, you'll be notifying everyone within a mile of your house for the rest of your life."

The man sneered. "Might be worth it."

Peter tensed beside her. He faced the man, hands curled into fists. Nia pulled his arm and his attention back to the bar.

"Aubrey!" She yelled over the crowd. "Aubrey!"

The men towered over her. Body heat clouded the air above. She turned to face Peter.

The music and hooting forced her to scream. "I need you to lift me!"

She turned her back toward him. Hands pressed into her armpits. She grabbed his wrists and pushed his grip down to her hipbone. Fingers tightened around her pelvis. She jumped as he lifted, helping him raise her torso above his head. She lowered herself onto his shoulders. He gripped her legs. Aubrey performed a deep backbend to pick up yet another shot. Nia waved frantically. "Aubrey!" The screams cut into her throat. "Aubrey!"

The girl made eye contact. She pointed to the door and then dismounted from the counter, wisely choosing to land behind the bar rather than in the arms of the crowd. The men whined for her to return. She pointed at Nia.

The crowd parted for the strange man with the other woman on top of his shoulders. Perhaps they believed Aubrey's fellow performers were coming to join in.

When they hit the bar, Peter reached above his head to her waist. He placed her on the counter. A few men whooped, anticipating a second act. She quickly hopped down to where Aubrey stood. Backlit shelves of bottles cast a blue hue across the girl's fair skin.

"What are you doing here? This is a night club."

Aubrey slapped her palm against her forehead. "Shit. I thought it was book club."

"We're taking you back with us."

Aubrey smiled. "That's awesome. I took the shuttle bus here and thought I would have to bum a ride with one of these assholes. You two are much better."

Aubrey grabbed Nia's arm like they were BFFs. She skipped while Nia strode around the bar toward the safety of her six-foot-plus date. Peter grasped Nia's free hand and led them through the mix of awed, bewildered, and pissed-off faces. They burst outside and past the doorman.

"The car is this way," Peter said.

"Nee-aaah." Aubrey cooed her name as if it were a piece of juicy gossip. "Dating Professor Andersen. Nice. The female contingent of the poetry club is going to swallow a box of aspirin and disappear into the lake."

So much for avoiding the rumor mill. Nia dropped Peter's hand. "We're two colleagues who met for dinner."

Aubrey stopped walking as if she had slammed into a wall. She released Nia's arm. "I saw you two on the dance floor." She winked.

Nia ignored her. "Those men are much older than you."

Aubrey laughed.

Nia wanted to slap the stupid, smug look off of Aubrey's face. Didn't she understand that she'd put herself at risk performing on a bar for a bunch of drunken men twice her age? Did she have an alcohol problem?

"Aubrey, you have to be more careful. When we get back, we can get together with your mom and some people."

Aubrey kept laughing. "Are you kidding me? I don't need an intervention. Ask your 'colleague.'" Aubrey scrunched her fingers into air quotes as she said the last word. "I'm Wallace's superstar student. I just like to have fun. Right, Mr. Andersen?"

Peter cleared his throat. "This isn't fun."

Aubrey yawned. "I'm tired. Can we just go to the car? You guys can debate disciplining me on the ride back."

The girl inserted herself between Peter and Nia. She wrapped her arms around their waists and walked lock step, like they were all pals headed home from a night of partying. "I vote for spanking," she said.

Nia wrenched from the girl's embrace. "That is not an appropriate joke for—"

"What I saw you two do on the dance floor wasn't appropriate either."

"You don't seem to realize how serious this is," Nia said.

"Yes. Sex is very serious business." She giggled.

Peter touched Nia's arm. "She's drunk. Let's not stand here and argue."

Nia marched back to the valet station, Peter trailing her. Aubrey chuckled and skipped behind like they were all on some hidden camera show where only she had glimpsed the boom microphone.

Nia watched Peter pay the attendant to avoid seeing Aubrey's underwear as the teen climbed over the front seat into the back. Aubrey lay down.

Nia dipped her head into the car. "Are you going to be sick?"

"Just relaxing. Leather feels so good."

Nia settled into the front passenger seat and waited for Peter to start the car. A streetlight glowed over the parking lot attendant station. Peter stood beneath it, looking handsome, far away, and totally unavailable. Aubrey had killed the mood.

"The leather feels sooo good," Aubrey repeated.

Nia refused to take the bait.

Peter jumped into the driver's seat and sped out of the lot. He leaned over to Nia. "We'll be home in ten. No traffic."

"Thanks." She placed her hand over his. "I'm sorry," she mouthed.

"It's not your fault." His eyes rolled toward the backseat where Aubrey gyrated to mental music.

Peter sped through farm country as if fleeing a crime scene. If a drunk teenager hadn't been sprawled in the backseat, Nia might have believed he wanted to get back to tear her clothes off. But Aubrey's presence had shifted them both back into work gear. She guessed he simply wanted to return home.

She understood the desire. The lack of sexual anticipation sapped her energy. The wine weighed on her eyelids. Still, she wished Peter would pay some attention to the speed limit. She didn't want to explain why a teacher and an assistant were racing home with a scantily clad minor that smelled like lime and liquor in the backseat. She also doubted Aubrey would back them up with the truth.

Peter turned the air conditioning to full blast. He either needed the cold to stay focused on the empty road or hoped the rush of air would drown out Aubrey's stream of inappropriate chatter. The girl moaned every time the car hit a pebble. She made kissy faces at the rear-view mirror.

Nia whirled to face the backseat. "Enough. Stop it."

"Stop what?" Aubrey scoffed. "Don't tell me what to do. You really think that our five- or six-year age difference makes you so much more mature than me? In a couple years, it won't matter at all. Why don't you let me enjoy myself?"

"Because you're hurting yourself."

"I didn't know you cared." Aubrey leaned forward, shoving her head between the seats.

"You want to save me? There are all these sad girls in our school that cut or regurgitate their food or snarf Adderall because they can't take the competition at Wallace. Why don't you save one of them instead of bothering me?" Her arms jutted into the space between the front seats, palms out as if praying. "Go ahead and touch. No scars. I'm just fine."

Nia returned her attention to the darkness enveloping the car. She folded her arms over her chest. Aubrey slunk into the backseat.

Maybe Aubrey was right. Her tragic past hadn't stopped her from achieving considerable success. Still, Nia was Aubrey's RA and teacher. She couldn't stand back while the girl sneaked into clubs and got bombed.

Peter turned his attention from the road. He whispered. "Let's just get her to the dorm. I'm tired. I really don't feel like spending the night explaining anything to Stirk."

Nia swallowed her protest. Turning Peter into an unwilling witness before his boss might squelch whatever burgeoning feelings he had for her. And for what? Finding one dead teen didn't mean Nia had to go around trying to save people who didn't want saving.

Nia again twisted toward the backseat. Aubrey's face peeked into the glow from the dashboard. Nia met her fierce blue eyes.

"Telling you to respect yourself won't make you do it. You're going to have to want that. Someday, you will. I just hope that day comes before you run into the wrong guy."

Aubrey's lips spread into a smile. "The wrong guy better hope that, too."

17

En Avant [*ah na-VAHN*]

Forward. Used to indicate that a given step is executed moving forward.

J oseph stretched alone on the far side of the classroom, glowering at his reflection in the mirror. An aura of angry energy surrounded him. It warned against approach as clearly as bared teeth.

He'd ignored Aubrey all class—not that the girl had exactly tried to talk to him. Word traveled fast on campus. Maybe he'd heard about Aubrey's night—or, at least, that she'd left campus without him. Nia wondered who would have ratted her out. She and Peter certainly weren't sharing a story about bringing back a drunk, underage teenager and then failing to report her behavior to the dean.

Aubrey had surprised Nia by sweeping in five minutes early, arranged like a perfect bouquet of cream and pink, skin rubbed clean, a hint of gloss moistening her lips. She had walked toward Joseph, as usual. He'd immediately crossed to the other side of the room. Aubrey had then continued on toward Marta, as if the virtual stranger had been her intended target the whole time. She'd settled down beside the girl and said something to make her smile. During class, she'd whispered what appeared to be pointers, resulting in one of Marta's better practices. Aubrey would say something and the girl's stomach would tighten in, her butt would lift.

Aubrey had also been extra nice to Lydia. After Ms. V left the room in Nia's care for stretching, Aubrey had offered to push Lydia's leg higher to aid with the arabesque. Lydia had eagerly taken her up on the offer.

Aubrey's helpfulness annoyed Nia. She wanted the teen to be so overtly disrespectful that Battle or even Ms. V could easily believe their prima-in-training's self-destructive behavior. As it stood, Aubrey's in-class attitude made the prior night's events sound like exaggerations at best and fabrications at worst.

Nia glanced at the clock. Two more minutes until class ended. She wouldn't have to stomach Aubrey's false alter ego much longer.

Talia struggled with a full split against the wall. Nia knelt beside her and pushed her palms against the girl's back, forcing Talia's long legs to spread along the painted cement. "You almost have it."

The girl grunted as her pelvis pressed closer to the wall. Her breathing quickened. A small "ow" escaped.

Nia patted her shoulder. "All right." She looked around the room for anyone else that needed her help. Alexei and June gossiped as he pushed a bony knee into her back, forcing her legs into a wider split against the mirrors.

"It's the lamest excuse. You're in Claremont to meet with some girl during move-in weekend? I don't think so."

"Well, maybe he was. She was killed Saturday evening, right? Her roommate last saw her around four, I think. Saturday night is date night. Theo could have gone to Claremont, even though it's a bit far. It's a cute town. It has nice restaurants. The train from the city goes straight there."

"You are hopeless. If he was there meeting someone, don't you think they would have come forward?"

Nia moved away from them. She could only hear so much about Theo's arrest. The media loved the case, but Nia had yet to watch a program that really delved into the facts. Most flashed pretty photos of Lauren and let "experts" pontificate about teenage privilege and rage. To her knowledge, the police hadn't released an official time of death. But Saturday made sense. Peter had said that Theo's inability to prove his whereabouts Saturday evening had been one of the reasons for his arrest.

Nia glanced at the clock. The next period would start in ten minutes. She clapped her hands. "All right. Good practice, everyone. Good stretching. See you all tomorrow."

The students rose from various positions on the floor. They put away their ballet shoes and began shuffling from the room. Joseph went first. He clearly didn't want to spend any more time in Aubrey's presence than necessary. Surprisingly, Aubrey followed him. She sped up, squeezed in between the T twins and ran out the door behind him, as if late for a class.

Marta watched, undoubtedly aware she couldn't slip between the twins fast enough to catch her new friend. She fidgeted with her pointe shoes, bending the front of her foot as if breaking them in, as if she'd never expected to walk out next to the girl with whom she'd spent nearly the entire class.

Lydia, Kim, and Suzanne followed the T twins out the door. June and Alexei whispered as they walked behind. The boy folded to say something in June's ear as they entered the doorway. She responded with a glance around the twins' shoulders and then pressed her lips together to keep from laughing. Nia wondered whether it was about Aubrey and Joseph. Anyone could sense the tension between them. Alexei would probably know why by morning. The boy was a node in the gossip network.

Too bad Theo hadn't been nice to him. If Theo really had gone to Claremont Saturday—and not the boathouse— Alexei would be able to sniff out someone who'd seen him. But he wasn't motivated to confirm Theo's alibi.

Marta finished swapping her toe shoes for navy trainers. She started out the door. She looked thinner now than three days ago. Still not like a dancer, but much less swollen. Amazing how fast the weight came off. When had she had the abortion? Just Saturday.

The realization tingled through Nia's body like a coming cramp. Marta had been in Claremont at the same time as Theo. He'd been the student she'd seen at the bus stop outside the clinic.

"Hey, Marta, can you wait a second?"

The girl stopped feet from the doorway. She pivoted just enough so Nia could see the side of her face. "Um, I have class."

"I know. I just have a question." Nia lowered her voice. Ms. V sat in her adjoining office. The instructor's door remained open.

"Did you see Theo that Saturday night when—"

"What?" Marta's eyes darted around the room. She grabbed her forearms and rubbed as though she were cold. "Why would you ask that?"

Nia stepped closer and dropped her voice another decibel. "He says he was off campus on Saturday when Lauren disappeared, and some people are saying he went to

Claremont. You'd told me that you saw a classmate at the bus station that night so you had to walk to a farther one. Did you see Theo?"

Marta's eyelashes fluttered. She shook her head no. The jitteriness of her movements said otherwise.

"Marta, if you saw him, you really should come forward." The girl's bottom lip trembled. A hinge creaked somewhere behind them. Ms. V had opened her door wider.

"Did you see him?"

Marta stared in the direction of the dance teacher's room. "I've really got to go to class. Can I talk to you later?"

"When?"

"Tonight. Around seven o'clock? When people are at dinner."

Nia tried to read Marta's tense face. Had she suggested a meeting because she wanted to confess to seeing Theo or because she feared any mention of the abortion in public? Nia looked over her shoulder at Ms. V's cracked door. She wouldn't get the answer now with the dance instructor able to poke her head into the room at any moment.

"I have a choreography meeting during dinner. How about eight?"

"Fine. Eight."

Marta ran into the hallway. Nia turned back to the cubby where her duffle bag lay and sat beside the stack of wooden boxes.

Ms. V emerged from her office. "Marta was here late."

"She's trying hard to get back into shape."

"And she wanted pointers?"

Nia pulled off her pointe shoes. She examined her toes through the white dance stocking. "She hopes we will give her a few more weeks before we make any decisions about casting the fall show."

Ms. V frowned. Her skin fell into deep crevices around her mouth, as though practiced in the expression. "I'm afraid that, after we cast, that's it. She shouldn't have let herself go during the summer. Dance isn't an elective. It's a lifestyle."

The teacher returned to her office. Nia slipped her fingers in the nylon's oval opening beneath the arch of her foot. She pulled the stocking back over her toes, exposing her foot to the air. She separated her scrunched toes from one another.

Nia relished the familiarity of the tights and leotard. Dance pants and tank tops didn't allow the same freedom. She'd run out of clean leggings and hadn't had time to do the laundry. Fortunately, when she'd shown up to class in the traditional gear, Ms. V hadn't said anything about it being too revealing. Hopefully, she wouldn't say anything to Battle.

She slipped the stocking back over her foot and shoved it into a sneaker. She put on its mate and then stood, ready to return to her lonely dorm to eat a solitary salad. Maybe she should invite Peter to grab something with her. He would be awake. He taught that poetry elective on Mondays, Wednesdays, and Fridays. Of course, if he didn't want to see her romantically again, suggesting lunch risked face-to-face rejection. She imagined how he would do it. *Sorry, Nia. All of Aubrey's talk last night made me realize that it's not wise for us to date. It's a distraction for the students. But I really like you and want to remain friends.*

Nia caught her reflection in the mirrored wall. She admired her long, defined legs and tiny waist, the ample chest pressed between sloping shoulders. She wanted someone to appreciate her body as Dimitri once had, someone who would be excited by the sight of her lean muscles and what she could do with them. Not Dimitri, but someone like him. Someone more mature. She wanted Peter.

She pulled the pins from her bun. Waves cascaded down her back. She tousled her mane until it took on the unkempt yet done appearance of lingerie model hair. She headed out the door. Maybe Peter didn't want to see her again. But she'd do what she could to make that hard on him.

Last night's warmth had melted into a cool morning. She jogged to shake the chill.

The stone buildings of the boys' quad resembled a fortress. She walked into the grassy square. A few male students rushed across the lawn, backpacks weighing on their shoulders. They were nearly late. First period would start in five minutes.

Nia approached the boys' dorm. As she ascended the stairs, she realized a flaw in her plan to surprise Peter: she couldn't open the door and there was nobody around to let her in. She had to phone him.

She dug into her purse. Her fingers passed a compact, lip gloss, and eyeliner, all thrown in last night. She touched the hard plastic of the wallet that held her ID, credit card, and a single folded twenty-dollar bill. Finally, she hit the smooth screen of her phone.

The door flung open. A young man burst from the entryway and shot past her. She caught the door just before it closed.

The inside of the boys' residence was only slightly less dim than she remembered. A few artificial lights lay embedded in the ceiling like insect eyes. They couldn't make up for the lack of natural light. She navigated down the hallway from memory. Peter's room was on the right, just before the hallway ended in a T.

A girl's giggle echoed somewhere beyond her. The ID rules really did fail to separate the sexes.

A familiar male chuckle answered the young laugh. Peter rounded the corner with a student behind him. The girl looked maybe fifteen, with long dark hair and a body that Nia swore could fit inside her own. Puberty had yet to spread the girl's hips and widen her torso into anything resembling adult sized. The girl tilted her head as she gazed at Peter like he was a teen pop star instead of an unpublished English professor, nearly two decades her senior.

"When Emerson writes, 'Little thinks, in the field, yon red-cloaked clown, / Of thee from the hill-top looking down,' he is saying that animals are not thinking about how others will see their actions and implying, of course, that neither should we. We should enjoy the beauty around us."

The girl stopped and tossed her hair. "I totally agree," she said.

"Now what do you think he meant when he said, 'Beauty is unripe childhood cheat'?"

The girl's tongue peaked from above her bottom lip, a deep-thought reflex or, perhaps, another Lolita gesture. Either way, she held Peter's attention. The girl glanced away while she searched for an answer. Nia met her blue eyes.

The teen almost blushed. "Oh, um, I think my RA is here."

Nia didn't know the girl. But she wasn't surprised at the recognition. A JPEG of her ID photograph had been included in the grief-counseling e-mail.

Peter's head snapped in Nia's direction. She became aware that her hands rested on her hips. She wondered whether anything besides her stance betrayed her disapproval.

"Well, think about that, Megan. We'll discuss next class."

"I think he meant—"

"You better get going." Peter stepped away from the student toward Nia. "Class has already started."

The girl's tongue retreated. She gave each RA a hard stare and then tossed her head back in Peter's direction. "It's cool. I have your note."

"The note excuses a little lateness, not a missed period. We'll talk in class."

The girl's head straightened from its coy tilt. She raised the book bag strap from her forearm to her shoulder. She strode past Peter.

He smiled. The expression had a sheepish quality. "Hey, you," he said.

The door slammed. He rubbed the back of his neck. His bicep flexed from the short sleeve of a navy shirt. The color, coupled with the light khaki pants, made him resemble the students. Was that his goal? To appear like just another Wallace kid?

"I hoped I might see you," he said. "I didn't get to say a proper good-night."

"I wanted to ask if you could grab a bite before your afternoon classes. But I can see you're busy."

Nia pivoted like one of the Nutcracker's toy soldiers. She headed toward the door.

"Don't be that way. That's not fair."

Fingers curled around her bicep. Peter pulled her toward him. The pressure of his hand nearly hurt.

"Come on. What? You think I like prepubescent girls?" Two lines cut into the space between his brow. "Poetry class attracts some young romantics, and some of them develop little crushes on the male teacher reciting their favorites. That's all."

"You're hurting me."

He winced. His hand fell from her arm. The anger melted from his face. He looked sad.

She'd made him that way. Why? What had she really seen? A teacher doing his job? Guilt swelled inside her. "Peter, I—"

"You know what? Just go."

"I'm sorry."

His brow lowered as if waiting for some sarcastic punch line: *I'm sorry you're such a terrible person. I'm sorry I'm such a bad judge of character.*

"I get that she was the one flirting. After last night with Aubrey throwing herself at you—"

"I don't want little girls."

"What do you want?"

He grabbed her waist. His lips pressed against her mouth. His tongue forced its way inside.

She closed her eyes as she returned the kiss. He tasted of bergamot and black tea. His skin smelled of grass, herbs, and a citrusy-mint. She didn't recall the cologne from the prior night.

His hands slid beneath her butt and lifted. She wrapped her legs around his waist. They continued to kiss as he carried her to his room.

Her back hit the door. Light enveloped her as the wood gave way. He pulled at the fabric clinging to her skin, searching for a button or a zipper. She lowered a pointed foot to the ground and then unwound the leg remaining around his waist. His hands fell on her shoulders. He pushed the leotard to her forearms. Her breasts burst from the Lycra, assuming their full, round shape. His thumbs brushed her ribs and then slipped beneath the seam of the tights. His lips grazed her neck as he pushed the clothing to her hips.

She stepped back from him into the free space between the couch and the bed. She slipped out of the clothing, leaving only a black thong covering her nakedness. His eyes rolled over her body then returned to her face.

"God, you are beautiful."

His fingertips caressed her chest, then her stomach. They traced her ribs and the sharp indent of her waist. His hands slipped beneath the strings fastening the thong to her body. "You're still dressed," she whispered.

He unbuttoned his collar and ripped the shirt over his head, exposing a defined chest with developed pectorals, more pronounced than those on the average male dancer's body. He unzipped. His boxer shorts, pants, and shoes fell to the floor in one fluid motion. A line cut into both his thighs, dividing the lateral muscle from the thick femur.

His hands returned to her thong. He pulled down the flimsy material and kissed her where it had covered. The act electrified her body. She moaned.

His hands pressed into her buttocks. She threw her head back as his thumbs moved to her inner thighs. She ran her fingers through his hair, freeing the strands that always fell into his eyes. Her body shuddered as he continued to work between her legs.

She touched his face and pushed against his chin, encouraging him to rise before dropping to return the favor. Her breasts pressed against his muscled thighs. She didn't need to excite him. He was ready.

"No," he said. "I want you."

She draped herself on Peter's bed while he ripped a condom free from its wrapper. A moment later, he was on top of her. The first time was a release, after the prior night's sexual frustration and Nia's year of forced celibacy. The second round was for showing off. Nia got him excited and then tried out different positions, displaying the flexibility she'd earned from fifteen years of dance.

When they'd finished, Nia felt girlish, giddy, and tired—the good kind, like after a particularly satisfying workout.

Peter touched her hair, a goofy look on his face. His lips pecked her nose.

"You must have class soon," she said.

Peter kissed her neck. "I'll call in sick. I'm sick."

She rose from the bed and onto the floor. She bent to retrieve her thong. It lay just under the bed, discarded like a dust cloth. A hand squeezed her butt.

"Don't go."

"You have to teach and I have a choreography meeting for the fall show."

His arms wrapped around her waist. He rose to his knees. "I know. You're right," he whispered. "When will I see you again?"

She scanned for her clothing. The leotard lay in a tangled heap beside the couch.

"Tonight? Can I come tonight?"

She laughed. "Haven't had enough?"

He swept her hair to the side. His nose pressed against the base of her neck. Warm breath tickled the baby hairs at the nape.

"Can't get enough."

"I can't come here at night. The students will see me."

"I'll come to you. I'll be discreet."

She tossed her hair as she finished dressing, knowing he watched her. "Everyone is in their dorms, asleep by ten."

"Then I'll see you at ten."

18

Épaulement [*ay-pohl-mahn*]

Shouldering. A term used to indicate a movement of the torso from the waist upward, bringing one shoulder forward and the other back with the head turned or inclined over the forward shoulder.

N ia swallowed the protein bar and rose from the couch to grab another. Dinner would consist of whatever she found in the cardboard boxes stacked beside the kitchen sink, plus the grapefruit on the counter. She'd planned on eating the fruit for breakfast tomorrow, but the choreography meeting had run long, and she hadn't wanted to grab dinner and risk missing Marta.

She grabbed a knife from the drawer beside the sink and stabbed the center of the grapefruit. She forced the blade down to the counter, splitting the fruit open. The two parts fell away, exposing the bright pink inside. She grabbed a spoon drying in the plastic dish rack beside the sink and wedged it into the flesh.

A knock sounded. She shoved the spoon into her mouth as she crossed to answer the door.

Marta entered the room like a thief diving into an alley. She clearly didn't want anyone to see her visiting. Talking to the RA was certain to provide grist for the Wallace rumor mill.

"Thanks for coming." Nia gestured to the couch.

Marta sat on the cushion like a kid waiting outside the principal's office. The girl tucked her knees to her chest. She pulled her extralarge sweatshirt over them, like a blanket.

"Want some grapefruit?"

Nia needed to put Marta at ease. Sharing food did that. But part of her hoped that Marta didn't take the offer. She needed the acidity to break up the sugars from the protein bars. Alone, the soy sitting in her stomach would become a lead weight.

"I never really liked grapefruit. But I guess it keeps you thin."

Marta was ten pounds lighter than when they'd first met three days ago. Disappearing water explained some of the postpregnancy weight loss, but probably not all of it.

"I don't have much else. Would you like water?"

"No, thank you."

Nia left her grapefruit and settled on the end of the couch. Her stomach rumbled, the churning acids kicked into high gear by the long-awaited presence of food. She longed for vegetables, steamed, over brown rice. Better yet, cucumber salmon rolls. Why didn't the boondocks ever have sushi restaurants?

Marta chewed on her thumbnail. Nia didn't remember that habit from their first meeting. Evidence of hunger? Frayed nerves?

"So you wanted to talk?" Marta examined the bleached, peeling skin beneath her nail instead of making eye contact.

"Yes. I wanted to know if Theo Spanos was the student you saw when you were in Claremont on Saturday."

Marta gnawed on the end of a finger. She shrugged. "I don't know."

"Well, how did you know that the person at the bus stop was from school?"

"Um, I guess I didn't, really. I just thought that I kind of recognized him."

"Who did you think you recognized?"

Marta pulled the sweatshirt lower, folding more of her body inside, turning herself into a ball. "I don't know. He just looked like someone who would go here."

"Do you remember hair color or anything about his clothing?"

Nia waited for a response. A digital clock hummed somewhere in the room. Air hissed from floor vents. The girl continued to peel the skin from her finger with her teeth.

Nia placed a hand on Marta's shoulder. "If you saw Theo, you have to say something. You don't want one of your classmates to go to prison for a crime he didn't commit."

Marta tucked her hands beneath her armpits, shrugging off Nia's hand and creating a shield of arms across her chest. "Even if I might have seen Theo, it doesn't mean he didn't kill Lauren. I mean, you and Director Battle found her body Monday, right before classes started. Theo had all Sunday to do it."

"You should still come forward. The police think Lauren was killed Saturday evening, and they don't believe that Theo was off campus then. It's a big reason why they arrested him."

A shriveled thumb sneaked back toward Marta's mouth. "The police will want to know what I was doing in Claremont.

They'll know I had an abortion." Tears muddied Marta's dark eyes. "They'll tell my parents."

"I don't think they would need to tell your parents."

"What if I'm asked to testify to Theo's whereabouts? I'll have to get up on the stand and say I saw him in Claremont. Then the attorney will ask why I was there. I'll have to talk about aborting my baby in front of my parents, my classmates, maybe the whole world. The case will probably be televised by, like, CNN. My grandparents will see it in Armenia."

Marta buried her head in her knees, reverting from teenager to toddler.

"I know it would be difficult. But if you saw something that could prove one of your friends is innocent—"

"Theo's not my friend." The sweatshirt muffled her voice. "I'm sure he barely knows I exist."

"Well, he's still your classmate."

Marta raised her head. Her brows pulled down into a deep V. "And he might still be a murderer. I don't know that he didn't do it. I just saw him Saturday after I got out. It was already five. Maybe he strangled Lauren super quick that afternoon."

Marta had seen him. That meant, in all likelihood, Theo was innocent.

Nia had traveled to Wallace by first taking the train from Manhattan to Claremont and then grabbing a bus to the school. If she remembered correctly, it had taken her ninety minutes to get to campus from Claremont. Round trip to the town would take three hours. Assuming Theo had waited at the bus stop for someone for an hour or so—or maybe even seen this girl—he would have spent nearly the whole evening off campus.

"The police can pinpoint time of death with forensics. If they have the time that you saw Theo, they can compare that to the window when they think Lauren died. That could exonerate him."

"And ruin me." Marta's brows retreated into a straight line. Tears again clouded her eyes. "My parents will never speak to me again. My grandparents will never speak to me again. I will be a baby killer. Nothing else will matter."

"Your parents love you."

The girl rubbed her forehead with her chewed fingers. "They won't if they find out."

"I know it must be scary. But you can't let an innocent person spend their life in jail."

Marta's legs burst from her sweatshirt cocoon. She stood from the couch and stepped toward the exit. "Theo's dad is a rich lawyer. He won't let him go to jail. I'm sure they'll subpoena bus stop tapes or traffic cameras, something to show he was there."

"But what—"

Marta grabbed the doorknob. "I can't destroy my life to save his."

"Marta, wait."

"I'm sorry. No."

The door clicked closed.

Conflicting emotions roiled Nia's insides. She didn't want to hurt her student, but she had to go to the police. Theo must have told the detectives where he'd gone on Saturday. The officers wouldn't have arrested him if they'd been able to confirm his alibi with a bus driver or a closed-circuit camera. He needed Marta's testimony.

She would give Marta the night to think about what she had said and then talk to her tomorrow. Perhaps she could convince her to come forward without revealing her motivations for heading to the clinic. Marta could admit to some lesser offense, like wanting to obtain birth control. The clinic couldn't be forced to divulge the procedure.

Nia glanced at the time. The clock almost read nine o'clock. Peter would arrive in another hour.

*

Someone knocked just as she exited the bathroom. Nia held her breath, waiting for another sound. Maybe Marta had already decided to come forward. She tied the towel over her breasts. The knock sounded again—a short, quiet rap. Almost timid.

Peter stood in the hallway. He wore jeans and a T-shirt that made him resemble a Gap model. A bottle of red wine dangled from his fingers.

Nia felt a flush of embarrassment. She didn't have wine glasses or food or even a bed big enough for two people.

"Come on in." She shut the door behind him. "Welcome to my very humble abode."

Peter winked. "I think I know your decorator."

He placed the bottle of wine on the kitchen counter. "Did they give you the standard issue water glasses?"

Nia followed him into the kitchen area. She opened a cabinet and withdrew two of four skinny, ribbed glasses. "Most of my stuff is at my mother's house. I took the train here, so I packed light."

"No worries." He pulled a steel utility knife from the front pocket of his jeans and flipped a corkscrew from the back. "I came prepared."

"You did. How did you even get in? I thought your ID didn't work in this building."

"Some girls are smoking in the courtyard. One of them let me in after making me promise not to report her."

"You promised?"

He twisted the screw into the bottle. "I told her lung cancer is a shitty way to die, like a proper authority figure. Then she said she was sure science would clone new lungs by the time she had to worry about it, like a proper spoiled Wallace student. Then I said she was probably right."

He yanked the cork out of the wine. A triumphant grin spread across his face as he filled both glasses. The vessels made the wine resemble grape juice.

He handed her a glass. His fingers fell onto her towel.

"Have a thing for terry cloth?" she asked.

The smile turned devilish. "I like to take it off."

19

Changement De Pieds [*shahnzh-MAHN duh pyay*]

Change of feet. Springing steps in the fifth position in which the dancer changes feet in the air and alights in the fifth position with the opposite foot in the front.

N ia's phone buzzed across the kitchen counter like a fly. The sound woke her from the light sleep she'd eventually eked out on the couch. She buried her head beneath the thin throw blanket, hoping the noise would stop.

Peter didn't know how to sleep in a small bed. He lay on his back in the center of her twin mattress, one arm flung across it, the other jammed against the wall. He had started on his side, hip bones pressed against Nia's pelvis, arms draped over her back, but the position had led to another athletic round of intercourse that left them both too sweaty for close quarters. Afterward, he'd rolled onto his back and fallen into a dead sleep, apparently unaware that his broad body left her a four-inch-wide rectangle of mattress.

The phone continued vibrating against the counter. She must have forgotten to turn off her alarm. Ballerinas shared God's work ethic—they rested just one day a week. Since Ms. V was Jewish, Nia's Sabbath was Saturday. Having class Sunday also worked better since some kids went home Friday night and returned Sunday.

Nia stumbled over to the counter to silence the buzz. Her temples throbbed from a mild hangover. Her muscles felt tight. She wanted to crack her toes.

A text from Dimitri blared on the home screen:

> *Just took the exit for Wallace. GPS says I should be there in ten. Where should I park?*

Brunch. She'd forgotten.

The room smelled like stale sex. She couldn't meet Dimitri like this.

Peter's pupils moved beneath his thin lids, a sign of REM sleep. Air rumbled through his nose.

She tiptoed to her bathroom, shutting the door behind her before turning on the shower. She avoided wetting her hair in the stream. Not enough time for the blow dryer. Barely time for soap. And zero time to explain to Peter about brunch with her ex. She would let him sleep and text him that she'd had a meeting. They could meet up later.

She applied light makeup: lip gloss, a little blush, a neutral eye shadow. She wanted to look good without seeming like she'd made an effort. Getting dolled up for the guy who'd dumped you was desperate, and she wasn't desperate. She'd met a very nice guy. A great guy, in fact.

Still, she wanted Dimitri to want her. She just didn't know if that desire stemmed from unresolved feelings or a demand for revenge.

She slipped from the bathroom like a cat burglar and made her way toward the closet. It creaked as she opened it. Peter stirred in the bed, a slumbering Goliath on David's pillow. She pulled a blue sundress from a hanger. The dress was summery, not fancy. Not trying too hard. She slipped it over her head and shoved her feet into her ballet flats.

Dimitri would need to leave the car in lot A, beside the football field. She texted parking instructions as she crossed the room to the exit. The girls' quad was a short walk away. She would see him in five minutes.

"That's not a leotard."

The bed springs groaned as Peter rose from the mattress. His eyes were still swollen from sleep. "So," he yawned. "Showered, nice dress. I was thinking faculty dining hall, but I take it you want to go out for breakfast."

He lumbered over to her. Lips landed on her cheek. Nia stood paralyzed.

He stretched his arms as he walked into the bathroom. The door shut. The toilet flushed. The sink faucet blasted.

She called through the door. "Actually, I have—"

"What? I can't hear you over the water. Just a minute."

Her phone buzzed again.

Parked. Walking to girls' quad. What building are you in?

Nia felt panicked. What if he somehow made it into her building and knocked on the door before Peter left? Meeting Dimitri with another guy would seem deliberately mean, as though she'd orchestrated Peter's departure to get back at him.

She texted,

I'll come out. Boys aren't allowed in the building.

Peter rubbed his face and hair with the hand towel as he reentered the living room. Blond strands flopped across his forehead. Stubble dotted his jawline. "There's this little country kitchen–type place in town. It's on the first floor of a bed and breakfast. Great apple muffins."

The back of her neck grew hot. "I'm sorry. I have plans. I'd told a friend that I would have brunch with . . ." she trailed off. No need to add a gender identifier. "It was before we had Friday plans."

"Oh. Should we all go together? Just let me get on some clothes."

Peter flung back the covers, revealing his wrinkled jeans and boxers from the prior night. He shook them out and then slipped them on. He peered behind the bed, hunting for his shirt.

"Actually, 'friend' might not have been the right word. A professional contact." She feigned nonchalance, as if she wasn't struggling to find gender-neutral pronouns. "Just someone I used to dance with who works at the New York City Ballet. I need to keep up my connections. There's a lot of crossover between NYCB and some of the companies that I hope to audition for this winter."

Peter continued searching for his shirt.

"Anyway, we were just going to talk shop. Ballet gossip. You know, who is dancing where, which choreographers are being groomed, kind of inside-baseball. It's really more of a professional meeting than friends catching up."

She was talking too much, but she couldn't stop. Words vomited from her nervous gut. She wasn't practiced in lying.

"I should probably go. I said we'd meet on the quad at ten."

"Okay." Peter smiled. It looked forced. "Would you like to grab dinner later?"

Nia couldn't imagine Dimitri staying until dinner, but she didn't want to risk it. What if they decided to eat in Claremont? She might not make it back in time. She didn't want to tell Dimitri that she needed to return for a dinner date.

"I don't know. Can we play it by ear?"

He found his shirt on the side of the bed and slipped it over his head. "Yeah, sure."

Nia's phone buzzed again. She glanced at the text:

Here.

Peter grabbed her waist. He pecked her lips. "Talk to you later."

"Yeah."

He opened the door and then turned back toward her. Another kiss landed on her mouth. More passionate than the first.

For a moment, she forgot about Dimitri.

The door closed behind him. The phone buzzed.

★

Nia descended the steps into the girls' courtyard. It was a fall morning. Goosebumps broke out on her shoulders and upper arms as she stepped into the shady quadrangle.

Peter was still walking across the courtyard. She watched him pass the magnolia trees. A door slammed. A couple girls hustled down the steps of a neighboring building. They waved to Peter as they turned in the direction of the dining hall. He was a popular teacher. He must be good at it.

"Nia."

Dimitri's voice. She searched for the source. He sat on a metal bench pressed against the side of her building, beside the stairs. The wind jostled his wavy dark hair and loose button-down shirt. Tan forearms, slender yet muscular, peeked from beneath three-quarter sleeves. The memory of her body in those arms—the way they had cradled her, thrown her, supported her—sent a shudder down Nia's back.

She walked down the remaining steps. Dimitri ran over and threw his arms around her waist. Her feet left the ground as he spun her around. "I've missed you."

The embrace felt like returning home. She wanted to relax into it but couldn't. He wasn't her home anymore. Moreover, she worried Peter would glance over his shoulder and see that her "friend" was more than that—or had been. He hadn't yet made it off the quad.

She pushed both hands into Dimitri's chest. He dropped his arms from around her waist. She stepped back.

"Hey," she said.

The warmth left Dimitri's smile. The expression froze on his face, toothy and awkward. "Something wrong?"

"No. It's good to see you. It's been a while."

Dimitri followed her gaze over his shoulder.

Even though Peter had made it to the edge of the quad, she could still tell his clothing was rumpled and used. The walk of shame wasn't as obvious as a woman in a cocktail dress on a Sunday morning, but it was close.

"I thought guys weren't allowed in the girls' building."

Nia squinted as though she couldn't quite see the subject of his curiosity. "Oh. That's Peter. He's a teacher."

Dimitri tilted his head. "And he's on the girls' quad on a Saturday morning?"

She felt a flush of guilt. She told herself that the emotion wasn't warranted. Dimitri couldn't have expected that she'd spent the past year without any romantic relationships. He'd undoubtedly seen many girls since their breakup.

Hurt crackled through Dimitri's chestnut-colored eyes. He knew. There was only one reason a thirty-something guy would be on the girls' quad on a Saturday: to see a woman. And she was the only woman around.

His mouth twisted in disappointment. "He came from your room?"

This was not how she'd imagined the reunion with her ex: him in the self-righteous position and her struggling to explain herself. He'd ended things. Why should she be on the defensive?

"Wait a second. You break up with me a year ago, then call out of the blue, and you want to start with the third degree?"

"Well, I didn't think you would have some dude with you."

"I didn't have him with me. He's across the courtyard."

"You're sleeping with him?"

She folded her arms across her chest. "Honestly? You've got to be kidding."

"I'm kidding about you sleeping with some guy?"

"No. You must be kidding coming here and acting like you have a right to know. You wanted to see other people. And now you're acting possessive, like I'm wronging you by seeing someone?"

Anger made her theatrical. Her hands flitted around like a hummingbird, brushing her brow, flying out toward him. She pivoted toward her dorm. "You know, this was a bad idea. You should just go."

He grabbed for her hand. She pulled both into her chest. "Okay." Dimitri's stance softened. "I'm sorry. You're right. I just wasn't prepared. Where would you like to go for brunch?"

"I don't know the area too well yet. There's a pay cafeteria—"

"I was thinking someplace more private."

"Apparently, there's a brunch place in a nearby bed and breakfast. I don't know the name, but we could search for it."

"Sounds good. My car is in the visitors' parking, down the hill."

He again reached for her hand. She kept it at her side. She felt the warmth of his presence behind her as she led the way down the sloping path. A pink blush crept up the tips of the broad-leaf maples lining the walkway. Soon the green landscape would turn red and gold.

"It's nice here," Dimitri said.

His fingertips brushed her thumb. She stopped walking and kept her hand steady. He read the signal. His palm engulfed her fingers.

"You look beautiful."

She turned toward him. He smiled. The expression seemed sad.

"Thanks. You look good, too. The same."

"I've missed you." He reached for her other hand. His thumbs stroked her wrists.

She steeled herself with a shrug. "Well. You wanted to see if you would."

His full lips curled inward. He nodded slowly. "I'm sorry. I should never have asked for space. It was the worst decision I've ever made."

The words cut through her. Distance had dulled the pain of their breakup. Dimitri's sudden proximity sharpened it into a stabbing sensation.

His chocolate eyes took on a syrupy quality, threatening to melt her anger. She held her breath, trapping the hurt, and forced a sarcastic snort. "Why?"

His pectorals lifted and fell, highlighting the crevice where her head had once fit perfectly. She tore her gaze away.

"I was stupid. I'd felt overwhelmed and everyone kept saying, 'You're young, you can't know what you want.'" He touched her chin, forcing her to look up at his deep brown eyes. "But I did know. I knew I wanted to be with you the first time I saw you."

She coughed, clearing a way for speech in her cinched throat. "I mean, why do you know this now? Did you break up with someone or—"

"No. I mean, I dated. But no one came close to you. I thought about going to see you, but I didn't know what it was like for you on the road . . ." He rubbed her hands again. "That's no excuse. I should have come sooner."

She blinked at the sky to keep the tears from falling. It was a smoky blue today. Gray blue. Like Peter's eyes.

"You're right. You should have come sooner. I'm seeing someone right now."

"It can't be like us."

"It's new. But I'm not going to break it off just because you've decided you made a mistake. All I can offer right now is friendship."

He looked away. She braced for his response. Maybe friendship wouldn't be good enough. Maybe he'd decide that coming to see her had been a mistake. Maybe she was blowing her one shot to make things work with him again.

She pressed her lips together, stopping herself from proposing anything more. She couldn't run back to him. It wouldn't be fair to Peter, and it certainly wouldn't be fair to her.

"Okay. I understand. I'll take it." He sighed. Another sad smile creased his face. "Where are we going to brunch?"

"I don't know. I'm not that hungry."

"Yeah. Me neither." He jostled her arm playfully. "So, want to dance?"

20

Exercices Au Milieu [*ex-ahr-CEE-SAYS O mill-eww*]

The name given to a group of exercises performed
in the center of the room, without the support of
the barre.

D imitri stood in front of the wall of windows overlooking the lake. He jumped in a perfect stag leap—front
leg bent, back leg extended behind him. For a moment,
he looked as though he were floating in air. He landed,
perfectly, on the pads of his sock-covered toes. He hadn't
brought ballet slippers, and street shoes were not permitted
in studios. Hard soles scuffed floors.

Nia fiddled with the computer on the wall. A gentle
waltz slipped through the speakers. She twirled into him. He
grasped her waist. She rose to the tips of her satin-wrapped
pointe shoes and, facing him, extended her back leg into
arabesque. He rotated her sideways and slipped his hand
beneath her raised thigh. She readied to fly.

He lifted her high above his head. She bent her knee and pointed her foot to her thigh, confident that the movement wouldn't upset his hold.

After a moment, he placed her pointed foot back on the floor. He stepped to the side, hand still outstretched, offering his physical support for whatever she wanted to do next. She dipped forward and extended her raised leg behind her into a straight line with her standing leg—scratching her earlier itch to showboat during penchée practice.

"Nice. You can balance that on your own now."

"Ruban taught me some things." She lowered her leg and traveled forward on her toes as she talked.

He followed behind. She caught a flick of his heel in the air. She copied his pas de chat, leaping from one foot to the other, bringing her knees up to form a diamond. They leapt across the room, alternating between the "cat's step" and the foot-fluttering entrechat.

They landed each jump at the same time, completely in sync. He'd always been the perfect partner. She could read the step he wanted from the micromovements of his body: the flick of his wrist, the slope of his arm. He could stare at her face while following her footwork, always in the right position to execute the next lift or turn.

She twirled around his muscled body and then slowly lifted a leg in front of her. Suddenly, she tossed herself backward. He caught her and lifted her horizontal figure to his chest. She might not trust him as a lover, but after years of dancing with him, she would always trust him to catch her if she fell.

He lowered to one knee. She dismounted and his hands encircled her waist. He spun her in front of him, then pulled her into his body.

His chest rose and fell against her own. They were too close to dance anymore. She looked up at his lowered head. His chin tilted to the side. His nose grazed her cheek.

Too close.

She jumped backward, freeing herself from his embrace. No more dancing.

"The students might need this room soon," she lied as she shut off the music. "We should probably go."

"Okay. If that's what you want." He grabbed his leather loafers from the side of the room and slipped them onto his feet. "So how is teaching going?"

"Good. The students' levels are pretty varied. But there are two girls who are really, very good. One was at ABT for the last two summers."

"Must be fun to choreograph for them."

Nia grimaced. In her attempt to sound more important during their phone conversation, she'd inflated her job description. Her earlier excuse for needing to leave the studio was already one lie too many.

"To be honest, my role has been more about demonstrating Battle's choreography suggestions. He likes to see his ideas in action."

"Oh." He tied his shoe. The silence that followed dwelled on her lie. She needed to break it.

"The school has been in the news a lot lately."

"Yeah. I saw. I meant to ask you about that. Did you ever meet that boy who killed that girl?"

Whatever happened to innocent until proven guilty? Nia figured she couldn't fault Dimitri for the assumption. Until last night, she'd also thought Theo did it.

"I did, and I doubt he did it. There's a student who might be able to place Theo off campus at the time of Lauren's death."

"Might just be one of his buddies trying to cover for him."

"I don't think so. The student doesn't really know him. She just saw him."

Dimitri stood. "Well, that's not good."

"Why? He's probably innocent."

Dimitri walked toward her. Concern creased between his brows. "Because it means the real murderer is still walking around."

21

Temps Lié [*than lyay*]

Connected movement. An exercise used in centre practice composed of a series of steps and arm movements based on the fourth, fifth and second positions.

N ia stood at the side of her bed and considered the man sleeping in it. His defined chest rose and fell with long breaths. He was out. She'd have to wake him. Though Peter could sleep in on a Sunday, she didn't have that luxury. And she didn't want to make a habit of sneaking out in the mornings.

She'd invited him to dinner last night in the teacher's quad. After spending the day with Dimitri, she hadn't burned with desire to see another man. But she'd wanted Peter to know that her "friend" hadn't stayed the night.

She'd already showered and dressed, hoping the sound would stir him before she needed to leave. She'd made coffee too, but the smell of French roast had no impact on the tea drinker sprawled atop her mattress. The long hand of her clock flirted with the ten. She had to walk to the dance building now or she'd be late.

She leaned over him. The presence of another individual, inches from his face, had no visible impact. Her lips grazed his forehead. Peter moaned and reached for her. She slipped from his grasp.

"I'm sorry. I have to go to class."

"It's Sunday," he whined.

"I know."

He opened one eye and frowned. "You're dressed."

"Class is in ten minutes. I made coffee. I'm sorry. I don't have tea."

He rolled over onto his side. His legs flopped off the bed. "I gotta pee," he mumbled.

She kissed the top of his head. "I gotta go."

He scratched the stubble on the side of his face. "Leave the cash on the dresser?"

"I'm sorry. But I can't be late. It's still the first week of classes."

Peter stood like a lazy giant, hunched posture hiding his height. "I'll walk out with you. Let me just hit the bathroom first."

"You don't have to rush."

"It's better I leave before the students start buzzing around the hallways."

Peter lumbered to the bathroom. She admired the muscle definition in his apple-shaped, bare bottom. The toilet flushed. The faucet ran.

He returned and fished his boxer shorts from the twisted sheets at the edge of her bed. Nia poured him coffee as he jostled back into wrinkled jeans and a crumpled shirt. The worn outfit again advertised his night as clearly as a hickey.

He smoothed his shirt. "Ready for ballet."

"You mean ready to roll back into your own bed."

"No. I'm up now." He tilted his head toward his armpit. "But I need to shower."

She handed him the coffee cup, relishing the routine of the gesture. *Good morning. Here's your coffee. I'm heading to work now.* It was nice to wake up with a man.

Peter's nose wrinkled as he sipped. She'd have to buy some tea.

"Okay. So let me walk-of-shame it on out of here, then." He scratched his head where the hair lay matted in the wrong direction. "Want to grab some dinner tonight?"

The force of her smile fought against her cheeks. To think a couple days ago she'd thought he would reject her. Now he couldn't get enough of her.

"Where were you thinking?" She sipped her coffee, hiding her grin behind the ceramic mug.

"I'll cook at my place. I'll sneak you in." He guzzled the remainder of the drink like taking medicine and set the cup on the counter. "My RA is totally clueless."

"I wouldn't say totally."

His eyes sparkled. She took the expression as a green light to offer a taste of the coming night. She kissed him. The coffee masked the odor of stale breath.

He pinched her butt. "Let me walk out with you. Then I'll leave you to your day."

They slipped from the door. Nia suppressed a self-satisfied grin as they swept past Aubrey's room. There weren't rules against RAs having sex with another consenting adult. The handbook advised discretion.

*

Nia entered the studio to stares and suppressed giggles. Aubrey stood in the center of Alexei's gossip circle. Her presence in the group surprised Nia. The T twins had always seemed to resent Aubrey's talent, and June hadn't said a word to the girl since the semester's start. Alexei clearly didn't like her. He'd been all too eager to share stories that painted her as loose.

It didn't take Nia long to figure out how Aubrey had ingratiated herself into the group. The girl covered her mouth and whispered loudly. "Listen. I bet she's hoarse."

Alexei waved as though he tried to grab Nia's attention across a crowded street. "Hi, Ms. Washington. How was your weekend?"

The group snickered. What had Aubrey told them? Why would she be hoarse?

Ms. V cleared her throat. She admonished the group with a laser-beam look. "Ms. Washington. May I have a word?"

Overenunciated consonants broadcasted Ms. V's annoyance. Nia felt guilty. Of what, she wasn't sure.

She followed her boss into the office. Ms. V shut the door and took a seat behind a metal desk. Her expression multiplied the smoker's lines around her mouth.

"Unfortunately, I must bring a rather uncomfortable matter to your attention."

This was not a good start to a conversation. Nia scanned her mental database of Aubrey encounters and imagined how her actions could be mischaracterized. Had Aubrey mentioned the club? How could she without admitting that she'd been in an adult-only casino?

"I understand that you have been having a male visitor."

The statement felt like an assault. "V-visitor?"

Ms. V held up her hand. "While there isn't a rule against fraternization, we do expect teachers to be examples of proper behavior and etiquette. Carrying on in a way that can be heard by the students is, at best, unbecoming conduct. At worst, it's detrimental to the well-being and safety of our students."

Fear hollowed out her insides. It sounded as though Ms. V were gearing up to fire her. Nia thought of the pain in her heel. She still didn't have health insurance.

She struggled to keep her tone and volume steady. "I don't know what was said to you, but I have not behaved in any inappropriate way. I have kept—"

Ms. V again held up her hand. The way she did it dismissed rather than surrendered. "I don't need to know the details, Ms. Washington. But you should know that our students observe their teachers. We cannot broadcast our private lives. Moreover, your behavior is interrupting the sleep of our students."

So Aubrey was the victim? Nia burned with the temptation to spill all of Aubrey's recent transgressions: sneaking into a club, drinking, performing suggestively on top of a bar, flirting with men twice her age, and more. But Ms. V would never believe her. The girl was the dance program's mascot.

Nia swallowed her anger. "I am very sorry and embarrassed that anything I said while in the privacy of my home was overheard. Thank you for bringing this matter to my attention. Now that I am aware, I will make certain my boyfriend and I do not stay at my place."

Ms. V settled into her chair. "That's probably for the best. Off campus is preferable for certain kinds of activities."

"Of course. I'll also make sure to apologize to my neighbors." As she said the words she thought about how she could have it out with Aubrey without getting drawn into petty bickering.

"I'm sure that would be appreciated," Ms. V said.

Nia kept her head high as she exited the room. The students watched her, undoubtedly looking for signs that she had been scolded, or worse. She walked straight to where Aubrey stood, beside Joseph. The pair must have made up.

"Aubrey."

The girl batted her cartoonish eyes. "Yes?"

The other students watched the exchange. Good. She wanted witnesses to this confrontation.

"I've been made aware that I kept you up last night. I apologize for that. I was with my boyfriend, Peter."

"Oh, he's your boyfriend?" Aubrey tilted her head and glared. Her arms folded over her chest.

"We didn't realize that our conversation could be heard through the thin walls," Nia continued. "We will be more discrete in the future."

"I understand that we all need to have a little fun."

"Within reason." Nia raised her voice. "As neighbors, we have to respect each other. I'll keep it down. I'll also make sure any business that I overhear or see is kept between us. I'm sure that you wouldn't want any of your friends hearing excruciating details of what you do in your free time."

Nia cast Joseph a pointed look. Alexei chuckled. This time, Nia wasn't the butt of the joke.

22

Ballon [*ba-LAWN*]

Bounce. The light, elastic quality in jumping in which the dancer bounds up from the floor, pauses a moment in the air and descends lightly and softly, only to rebound in the air like the smooth bouncing of a ball.

N ia took the students through the usual stretch regimen of pliés, arabesques, and grand battements without suffering pointed stares or whispers. She then, per Ms. V's instruction, spent another ten minutes reviewing fouetté turns, correcting hip position and toe points as the students attempted multiple twirls. Ms. V was giving her more responsibility, prepping her for when she would take over corps practices for the fall show.

Lydia and Aubrey had the turns down, so much so that they could perform several sets without stopping. June could do two sets but frequently spun away from where she started. The T twins had trouble with one.

Surprisingly, Alexei and Joseph proved very capable with the male version of the turn. Unlike a woman, a man only rose onto the pad of his foot and kept his leg extended through the rotation. Both boys boasted strong thighs and abs that easily supported the weight of their raised leg.

After class, Ms. V called attention to the lesson schedule. They had decided to start with the most promising students rather than the struggling ones. Ms. V had explained that, after hours of correcting basics like keeping toes pointed, arches flexed, knees turned out, and backs straight, Aubrey and Lydia would seem beyond reproach. Without corrections, the best couldn't get better. Even principal dancers had choreographers to criticize their forms.

As the students slipped on their street shoes, Nia overheard Alexei tell June something about the police. "I got Detective Ed somebody. How about you?"

"They didn't get to me yet. But I hear they're interviewing everyone except freshmen," June said. "What'd he ask?"

"He wanted to know if student cell numbers were listed anywhere publicly."

"Like on a bathroom wall?"

"Or a Facebook wall," Alexei said. "Of course, I told them no. People don't just give out their cell. That's private."

"But Lauren's number wouldn't be difficult to find. She probably gave it out to friends or study groups . . ."

"You just want Theo to be innocent."

"Well, it's true. When they get to me, that's what I'm going to say."

Alexei and June continued debating out the door. Everyone filed behind them except for Aubrey and Lydia. Ms. V took Aubrey onto the stage to rehearse. For once, the teacher's favoritism worked in Nia's favor. She would get an hour with Lydia.

Nia started the music. Drums crept into the room like a far-off war cry. Battle had chosen a fusion of eighteenth-century classical and modern alternative by an Icelandic "postrock" band. Guitar strings, scraped by a violin bow, screeched into the room, followed by the male singer's haunting falsetto.

Lydia bounced on her toes. "I love this band."

"This is the music for the soloist in the fall performance," Nia continued. "Ms. V and I are teaching the routine to both you and Aubrey, as you each demonstrate superior technique. Only one of you will get it. The other will be the understudy and also learn a pas de deux to perform with either Alexei or Joseph."

Lydia's big brown eyes grew serious. Her pixie chin lowered. "I want this solo."

Nia admired the ferocity in her look. She wanted a competitor for Aubrey and she had gotten a good one. "And I want you to win it."

They listened to the song twice before Nia demonstrated the first movement. She watched Lydia absorb the dark melody that exploded into a triumphant march during the refrain, only to be drawn back into the depths during each verse until it finally wrested free in a joyous coda.

Lydia took direction like a professional. Nia never needed to give the same correction twice. If she told the girl to raise her leg higher or keep her hip down, the leg stayed up and the hip lowered each time the step repeated. The petite prima also memorized choreography at first sight, often imitating Nia's demonstrations before she had completely finished.

Still, there was work to be done. Lydia had an impressive arabesque, but not the jaw-dropping full split that Aubrey flashed with such ease. Nia was certain she could get Lydia there. The girl could perform a split in multiple directions, and a standing split utilized the same muscles and ligaments. Lydia also lacked the power of Aubrey's leaps, but Nia couldn't fix that as easily. Innate Achilles strength determined jumping power as much as training. Lydia was already well trained.

What Lydia lacked technically, she compensated for with something that couldn't be taught: she internalized the music. The girl breathed the rhythm until her rib cage rose and fell in time with the song. She never needed Nia to clap the tempo for pointe work. She danced as if the music compelled her legs to rise, her toes to point. She heard the beat, no matter how intense, dissonant, or distracting the melody. And she translated every step, even the new ones, into seemingly effortless expressions.

By the end of practice, Nia knew Lydia could beat Aubrey. The only question was, could Nia instruct as well as Ms. V did?

The other individual sessions were a letdown. She'd pulled Talia, June, Joseph, and Marta. Ms. V took the two Russians, Tati and Alexei, as well as Kimberly and Suzanne.

The dancers in her group weren't poor. On the contrary, most were solid for a preprofessional program. But the corps steps bored Nia. They didn't challenge and so were less interesting to demonstrate and more of a pain to instruct. The students felt they knew the quick toe sweeps and little jumps. As a result, they got lazy. Toes weren't pointed to the extreme. Knees slipped into the forward position.

Pas de deux practice with Joseph was the exception. His movements were polished. His jumps showed real power. He'd even proven adept at the lifts, which Nia had demonstrated by playing the role of his partner. Unfortunately, there was a downside to his talent. He didn't appreciate direction. Joseph felt he knew the "man's role," and he clearly didn't want his female partner telling him where to put his hands.

By the time Marta entered the room, Nia was relieved to bid Joseph good-bye for the day. His overconfidence would lead to mistakes. She didn't want to be propped above his head when he made one.

Nia welcomed Marta into the studio, holding her tongue about Theo, for the moment. First and foremost, she had a job to do. She couldn't have Marta running away before her lesson started.

The practice went well. Marta's weight loss had helped her regain her center of gravity. Now she moved fluidly. Her posture remained erect. She had a beautiful straight line when she pliéd. Her flexibility surprised Nia. Marta could almost pull her foot to her head.

"You've been holding out on me." Nia meant the compliment, though she said it to put Marta at ease. Now was her chance to bring up the police.

Marta completed a pretty arabesque followed by a deep bend to one knee.

"The you-know-what gives you this hormone that stretches your ligaments," Marta said. "I guess it helped in one way."

"The way you look now, you could land the other pas de deux part."

"Yeah, right." Though the words were clearly intended to be sarcastic, Marta couldn't cover the hopeful rise in tone that turned her statement into a question. *Right? Do you really think so?*

"I mean it."

Marta pulled her leg to her side. "Suzie always gets the partner dances. Ms. V thinks she and Alexei look good together. Aubrey usually dances with Joseph and does the solo."

"Well, whoever dances the solo won't get the pas de deux this time."

"But we have Lydia now."

Nia crossed the room to the computer. She turned off the band that had screamed from the speakers for most of the day. It was a credit to the musicians that she could listen to the singer's wail on repeat for five hours without tearing her hair out.

"Well, I still think you have a chance. Your movement shows a lot of emotion."

Marta shrugged, demonstrating the nonchalance that teenagers strived so hard to perfect. The teen picked up her street shoes and then tucked into the corner and pulled off the slippers plastered to her feet. Her body language didn't invite conversation. But Nia didn't have a better time to talk to her.

She cleared her throat. "I've been thinking about what you told me. You got contraceptives when you went to that place, right?"

Marta froze like a lizard trying to camouflage itself against the background. Her fingers hovered above her shoe, still grasping the laces. She didn't look up. "Yeah."

"You could potentially tell the . . . people that you went into the city to check out birth control options and saw Theo waiting for the bus."

Marta's legs retreated toward her chest. "My parents would be really upset if they knew I was even sexually active."

"But if Theo's innocent, you wouldn't want—"

"Shouldn't you both be done by now?" Aubrey's head ducked into the room. She looked like a disembodied doll.

Marta jumped into standing position. Her right shoe remained untied. "I'm good. Let's go." She ran from the room.

Marta's speed showed Nia what she needed to know. The girl's fear of her parents would prevent her from admitting going anywhere near an abortion clinic. Nia couldn't appeal to Marta's desire to do the right thing, and she couldn't let a teen's cowardice put an innocent boy in prison.

Nia headed home. The detective's card was on her dresser.

*

The phone rang, a shrill siren that reminded Nia of her first day on campus six days ago. Detective Kelly hadn't wanted to hear her theory that Lauren had been strangled. Would he want to hear her share another student's alibi for Theo? Wasn't that hearsay?

She had to try. Peter's description of his favorite student replayed in her head. The boy was a promising, sensitive poetry student and she, like everyone else on campus, had convicted him just because he'd dumped, and possibly cheated on, his girlfriend. Infidelity was not in the same realm as murder. She'd been wrong to assume the worst.

The gruff, Massachusetts accent picked up on the fourth ring after a pause, as though his work line had forwarded to a cell phone. "Detective Kelly, Connecticut State Police."

"Hi. It's Antonia Washington. We met on Monday."

"Yes. I remember."

Cheering overwhelmed the speaker. A woman screamed for someone named Mikey to "go, go, go." People clapped.

"Excuse me." Kelly seemed to shout. "Little league game. Just give me a moment."

Nia heard the sound of shuffling and walking. The cheering died down, though she could still hear yelling in the background.

"Are you still there?"

"Yes," she answered.

"How can I help you?"

"You'd said to call if I thought of anything or learned anything."

"And . . ."

Marta's face filled her vision. Nia winced away the image. The girl would have to understand. An innocent teenager's freedom was on the line. "A student recently told me that she saw Theo in Claremont on Saturday."

"Did you give her my number?"

"She's afraid to talk to you."

"She can bring her parents."

"No." The word came out too quickly. Nia fumbled for an explanation that wouldn't require too many details. "She is pretty unwilling to come forward."

The background noise intensified. It sounded enthusiastic. The home team must have gotten a hit.

"Why don't you come on in tomorrow and we'll talk? I'm at the state police barracks in Claremont. Bus drops off at the station."

23

Rat [*ra*]

A slang term for a child dance student at the Paris Opéra. The term, coined early in the nineteenth century, was derived from the children's appearance: always in movement, with lean faces, and incessantly nibbling at food. The "petits rats" are the lowest rank of dancers in the cadre of the Paris Opéra ballet.

The bus pulled away, stranding Nia in Claremont. Even though it was Monday, the bus didn't run regularly at midday. The next one wouldn't come for two hours. If she didn't time her conversation with Detective Kelly just right, she'd risk missing her individual lesson with Lydia. Nia didn't want to disadvantage her student. Moreover, she couldn't miss her afternoon class and give Ms. V a new reason to believe her irresponsible.

She briefly regretted not asking Peter to drive her, but the decision was for the best. She couldn't spill Marta's secret to anyone else, especially not to someone inclined to repeat it at school in order to clear his favorite student's name. She felt bad enough telling the cops.

Nia rounded the corner to the address on her phone. The state police complex lorded over a four-lane road, more minicity than office building. She jogged up the steps to brick columns flanking a glass entrance. Words etched into the double doors read, "Connecticut State Police."

She approached a long, mahogany countertop in front of a glass wall cordoning off uniformed officers from visitors. A heavyset policewoman sat at the counter. She wore her hair pulled back in a severe bun. The style suited her unfriendly expression.

"Hi. I'm here to speak to Detective Kelly about the Lauren Turek murder."

The officer examined her face, staring into her eyes, a pit bull challenging a Pomeranian. The reaction took Nia off guard. Wouldn't the police be happy that someone was coming forward with information?

"He gave me his card and said to talk to him if I thought of anything."

The female officer sat back in her chair. She picked up a clipboard from the desk and handed it to her. A pen rested on top.

Nia expected the attached form to resemble the documents she'd filled out at doctor's offices. *Name. Age. Social Security Number.* Instead, the first question asked that she check a box if the crime involved a minor.

"I'll page him," the officer said.

Nia spied gray plastic chairs in the corner. She moved to one and read the form. Most of the questions involved a suspect. She didn't write anything on it.

Detective Kelly stepped from behind a frosted-glass door at the end of the hallway. He wore a navy-blue suit with a red tie. He'd cut his gray hair shorter since she'd last seen him. It sat close to his head, military style. Maybe seeing himself on the nightly news had encouraged him to get a cleaner cut. Nia felt suddenly underdressed in the zip-up sweatshirt covering her leotard and leggings.

He held the door open and motioned for her to come through, as if directing a reluctant car into an intersection. "The dance teacher that made the awful discovery. Good to see you again."

How was she supposed to respond to that greeting? "I hope I can be of some help."

She handed him the clipboard as she entered. He tucked it under his arm, apparently unconcerned about the contents.

"Sorry about the quiz. The media attention has attracted a lot of fake information."

Nia followed him into an open room lined with blond wood desks of the IKEA variety. Papers and manila file folders were stacked atop most of them. The air smelled like newspaper.

Kelly settled in a rolling desk chair. He motioned to an empty one beside him.

"So, you said on the phone that a student told you that she saw Theo, but she doesn't want to come forward?"

Guilt hollowed out Nia's insides. Marta was a very troubled teen. But she still couldn't stand by with information that could establish someone's innocence. She'd help her deal with the fallout.

"Yes. I'm the RA in the junior and senior girls' dorm. A girl on my floor told me that she saw Theo at a Claremont bus stop on the Saturday evening when Lauren went missing."

Kelly's eyebrows rose in an inverted V. "What time?"

"Sometime around five o'clock. She'd be able to narrow it down."

"Who's the girl?"

Nia swallowed her guilt. "Marta Hovnanian."

He scratched at his temple and leaned forward in the chair, ready to share a secret of his own. "Maybe this girl is just a friend of Theo's trying to help his reputation at school. I mean, if she really saw him, then why wouldn't she tell us? Maybe because it's not true."

Nia scooted forward another inch on her seat. She needed Detective Kelly to take her seriously and he didn't want to. The police had a suspect. News that they'd charged the wrong guy would not be welcome.

"No. It's true. Marta was in Claremont to visit a family planning clinic. Her parents don't know that, um, she's become active in that way. She is very concerned that, if she comes forward, the police may tell them."

Frown lines pulled down Kelly's lips like puppet strings. "How old is she?"

"Sixteen."

He brushed the top of his head, as if dusting dandruff off his crew cut. "Well, unfortunately, we would probably have to talk to her parents. We typically can't question a sixteen-year-old without at least trying to involve the guardians."

"Maybe you wouldn't have to say why she was in Claremont."

"We always try to be discrete." He shrugged, advertising that he didn't really care about protecting a kid's reputation.

"She's really vulnerable. When she came to me, she was extremely broken up about it, and she's very afraid of her parents' reaction. Could you, maybe, not ask too many questions about why she went to Claremont?"

"Like I said, we'll try."

Kelly pulled a notebook from atop a stack of files. He removed a pen from a coffee cup that read, "World's Best Dad." Nia wondered whether a father would be more or less likely to help a kid hide her sexual activity from her folks. Probably less.

"Okay." Kelly exhaled as if his day had just gotten a lot longer. "Tell me everything from the beginning."

24

Pas tombé [*pah tawn-BAY*]

Falling step. Pas tombé is used as a preparatory step. It is a movement falling forward or backward on one foot in a demi-plié, transferring the weight of the body. It is used with such steps as développé, ballonné and so on.

"Okay, you really have to listen to me this time." Nia spoke with her hands, emphasizing each word like a conductor hitting the downbeat. Joseph paid more attention to movement than to words. She needed him to hear her before they started practicing again.

"Boat lifts aren't like a press lift where you can be a little off and no one will notice. If your hands aren't right or you overarch your back, I could topple over your head."

Joseph folded his arms across his chest and leaned back, the picture of defiance. "I've done these before with Aubrey. She never had a problem."

Nia rubbed her forehead, staving off a coming headache. Aubrey was Joseph's answer to every criticism. *Aubrey was fine with it. Aubrey maintained balance.* It was as though he never expected to dance with anyone else.

"However Aubrey compensated doesn't change the fact that your hands are in the wrong position. They need to be above the hipbone."

"Maybe you're just top-heavy." He spoke under his breath, but she heard the insult.

Bickering with Joseph would only bring her down to his level. She looked out the dance studio's wall of windows and took a deep breath. Another gray September day. Northeastern autumns were either extended summers or wet and chilly. This one had morphed from eighty degrees to sixty in the matter of a week.

"Joseph," she started, but he cut her off.

"My hands are fine."

Nia blamed his attitude on her age and appearance. He didn't act this way around Ms. V. Joseph mistook her for a peer, probably because she didn't really look older than the schools' seniors. All the dancing kept her body relatively small compared to other women her age.

She put up a hand, mimicking Ms. V's *I'm done arguing* move, trying to emphasize her authority. "I'm not debating this. Your palms need to be flat, just above my hipbones. Put them there. Are you ready?"

His eyes rolled up to the ceiling. He opened his arms. "Yeah. I'm ready."

Nia put one foot in front of the other. She ran several steps and jumped, as though she intended to leap over him rather than into his arms. The forward momentum helped with the lift, for an experienced partner.

Thumbs dug into the soft area below her pelvic bone. Fingers pressed into her buttocks. Her hips grazed the top of his head.

"Wait, you don't have it—"

Joseph extended his arms. She was too off balance to maintain the look of flying above him. Her body pitched forward. She threw her head back, trying to reverse direction and not tumble onto the floor below.

Joseph's arms wobbled. She reached for his shoulders, hoping to brace herself and slide down his body to the ground. The shift in her weight seemed to throw him. He stumbled backward and released her.

Her feet hit the ground hard. A burning sensation, like an electric shock, went straight from her heel through her entire leg. She fell backward, putting her hands out just in time to soften the impact on her tailbone.

Nia writhed on the hardwood, pressing her fingers into her heel in hopes of squashing the source of her pain. Her eyes filled with tears. Had the tendon ruptured? No. She would have heard a pop. There hadn't been a pop. Had there?

"You were going to fall on top of me. I didn't—"

"Get Ms. V."

Joseph's hands dove into his hair. "I didn't mean to. I—"

Her breath came out in gasps. "Get Ms. V."

25

Sur Le Cou-De-Pied [*sewr luh koo-duh-PYAY*]

On the neck of the foot. The working foot is placed on the part of the leg between the base of the calf and beginning of the ankle.

Peter pulled the car into a massive parking garage. Each level connected to the six-story New Haven Center for Sports Medicine and Orthopedic Surgery. Peter parked the BMW in the first open spot on the third floor, a few feet from a glass elevator bank. A wheelchair sat beside the door, waiting for a patient. Nia's stomach dropped at the thought that it might be waiting for her.

Peter hurried around to her door and then slipped his arm behind her back and beneath her armpit. "Okay, just take it slow."

She leaned into him. The pain had subsided since the initial impact, though her foot still throbbed. Ms. V had run into the studio and insisted that she take a golf cart to the school medical facility. The staff nurse there had taken one look at her gnarled, calloused toes and urged her to see a specialist. Nia had then called Battle, who had made the appointment with "his guy." He'd told her not to worry that her health insurance hadn't kicked in. The school would pay a worker's compensation claim.

She leaned into Peter as they waited for the elevator. What would she do without him? If not for Peter volunteering to drive her ninety minutes to New Haven, she wouldn't have gotten to the appointment in time. The orthopedist had put her in that afternoon as a favor to Battle.

Silvery sunlight slipped through the parking ramp's open walls. It haloed the wheelchair's metal frame. She avoided looking at it as they stepped into the industrial-sized elevator.

Instead of numbers, the elevator buttons included fine print department labels. First floor: admitting, consultation. Second floor: diagnostics, testing. Third floor: pain management. Fourth floor: podiatry. Fifth floor: physical therapy. Sixth floor: surgery.

Nia double-tapped the first-floor button. The elevator descended. She relaxed with the motion. The farther away from the surgery department, the better. Surgeries had long recoveries. By the time she finished physical therapy, she might be too old to get a job with any company.

Inside, a woman behind a glass partition handed her a brown clipboard with several papers attached to the front. Nia had déjà vu from the police station. She brought the paperwork to one of several empty chairs.

The first page concerned billing. She filled out her details and initialed beneath a line stating that she understood she was responsible for the cost of all services rendered. Bill collectors used more affable language.

Peter paced in the lobby as she filled in the blank lines beneath "description of injury" and "history of past hospitalizations." Besides her Achilles tendonitis, she'd never had any notable health problems. She'd never broken a bone. She'd never suffered a serious infection or illness. She didn't take any medications.

She wrote a detailed explanation of her problem and then signed one more line acknowledging that she was responsible for any charges before returning the forms to the front desk. The secretary handed back her ID card with instructions to walk back to room 4E.

Peter followed behind as she limped past a series of closed wooden doors. The door marked 4E rested half ajar, revealing a leather chair with extended footrest covered with hospital-standard wax paper. She couldn't remember the last time she'd been in a real hospital. The campus facility didn't count.

Wax paper crunched as she settled into the chair. A male nurse, identifiable by the green scrubs that hung around his body, entered the room. He took her blood pressure then told them to wait for Dr. Murthi.

Peter walked to a counter with a model foot, cut open to show all the muscles and tendons. He touched the plaster cast. "So the Achilles is right there."

She didn't look to where he pointed. Her pain told her well enough where her Achilles was located. More than that, she didn't want to see a foot—even a fake one—cut open. It made the prospect of surgery more present.

A fit Indian man with thick dark hair and high cheekbones entered the room. He was younger than she'd expected for a surgeon. He was also better looking. The man looked more like a soap opera actor that played a surgeon on television than an actual doctor.

"Hello, Ms. Washington." Dr. Murthi even sounded like an actor. The man's voice was clear and accentless. Television news anchors aspired to sound like this guy.

The doctor scanned the documents on the clipboard. He pulled a swivel stool from beneath the desk holding the model foot and swung it in front of her chair. He sat level with her feet. Her reclined position suddenly felt as awkward as sitting in the stirrups in the OB-GYN office. She wanted to see his face.

He slipped her shoe off the injured foot. "I understand that you're a ballet dancer and you have Achilles pain in your right foot. Achilles ruptures are common in your field."

Her gut wrenched at his words. Tendon ruptures ended careers.

He pressed his thumbs into the back of her heel. She grimaced preemptively, anticipating the pain that came with the Achilles cramp.

"Does that hurt?"

Nia relaxed. The touch didn't bother her. "That's where I feel the pain most often, but not as much right now."

The doctor nodded. He slid his thumbs down her foot. He pressed into the arch. Flaming pins and needles jabbed into her nerves. She grabbed the edge of the chair.

"That hurt?" The question seemed sadistic. She pulled her foot from his grasp. The reflex nearly sent her knee slamming into her chin.

"I'm actually quite a fan of ballet. Mind showing me some of your footwork?"

Dr. Murthi extended his hand to help her out of the chair. She placed her good foot on the floor and walked into a small space in the center of the room. She brought her right leg into an arabesque *en attitude*, bending her knee behind her so as not to knock over any of the trinkets on the desk. She rose to the toes of her left foot.

The doctor smiled. "Beautiful. But I think I need to see you with the weight on your right foot. Can you take a few steps toward me and then do that again?"

Nia flushed with embarrassment. Of course the doctor didn't care for ballet. He wanted to see how her injured foot reacted when all her weight rested on its toes. She did as instructed, walking toward him before switching working legs and repeating the arabesque. Pain pulled at her heel as before. But this time, she became aware of a pricking sensation in her arch.

"Where does it hurt?"

"My heel still. But also where you pressed before."

The doctor motioned for her to sit back on the chair. "I didn't press hard enough to hurt it. I don't think you have a real Achilles problem. I think you have an inflammation of the tendon in the arch and, given the swelling on the side, a minor sprain from your fall today. Pain is funny. Sometimes our body sends signals that mask the point of origin. I'm pretty sure it's plantar fasciitis."

Latin. Latin wasn't good. Latin sounded like surgery.

"How do you treat that?"

"In very serious cases with surgery."

The ax fell. All sound stopped in the room. A scream curdled in Nia's head.

"Fortunately, I don't think that your case is that serious—though I have no doubt that you have considerable soreness and cramping. The tendon has been strained from all the dancing. But you don't have a heel spur and your toes don't show any upward inclination, which would indicate the need for more invasive treatment." He pushed back on his chair, scooting toward the counter with the sectioned foot. "We'll confirm with MRI, but I've treated the condition enough to eyeball it. I think you have a moderate case."

A tear dribbled down Nia's cheek. She brushed it with the back of her hand.

"How do you treat it?" Peter asked the question that she was too emotional to utter.

"You have to rest it for a few weeks. Take it easier on the dancing. There are also braces to wear at night that will stretch the tendon so it doesn't seize up in the mornings and orthotic inserts for your street shoes. I'll write prescriptions. But the brace is really the key."

The doctor pushed his chair by the desk. He opened a drawer. When he wheeled back, a tissue lay between his fingers.

Nia hadn't realized how many relieved tears had fallen from her eyes. The wetness of her cheeks surprised her. She patted the tissue on her face, too overwhelmed to say thanks.

"The night brace can be a little uncomfortable at first. It's like a sock, but it's made out of an Ace bandage–type material, so it compresses your foot and cuts down on swelling. It also has a strap in the front that pulls up on your toes at night, stretching out the arch."

Compared to surgery, a tight sock was nothing. Nia almost giggled.

"My guess is you've been massaging the heck out of your heel because you thought the pain came from the Achilles. It probably helped a little. But I bet the only thing that really helped was icing the whole foot, right?"

A hot blush filled her cheek. How could she not have noticed that only attention to her whole foot relieved her pain? Why had she seized on the Achilles?

The doctor tapped his pen against the clipboard. "So let's confirm with an MRI. You'll head up to level two. Then, if everything's as I think, you'll pick up the prescriptions at the front desk."

Nia could have hugged the man. Perhaps Peter sensed it; he tensed up beside her as she stood. "Thank you."

A grin lit the doctor's face. "Maybe you'll send tickets someday."

"You can count on it."

Peter stood by her side. His arm slipped around her waist. "Well, then. Nia, let's head to the next level."

26

Retiré [*ruh-tee-RAY*]

Withdrawn. A position in which the thigh is raised to the second position in the air with the knee bent so that the pointed toe rests in front of, behind, or to the side of the supporting knee.

Nia counted the steps from the girls' parking lot to her building's entrance. Each one sent a shockwave of pain from her injured heel into her calf muscle. She couldn't wait to sit on her couch and slip on the boot in her hands.

Peter had dropped her off. A true gentleman, he'd offered to take her to his place. She'd declined. According to Dr. Murthi, the first night with the brace was the worst. She didn't want her tossing and turning to disturb his sleep. Besides, he'd done enough for her. As nice as he was to offer, asking him to nurse her back to health after less than a week of dating was a quick way to be labeled "too needy."

She could take care of herself. To prove it, she'd even insisted on walking from the parking lot to her dorm alone.

She also hadn't wanted Peter anywhere near her room at night, lest his presence give Aubrey new ammunition. She could go over to Peter's tomorrow.

Only about ten more steps to go. Nia sucked in her breath and put the injured foot down again. The pain distracted her enough that she almost missed the student sitting on the top step. Dark hair hung over the girl's face. She hugged her knees to a bent chin. Her shoulders trembled. She wore a large boy's sweatshirt at least three sizes too big for her frame.

"Marta?"

The student raised her head. Red rimmed Marta's big brown eyes and the edges of her swollen nose. Tears streaked from her cheeks to her chin, like raindrops on a window.

"What's wrong?"

Marta flung back her hair. "Don't pretend you don't know."

The police had already talked to her. Did that mean they'd called her parents? "I'm not sure that I do. Do you want to go inside and talk?"

"I can't go inside. My mom and dad are arguing in my room."

"You told them?"

"I had to. It would have come out in court. That detective you told asked why I'd gone to Claremont. I couldn't tell him it was birth control and then repeat that answer under oath, swearing on a Bible. I had to tell the truth."

Nia swallowed the temptation to justify her actions. Marta knew why she'd told. The girl didn't need to hear that Nia thought Theo's freedom more important than Marta's relationship with her family.

"How did they take it?"

Marta snorted. She wiped her nose with the back of her sweatshirt sleeve. "My father doesn't want to keep me. I guess that's divine justice, huh?"

"Your parents can't stop being your parents."

Marta twisted the ends of her hair. "He can't even look at me. My mother blames the boy."

"She's right to. The boy was much older and more experienced."

Marta's eyes melted with tears. She seemed almost grateful to have Nia side with her mom.

"I already told Detective Kelly, but I'm going to give an official statement to the prosecutor and Theo's lawyer tomorrow."

Nia felt equal parts relief and guilt. She had helped keep an innocent kid from prison, but she'd also hurt a girl who had trusted her with a secret.

Marta pulled the sweatshirt tighter around her frame. The tugging only widened the neck hole, giving the chilly September wind access to her torso. She shivered.

It was too cold to be outside without a jacket. Nia saw an opening to undo some of the damage she'd caused—albeit for the right reasons. She could console Marta, give her a warm place to stay while her parents argued, prepare something to eat. The girl's cheeks had become sunken. Shedding so many pounds so fast could not be healthy. Starvation would damage her muscles.

"Come in and talk for a minute. It's better than sitting on the stairs."

Marta nodded. She watched her feet as she walked beside Nia into the dorm.

The door opened before Nia could place her keycard on the pad. Aubrey stood in front of them, still dressed in ballet gear. Ms. V must have let her get in some extra practice.

"Marta? What's wrong?" Aubrey's concern had a theatrical quality.

Marta's face pinched like a squeezed fruit. Fresh tears dripped down her cheeks.

Aubrey wrapped her arms around the girl. Her eyes accused Nia of something horrible. "Oh, honey. Come inside. We can talk in my room."

"It's really bad." Marta gurgled the words.

"It'll be okay."

"No. It won't. I had an abortion." Marta dissolved into sobs. Her head fell onto Aubrey's shoulder. "My parents hate me."

Aubrey rubbed Marta's back. She glared again at Nia. "Hey. Don't let anyone tell you that you're a bad person. I had one, too. It's okay."

"Really?" Marta asked.

"Yeah. An older guy I was with for a while." Aubrey rubbed one of her eyes, as if she too might cry. "I was totally in love, but he was married, said he'd get in big trouble if I had it. Then he broke up with me anyway."

Aubrey put her arm around Marta's shoulder. She opened the door with her free hand. "I know how you feel. We'll talk about it."

The girls entered the building. Nia reached for the door to follow them inside. Aubrey yanked the handle. The door slammed in her face.

27

Retombé, retombée [*ruh-t awn-BAY*].

Falling back. A term of the French School and the Cecchetti method. To fall back again to the original position.

Nia's feet hit the cobblestone walkway without a wobble. She picked up the pace. The gel pad inside her sneakers made her feel capable of running without hurting herself. Pride made her want to sprint.

She had to tell Peter. He knew the strange glee of helping someone else do their best. Now, thanks to Lydia, she did too. Her student had finally nailed the standing split.

It had taken a week of practice. Nia's sprained foot had prevented her from demonstrating her tips on balance and flexibility. But, fortunately, Lydia had been smart enough to follow along with Nia's verbal pointers. Nia had also shared a stretching regimen from her time at SAB that had proved helpful.

Finally, today, Lydia had gotten to the finale and stretched her leg straight in the air. Her student's arabesque penchée could now compete with Aubrey's own. Lydia had a solid chance of winning the solo during auditions tomorrow.

Nia hurried onto the boys' quad. A group of students burst from the door to Peter's building. They wore blue-and-white soccer jerseys with the Wallace crest on their breast pockets.

Nia waved. "Hold the door?"

They shouldn't have listened to her. Still, one of the boys grabbed the handle before the door shut. Knobby knees poked from beneath his dark athletic shorts.

She jogged up the steps. "Thanks."

The boy held open the door until she could grab it from him before sprinting to catch his teammates, already across the courtyard. Nia speed-walked to Peter's room. She knocked and entered. Peter always left it open and he didn't seem to mind her barging in. He probably preferred it to her hanging around in the hallway, advertising their relationship.

"It doesn't matter."

A boy's voice. Too young to be Peter.

The man she'd come to see sat on his couch across from a thin student. Dark hair hung beside the boy's prominent cheekbones. A masculine, Greek nose overwhelmed his gaunt face.

Nia's stomach clenched. She knew that face.

Theo looked like the undead version of the young man that she'd seen just a couple weeks ago. His dark eyes appeared sunken. His skin looked gray, as though it hadn't seen sun in weeks. Veins protruded from his neck.

Peter brushed his hair back. Nia now recognized the move as a nervous habit. Whatever he and Theo were discussing wasn't good.

"Of course it matters," Peter said. "You have your life back. You will finish school and go on to college. Maybe, someday, you'll even publish a book about what happened. This experience could make great fodder. Look at Cervantes or Dostoyevsky."

Theo looked away from Peter and toward the door. Nia gave a slight wave. "Hey, I'm sorry. I'll come back later."

Peter motioned her inside. "No. Come in. The police realized that Theo had an alibi and the prosecutor dropped the charges. We're brainstorming how to get the word out."

Nia joined them on the couch, near Peter but far enough away for the distance to appear professional. She gave Theo a weak smile. "I'm so sorry about what happened. I'm glad the police realized they were wrong."

"It doesn't matter that the police let me go. People want someone to blame and there's no one else."

"It must have been some sicko that sneaked in during move-in. That's what we'll tell people," Peter said.

Theo rubbed his palms over his gaunt face. He'd lost at least fifteen pounds since she'd first seen him, mostly muscle mass by the looks of him. He couldn't have been eating.

"I can't imagine how difficult it is to be falsely accused of something horrible," Nia said. "But Peter's right. You can put it behind you. Don't let other people's mistakes ruin your life."

Theo's head fell into his hands. "You don't understand. People don't think the police made a mistake. They think there's just not enough evidence to charge me. Everyone wants to believe that I killed Lauren because I'm some sort of psycho who couldn't handle rejection. They don't care that I broke up with her last June or that some girl saw me in Claremont when Lauren disappeared."

"Well, have you thought about switching schools?" Peter asked.

"The story's everywhere. Another school won't be any different."

Theo wasn't exaggerating. Nia hadn't been able to turn on the news without hearing of an "update" on Lauren's case.

"Maybe if students here understand why you went to Claremont, they'll believe you," she said.

Theo looked down into his lap. His head shook slowly back and forth. "That might make it worse."

"Why?" Peter asked.

The boy exhaled. His shoulders dropped another inch, hunching his back so that Nia could see the ridge of his spine through his white T-shirt.

"It was stupid. I went to meet up with this girl who was mad at me because I did something dumb. She said she wanted to talk about it, and I needed to apologize. But then she didn't even show."

"Whatever you did, it can't be that bad," Peter said.

Theo looked up at the ceiling. "I made a tape of me and her being, I don't know, intimate together. It was stupid. I'd been a virgin before so I sent it to my buddy to show him that, you know, I wasn't anymore. But he was a douchebag and sent it to a bunch of people. Then they sent it out, too. Next thing I know, it's on some website."

The sex tape with Aubrey.

Theo looked into his lap as he continued his explanation. His cheeks reddened. "People were talking about it during move-in week. She confronted me about it on Saturday, but then she asked to meet in Claremont to 'really talk' so people wouldn't see us arguing in the hall."

Peter rubbed away the wrinkles on his forehead. "Well, maybe you should talk about it. It's pretty unlikely that someone who went out to see another girl would then come back to see his ex."

"She won't back up my story. The police already asked her. She hates me." He fought back tears. "Everyone hates me. They all think that I agreed to meet Lauren because of some text I didn't even send." Theo's head again dropped into his palms. "I wish I'd died instead of Lauren."

Peter's hands landed on Theo's shoulders. He shook the boy. "You can't believe that. You are a good person and people will see. You just have to let the dust settle."

Theo continued crying. No amount of Peter's support would change things for him. People thought he was a murderer who'd gotten away with it. They wouldn't believe anything else until the police caught the real killer.

"Theo, how do you think that text message got sent from your phone?" Nia asked.

"I don't know."

"Did anyone have access to your phone?"

"No. It was in my pocket. I brought it with me to Claremont."

"Maybe someone had access to it before."

His shoulders shuddered as he shrugged. "Maybe my roommate, but he didn't do anything. He's one of the only people sticking by me. I'm not going to go blame him—"

"Someone sent a text from your phone. That person might have something to do with Lauren's death," Nia said.

Peter draped an arm around Theo's shoulders—inappropriate touching by school standards but a completely human reaction. If someone had ever needed a hug, it was Theo.

"The police don't have to find the killer for people to change their mind," Peter said. "I'll talk to Stirk. We'll get the cops to come and address the student body, explain that you had nothing to do with it."

Theo picked up his head. He looked like he'd been in a fight and lost. His nose and cheeks appeared swollen. His eyes were puffy.

"Do you think you guys could do that?"

Nia couldn't imagine Detective Kelly coming in to discuss an active investigation. But maybe, if the cops knew how poorly Theo was doing, they would release some kind of statement to the press. They wouldn't want a kid hurting himself because of a wrongful accusation.

"I actually know the detective," Nia said. "I'll give him a call. Tomorrow, right after class."

28

Battu [*ba-TEW*]

Beaten. Any step embellished with a beat is called a pas battu.

Nia read the score sheet with Lydia's full name printed in the right-hand corner. A single word shone in the center of the page: "Criteria." Beneath it, several bullet points were stacked atop one another: Movement skills. Articulation of body segments. Body integration and connectedness. Full-body involvement. Overall proficiency rating. An underlined space rested beside each line item, waiting for the judge to write a number between one and ten. The higher the number, the better the score.

She had memorized the judging criteria, but her eyes needed to focus on something besides her reflection in the mirrored wall. She didn't dare look at Ms. V's cinched face. The woman sat beside her, body language announcing annoyance like a loudspeaker. Her tense neck and shoulders reminded Nia of a corset. The woman's thin skin stretched like hosiery over unyielding bones.

Ms. V directed her posture at Battle. He'd overridden his deputy's request to see the dancers audition on the stage. Instead, he'd installed a folding table and chairs in the practice room. The mirrors, he'd insisted, would allow better evaluations of the students' lines.

Nia fought the temptation to tip her plastic seat against the barre behind it and balance on the back legs, just to keep moving. In moments, Lydia would face off with Aubrey for the principal role of the fall show. Her student's performance would not only reflect her teaching ability but also determine if Lydia received more of Battle's attention. He would teach the soloist himself. Learning under such a master would help Lydia perfect her form and get into the kind of prestigious summer intensives that led to a real career in dance.

Part of Nia also wanted Lydia to win for revenge. Aubrey needed to be taken down a peg after trashing her to Ms. V. Lydia could do it.

Lydia entered in the school's navy leotard and required white tights. She stood in the center of the room, all presence and poise. Nia followed her eyes as she acknowledged each teacher. When she looked at Nia, her mouth curved in a nervous smile.

Ms. V stiffened beside her, wearing a strict expression to which Aubrey would not be subjected. Nia smiled broadly. "You got this," she mouthed.

The music stole into the room like a whisper, interrupted by the screech of a bow scraping against a guitar string. Lydia ignited with the sound. A sly smile spread across her face as she sprang onto her toes. She traveled across the room, feet punctuating every beat of the tribal drum. She whirled as if swept by the wind of the background vocals. Her head whipped around when the singer's falsetto started. Her mouth parted with pretend fear, as if realizing a scary stranger watched from the sidelines. Then, just as practiced, her face softened as though she realized she might love this stranger. Finally, it hardened into something approaching aggression. She leapt across the stage, legs parted in a near split. Nia tried not to wince. Aubrey would, undoubtedly, have the height and full leg extension.

Lydia landed and spun into a beautiful series of fouetté turns. They weren't perfect, but they possessed emotion. The turns seemed to beckon along with the singer's call. Lydia carried the feeling throughout the dance, embodying the singer's passion, angst, and adoration. When the final note rang out and Lydia extended into the arabesque penchée, Nia was so moved that she nearly didn't care that her protégé's foot pointed above her head, just as she had taught her.

Nia beamed, hoping the smile conveyed the applause her hands itched to give. Clapping was forbidden, lest the sound intimidate any of the students waiting outside the room. Nia examined the reflections in the mirror. Battle suppressed a smile as he filled out his scorecard. The girl had impressed him. Ms. V's mouth seemed tighter.

Lydia held the door for Aubrey as she exited. "Good luck."

If Aubrey had said the words, Nia would have assumed sarcasm. But from Lydia, the encouragement was genuine.

Aubrey flashed a winner's smile. "Thanks." The tone of her voice almost sounded pitying.

Aubrey strode into the room in flesh-colored tights and her navy leotard. Classical ballet companies preferred white tights because they advertised mistakes. An opaque white should have covered her legs.

Ms. V and Battle didn't say anything. If the senior teachers didn't object, Nia couldn't bring it up.

Aubrey stood in the center of the room. She twisted her right leg behind her head and held it there as she zeroed in on each individual judge. The standing pose was not part of the planned choreography. It transformed Aubrey's legs into a snake's jaw, unhinged, awaiting prey.

The girl unfurled from the position as the music started. She performed like a predator, feet chasing unknown victims to the rhythm. Watching her, the vocal wind turned into a wail. Technically, Aubrey was perfect. Each turn possessed a feline grace and power that Nia could either admire or resent but not deny. The height of Aubrey's grand jeté beat Nia's own. Her legs extended in a full split in the air, creating a beautiful horizontal line.

Ms. V nearly moaned when the girl finished. She exhaled a satisfied murmur equivalent to a muffled burp after a good meal. Nia scrawled tens on the card above blank underlines. She wrote an eight under movement skills, docking Aubrey for failing to express the music's softer side. Her score wouldn't count much anyway. She and Ms. V would chime in, but, ultimately, Battle would make the decision.

Aubrey curtsied and thanked them before swaggering from the room.

The girl's departure changed the air temperature. Nia's skin tingled, as though sensation were returning to a frozen limb. Her breathing normalized as the door clicked shut.

Ms. V's hand fluttered to her heart. "I've never seen finer form."

Battle tilted his head. "She has a mastery of technique. It's a credit to you."

Ms. V beamed. "Well, she possesses such natural grace and flexibility."

"And, of course, ABT's summer intensives really polished the turns." Battle gestured toward Nia. "American Ballet Theatre wanted to take her away from us this year, but Aubrey insisted on returning to graduate."

The director would announce Aubrey's selection momentarily. Nia swallowed her disappointment.

Battle tapped his pencil against his paper. His brow furrowed. "However, Ms. Carreño danced with real feeling."

Nia's stomach dropped. Did she dare hope?

"Yes, but she doesn't have Aubrey's abilities. The grand jeté wasn't fully extended and the turns don't have the precision. She wobbled one."

"Even primas wobble one," Battle said. "She recovered so well I doubt anyone would notice. But they will notice how her movements convey the nuances of the music. She shows real tenderness during the romantic parts, which contrasts nicely with the darker moments. It makes them shine. Light and dark—"

"Aubrey will amaze the audience." Ms. V shot Nia a look. "There is no doubt that Lydia learned the choreography well. I notice she has recently acquired a one-hundred-eighty-degree angle on her arabesque, but she has not demonstrated in class that she can perform that consistently."

Nia cleared her throat. "We worked on her flexibility. I believe she can."

"Dancing isn't just about flexibility," Battle said. "I believe the parents and students will appreciate the new feeling Lydia brings to the solo."

Ms. V turned her whole body to face Battle. In the mirror, Nia glimpsed the teacher's lowered brow. "I should hope that parental response does not influence our decisions about ability. I am proud to say that parent interest, or lack thereof, has never influenced our decision before."

"Irina, I don't like what you're implying. It's not about donations."

"Then tell me why Aubrey, the superior dancer, doesn't deserve this part."

Battle slammed his palm on the edge of the table. "Attack. Attack. Attack. It's all she knows."

"But her technique—"

"Dancing is more than technique. It is feeling. This music has moments of tenderness and hope. Where is that in Aubrey's performance?"

Ms. V pinched the bridge of her nose. "Maybe the girl hasn't experienced much of that in her life. That's not her fault."

"Well, consider that your job, Irina. Work on inspiring her to show tenderness with Joseph in the pas de deux. The two of them have always had a close relationship. Perhaps you can get her feelings for the boy to translate into movement."

Nia pressed her lips together to avoid betraying her excitement.

"Okay. Let's call them back inside with our decision," Battle said.

Ms. V's plastic chair scraped against the hardwood floor like nails against chalkboard. She stood. "I wish to tell Aubrey myself."

"Understood. Send in Ms. Carreño, please, on your way out."

Nia pressed her belly to the table to provide Ms. V with a quick escape route behind her. The woman brushed the back of her chair as she passed without an "excuse me," another sign that her anger extended beyond Battle to her new assistant teacher. Nia couldn't care. She was too excited for Lydia and herself. Her dark-horse dancer had beat out the favorite.

Lydia entered the room, shoulders slumped, head down—the body language of the defeated. "Ms. V said you wanted to see me."

"Congratulations."

Lydia's head snapped upright. "What? I thought Ms. V went out to tell Aubrey."

"Aubrey will dance the pas de deux with Joseph. You have the solo," Battle said.

The girl bounced on the pads of her toes. "Really? I thought . . . thank you. Aubrey is such a wonderful dancer. I thought—"

"We appreciated the emotion you brought to the piece," Battle said. "You and I will work to refine your technique before the show. Jumps, as you may know, are something of my forte. I believe I can improve your grand jeté and help you land your turns with additional precision."

Lydia's eyes welled. "Thank you. I will work really hard."

"I know you will," Battle said.

The girl ran toward the table like a family member waited behind it. Nia staved off the coming hug with an extended hand. Lydia took it, and Nia shook like she mixed a drink, letting the number of times up and down express her excitement. "Congrats. You deserve it."

The door opened. Aubrey strode inside. Ms. V followed, head lowered like a chastised child. The girl turned a forty-five-degree angle to stare at Battle.

"Thank you for the opportunity." Aubrey's tone didn't betray disappointment or joy. She sounded flat. Disinterested.

Lydia broke away from Nia and stepped toward her taller, blond counterpart. "Aubrey, you're such a wonderful dancer. I know your pas de deux will be amazing."

Aubrey's blue eyes skewered Lydia. She tilted her head and smiled, an ear-to-ear grin.

"Good luck," she said.

29

Pas Jeté [*pah zhuh-Tay*]

Throwing step. A jump from one foot to the other in which the working leg is brushed into the air and appears to have been thrown.

Nia felt like blasting music and dancing in her room. Her student had beaten Aubrey, the same girl who had told Ms. V awful things about her, all the while pretending to be above reproach. A petty part of her wanted to celebrate, rubbing Lydia's win in her neighbor's face.

Nia stifled the urge by calling Detective Kelly. She'd promised Theo. Besides, she shouldn't gloat. Nia knew the pain of a failed audition better than most.

She settled on her couch and dialed the detective. Kelly answered on the second ring. "Ms. Washington? Calling with another student confession?"

The comment could have been sarcastic, but Nia thought his tone sounded genuine. "No. I'm actually calling because

Theo is in a pretty bad way and I was hoping there might be something you can do. Maybe talk to the students or—"

Kelly cleared his throat. "I'm sorry to hear that. But we can't comment until we close this case."

"The students here saw you arrest him. They don't believe that he's out now because he didn't do it. They think the police just didn't have enough evidence."

"Well, it's not just the alibi. You can tell students that we have other evidence that he didn't do it."

"Like what?"

"I can't really—"

"Saying you guys have something else isn't going to convince anyone. And Theo is suffering. He's not eating. I think he could hurt himself."

The detective's breathing became audible. "Did you tell his parents?"

"I don't think they can help. He needs the students to understand that he didn't do this. If you know he didn't, then maybe you can give a statement to the press?"

Air overwhelmed the receiver with static. "Look, I really can't say anything publicly until the case is over. But come to see me tomorrow. Perhaps I can give you something, off the record, that you could spread around."

Punishment for her good deed. Kelly's office was an hour away by bus. The meeting could take half the day. Maybe Peter could drive.

"All right. I'll probably bring a fellow teacher too. See you tomorrow afternoon."

Nia hung up before Kelly could object. The drive with Peter would be much more pleasant than the bus.

She'd tell him tonight at dinner. Perhaps they could celebrate Lydia's win with a picnic on campus. The third week of September had ushered in cold winds that had accelerated the foliage's costume change. The oaks had exploded in reds and golds during the past few days. It would be romantic to see the landscape around sunset.

Nia thought better of it. She didn't want beautiful scenery to encourage "the talk."

They'd never discussed the nature of their relationship or whether they were exclusive. The sheer amount of time they spent together made it clear that there couldn't be anyone else. She liked having a constant companion. She guessed Peter was the same. Maybe marriage had made him more comfortable with dating just one person.

Or maybe he *really* liked her. Problem was, she didn't know how she felt about him. She liked him, of course. But she was still reeling from the breakup with Dimitri and his recent revelation that he'd made a mistake. Until she resolved her feelings for her ex, she couldn't claim to have deep feelings for anyone else. She didn't want Peter to express any sentiment that she couldn't return.

Nia had just enough time for a bath before getting dressed for her dinner date. A pair of jeans and a top would work fine tonight. They had passed the point of impressing each other with appearance. After you saw someone naked in the morning a dozen times, what they looked like with lipstick or hair gel didn't matter all that much.

She walked into her bathroom and turned on the faucet. The dining halls served dinner from six to eight o'clock, and most of the students would be eating. Peace, quiet, and a satisfying soak followed by dinner with a handsome man. What better way to celebrate?

Nia peeled her shirt over her head. Something smashed against her wall. She heard the thud of the impact and then a sound like snapping wood. A profanity echoed through the plaster separating her apartment from the neighboring unit.

Had furniture fallen? Was someone hurt? She put her top back on and hurried out her door.

She looked at the hallway. Her bathroom shared a wall with dorm nine. Aubrey's room. Nia knocked. "Aubrey. Are you in there?"

Footsteps marched toward her. The door yanked back.

"Are you okay? I heard something break."

Aubrey held the door open another few inches, just wide enough for Nia to see inside. A wooden foot stretcher lay against the wall, splintered into pieces.

"Piece of junk," Aubrey said. Her eyes looked a shade bluer than usual. Eyeliner smudged at the corners.

"But you're okay?"

Aubrey still wore her ballet uniform. Frayed lines ran up her flesh-colored tights like slash marks.

"Yeah." She shook her head. "Ms. V had me focus on the wrong thing. All that pain perfecting my feet for nothing."

Nia could sympathize. It was awful to work hard to achieve something, to physically suffer for it, and then not get it. How many diets had she tried? How many times had she danced on swollen feet only to not get the part?

"You'll be beautiful in the pas de deux."

Aubrey smiled, a tight, closemouthed expression that didn't reach her eyes. The girl's blue irises targeted her like a pair of hunting scopes.

"I need to up my game. I'm losing too much to the competition."

Nia scrambled for some words of encouragement. Before she could find any, Aubrey started to shut the door.

"I better study."

The door closed in her face. Nia walked back to her room and the now-full tub. She slipped into the bath and dunked her head beneath the water.

∗

Hot air blasted against her bangs. Nia pulled the round brush through one last time and shut off the appliance. She examined her reflection in the mirror: clean, put together, ready to see Peter. She threw on a long cardigan over her jeans and stuffed a change of underwear into her handbag. She could don the same outfit tomorrow. She doubted she'd wear it for long anyway.

Her cell buzzed just as she walked outside. She fished it from the pocket of her sweater, now wrapped tight around her to ward off the chill in the late September air. She was always cold. Anything less than seventy-five-degree weather iced her bones.

Dimitri's number showed on the home screen. She waited a beat before she answered. They were friends now. But she didn't need to pounce on a friend's phone call as though she'd been counting the seconds to talk to him. She hadn't even thought of Dimitri much since he'd visited. They'd only spoken once or twice on the phone. He'd called more than that, but she couldn't answer when at Peter's apartment.

"Hi."

"Hi. How are you?"

"Good. My student Lydia got the solo."

"Wow. That's great news."

"Yeah. She dances with real feeling, and she was able to execute on some of the things she'd had trouble with before."

"Well, she had a great teacher."

Dimitri's compliment warmed her insides. "Well, I shared some of the tips that Ruban gave me."

"How are you feeling?" he asked.

"I'm good." Nia stopped walking and flexed her foot, verifying to herself that she told the truth. "That stretching boot I told you about is amazing. A little over a week and my foot feels much stronger."

"That's even better news."

"Yeah. I think staying off it a bit this past week has also helped. I've been talking through my corrections more than demonstrating. And now that auditions are over, I'll probably be able to take it even easier."

"Well, it's good that you're getting to rest it a little. Speaking of auditions, I have some news."

Nia braced herself. Dimitri's revelations always stirred up powerful and, lately, unwelcome emotions. She tried to read his tone. He sounded happy.

"I landed one of the soloist roles in *Agon*. They just announced. You're the first person I've told."

Longing tempered her enthusiasm. She'd dreamed of dancing in Balanchine's classic. *Agon* was one of her favorite ballets: a showcase of athleticism choreographed to Stravinsky's romantic and quirky score. It was one of the few ballets that gave men the stage for extended periods of time rather than employing them as lifts and props for their female counterparts. Men in the company would have competed fiercely for one of the four male roles.

"That's wonderful. Congratulations. You're perfect for it."

"You'll come to see me opening night? I have tickets."

"Of course. What day?"

"Next Saturday."

Ten days away. The fall show would be the following Friday evening. But surely Ms. V wouldn't have the students practice the Saturday before. The students who went home wanted one day with their parents, and bodies needed to rest. Besides, it was her Sabbath.

"I'm sure that will be fine. And, if not, I'll make it happen."

"Great. You're the only audience I want."

30

Entrechat [*ahn-truh-SHAH*]

Interweaving or braiding. A step of beating in which
the dancer jumps into the air and rapidly crosses
the legs before and behind each other.

etective's Kelly desk was in worse disarray than the last
time Nia had seen it. Once organized stacks now tee-
tered from the weight of overstuffed folders. Pinned
documents littered the attached cubicle wall like fliers on a
grocery store bulletin board.

The detective pulled a piece of paper from the top of
his desk and pushed it across to where Nia and Peter sat facing him.

"You know what SMS spoofing is?"

Nia picked up the sheet and held it out for Peter to see. It
was a printout of an online banner ad, blown up. The ad featured a picture of a phone with a text message "555" number
on it. Orange lettering beside the image spelled out the offer:

"SMStealer: Send text messages from any phone number. Buy credits now."

"I've never seen this." Nia turned to Peter. "You?"

Peter pushed his hair back. "No. What is it?"

"It's the latest way technology is making my job damn near impossible." Kelly's finger accused the paper. "SMStealer is an app that allows people to send a text message and make it appear as though it came from another number—basically, it lets you commit fraud."

He leaned back in his chair and folded his hands on top of his stomach. "Of course, they maintain it's a service for legitimate marketers who need messages to appear from a single company extension."

"So this is how the message was sent from Theo's phone?" Nia asked.

"All of this is off the record. You can't say it came from the police."

Nia nodded. "Sure."

"Once we confirmed that Theo was in Claremont, we launched a deeper investigation into Lauren's phone records. Turned out Theo was still in her contacts under, well—" Kelly cleared his throat. "Let's just say a not-so-nice name. But the text message didn't link with the name in her stored contacts. It came up as just his phone number."

Kelly held out his hand for the paper. Nia passed it back to him.

"We now know that's an indication of a spoofed text. If the text really comes from a number, it displays the sender information as the name stored in the phone." Kelly waved the paper. "We're pretty sure the text was sent using this app. It's one of the only ones that hasn't been shut down or sued out of business."

Nia felt Peter's energy change beside her. His back stiffened. He became still, like a squirrel sensing a dog. Nia read it as anger. He probably hated Kelly for not doing such due diligence in the first place.

"And you think you can find the person who did this?" Peter asked.

"There's a good chance that whoever used the app did so from a traceable cell phone or computer."

Kelly sat forward in his seat. He rolled up the SMStealer paper and slapped it against his desk. The act jostled some of the stacks and sent the smell of ink into the air. Much of Kelly's research must have been fresh out of the printer.

"We need cooperation from this SMStealer company," he continued. "As you can imagine, they're fighting us. The state attorney's office is working on a subpoena."

Peter sat back in his chair. He looked like he was on day two of the flu. Exhausted. Pale. In need of a bucket.

The text spoofing meant the murder was premeditated. That punched a big hole in Peter's theory of an opportunistic predator who had stumbled upon easy prey seeing Lauren by herself at the boathouse.

A digital desk clock sat half buried on the corner of Kelly's desk. Nia saw the number twenty-five. She needed to get out of here. Group rehearsal would start in ninety minutes and the drive took forty.

"So, bottom line, we can tell students that the text was faked," Nia said.

"I can't tell you what to tell anyone," Kelly said. "And everything I am telling you is off the record. You can't say the police told you. But if you were to tell students that these text spoofing applications exist, maybe they would form a different opinion about Theo."

"Do you think another student is responsible?" Peter sat on the edge of his chair as he asked the question.

Kelly rapped the paper against the desk. "I didn't say that," he said. "But whoever sent the text knew both Lauren's and Theo's cell phone numbers. I can't stop you from drawing your own conclusions."

31

Sous-sus [*soo-SEW*]

Under-over. A term of the Cecchetti method. Sous-sus is a relevé in the fifth position performed sur place or traveled forward, backward or to the side.

A bell's chime echoed in the auditorium rafters. The students froze on stage, as though time had stopped behind the curtain line. At Ms. V's command, they relaxed from their varied positions, shaking out limbs and descending onto flat feet.

"Good rehearsal, class." The Russian spoke in her regular faux-French accent. "They're all yours, Ms. Washington."

Finally. Battle had promised that Nia would lead the corps de ballet after roles were assigned, giving him and Ms. V more time to concentrate on the solo and partner dances. But Ms. V had been unwilling to relinquish control of the class. Nia had arrived ready to teach and been told to watch while her boss led the first practice on stage.

Fortunately, Ms. V never stayed for stretching. She watched the teacher exit, feeling particularly happy that she could have the students all to herself. She had something to tell everyone, and she didn't want Ms. V interrupting from the audience.

Nia clapped her hands. "Okay. There's no barre in here, so we'll stretch with partners. Everyone, please pair up."

She rose from her front-row seat in the empty auditorium. The air grew hotter as she approached the stage steps. Ms. V had wanted the spotlights blaring at maximum brightness in order to scrutinize movements.

The students moved around the stage to find their usual partners. They always broke into the same sets: the T twins, Alexei and June, Joseph and Aubrey, Kim and Suzanne. Normally, Marta, as the second least popular kid in class, would end up with new-girl Lydia.

Aubrey sashayed from the front of the stage to the center where Lydia stood.

"Be my partner?" She grasped the soloist's hand. "It's better to do this stuff with someone who shares your flexibility." Aubrey turned to Marta. "Help out Joey."

Marta nearly skipped over to Joseph. The boy looked at the floor, not concealing his annoyance.

Lydia flashed a toothpaste commercial smile. She seemed relieved to have a classmate talk to her. Since landing the solo, Suzanne and Kim had become less friendly. Nia guessed that, before Lydia's arrival, Suzanne had considered herself second best after Aubrey. Suzanne didn't like being bumped, and bulkier Kim seemed all too happy not to stand next to ballet's idea of the perfect body.

The rest of the class paired up in the expected way. Nia stood at the edge of the stage. "Okay. Stand back to back and then grab your foot and bring it up as high as you can toward your head. Use your partner's back for support."

The class transformed into five letter Ws. Nia moved toward Alexei and June. The pair talked to each other as they held their legs by their ears.

"So, super thin?" June asked.

"Basically emaciated." Alexei chuckled. "He's on the guilty diet."

Nia placed her palm on June's foot. She pushed it another inch higher. "Really try to attain maximum flexibility," she said.

The girl pressed her lips together. Nia let go. "Hold it there for a four count."

Nia rounded to Alexei on the other side. "Sorry to overhear. But if you're talking about Theo Spanos, he's not guilty." The auditorium acoustics made it easy for the whole class to listen in. Out of the corner of her eye, Nia caught the T twins watching. "Apparently, that text message to Lauren didn't come from Theo. It was just made to look that way."

Alexei's leg fell onto the floor with a thud. He put his hands on his hips. "How do you know?"

"Unfortunately, I can't disclose that." Nia assumed an authoritarian tone, trying to give her information more weight than Alexei's usual gossip. "But I have it on good authority."

Doubt clouded Alexei's face.

June's leg returned to the floor. "The police probably told you. Or Dean Stirk?"

Nia didn't respond. June didn't seem to care. She appeared excited to hear someone finally agree with her that Theo didn't do it.

"Good authority?" Alexei's eyebrows rose in disbelief.

"There's an app that allows people to fake sender information. Someone likely used it and entered in Theo's number. It's called SMS spoofing."

"So Theo really didn't do it." June spoke loudly. "I knew he didn't." She turned to Alexei. "He's really not a bad guy. If you got to know him, you would like him."

"What are you talking about?"

The question came from center stage. Aubrey had lowered her leg. Lydia's back no longer touched her partner's. She balanced by herself.

"Theo isn't guilty," June said. "Ms. Washington heard that the text message was faked using some kind of app."

Aubrey glared at Nia. "Who cares about an app? Theo is definitely guilty. He's the only one who would want to hurt that girl."

June returned Aubrey's annoyed look. "How much evidence do you need? The police already let him go. They know he was waiting for someone in Claremont when Lauren was killed. And now this text message is fake."

"He had motive," Aubrey said.

"Just because you messed around with him and he didn't care enough to keep it quiet doesn't mean he's a murderer," June said. "You made that tape. That's on you."

Alexei looked at June with an expression that could only be described as impressed.

Aubrey scowled at June and then transferred the look to the teacher that had started the whole conversation. The girl hated Theo for e-mailing that video to his friend. She probably had demanded the meeting in Claremont to punish him by wasting his time.

"I thought I should squash false rumors before they get out of hand," Nia said. She clapped her hands together. The sound reverberated on stage. "Now let's get back to it and stretch the other leg. Press your back against your partner and lift as high as you can. Really aim for a full split. Major companies want to see that straight line. Some even look for a reflex angle."

32

Temps Développé [*than dayv-law-PAY*]

Time developed, developing movement. A movement in which the working leg is drawn up to the knee of the supporting leg and slowly extended to an open position en l'air and held there with perfect control.

A subtle march crept from the auditorium speakers. The drummer played with a brush rather than a stick, suggesting the steady shuffle of footsteps rather than the pounding boots of war. Above the sound, bells shimmered, accenting the singer's sustained falsetto.

The class tiptoed from the wings in time with the recording. Cotton skirts swept calves as the girls swirled to center stage. The flowing fabric mimicked the ombré chiffon costumes that the female students would wear during the performance. Nia had unpacked the gown order, taking extra time as she placed the dresses on hangers to admire how the brilliant gold bodices melted into dusky pink hems. The program spared no expense with costumes. Once dressed, the women would resemble sunbeams in a Maxwell Parrish painting. Nia's job was to get the group dancing that way, light and graceful like sunshine sparkling atop water. After taking over the rehearsal Tuesday and Wednesday and then sitting in on Thursday, Ms. V had finally allowed her to fully take over instruction. Nia felt more relaxed than she had in weeks. It was freeing to teach without someone judging every comment.

"Alexei, Joseph. Stag leaps, in time with the girls," Nia shouted. "As their heads turn, you should hit the ground."

The boys tried to follow the command. Joseph jumped higher, but off the beat. Alexei hit the mark, though his height was less impressive.

"Fifth position," Nia shouted.

Heels descended in unison. Front legs raised into passé. Toes pointed just above standing knees.

"And onto devant." Legs extended in front of waists. "Plié," Nia commanded. Standing legs dipped. Nia scanned knees for desired angles. "Tati, more turn out. That ankle should point to the ceiling."

Tati's face tightened as she rotated her raised leg.

"Good. And close." Nia stood parallel to the line of students. She performed each movement as she named it on the beat, a staccato rap of broken French. "Pointe, lower onto devant, arms up, relevé. Hands down. Sweep the floor."

She stood and watched the line. The ghosts of teachers past criticized the group in her mind. She vocalized their more constructive comments. "As your arm lifts, so does your leg, as though they're connected by the same puppet string."

Legs rose. As expected, Aubrey and Lydia translated the instruction immediately into the desired movement.

June tried too hard. Concentration stiffened her body. Her leg rose to an oblique angle, a robot hitting a mark on a protractor.

"June, relax. Open your shoulders. Hear the music. Think graceful."

Tati's and Talia's long legs didn't achieve the angle she'd hoped for in time with the count. Nia clapped her hands beside them. "One, two, three, four. Five, six, seven, eight. Talia, Tati, to the beat. Step out, arabesque. As high as you can, everyone—except for Aubrey and Lydia. You two keep the legs in line with the class." The two starlets raised their legs 135 degrees, higher than their classmates but not enough to completely show them up.

"Good. And port de bras. Switch arms. And sweep arm, open and plié."

Nia clapped. "Okay. Very good. The opening is coming together. On Sunday, we'll work more on the second half and perfecting those turns. Thank you all. Massage those feet. See you then."

Nia sat and dug her knuckles into her arch as she watched the group split into their usual circles for warm-downs.

"Hey, Lydia, you're coming tonight, right?"

Lydia raised her head from her calves. Her big brown eyes scanned for the source of the question.

Aubrey batted her doll lashes. One of her arms draped over Marta's increasingly frail shoulders. The other arm was extended in welcome.

Nia wanted to step in front of the open limb, block the path to whatever door Aubrey held open. It couldn't lead somewhere good.

"She has to come, right, Mar?" Aubrey asked. "It's practically Wallace's official Halloween party."

"Um . . . yeah." Marta seemed uncomfortable with the invitation.

Nia's ears perked up. What were they talking about? Halloween wasn't for more than a month.

Lydia rolled up to standing position. Her left foot scratched her right calf. "Isn't it just for seniors? Senior Samhain, right?"

"What's Samhain?" Nia asked. She didn't like the fact that the party had "senior" in its title, or that Aubrey invited Lydia. That girl was not a good influence.

"It's the Gaelic shindig Halloween is based off of," Alexei piped up from somewhere behind Nia. No wonder that guy was the source of so much gossip. He heard every conversation, even those he wasn't involved in.

"Samhain marks the end of the harvest season," Alexei continued. "It's typically mid-October, but whoever started the party here picked September because it's still warm enough to wear cute costumes."

"We're not allowed to celebrate Halloween because it glorifies violence, so we have Senior Samhain," June said.

Alexei cleared his throat. He looked straight at Lydia. "And, yes, it is just for seniors."

Aubrey rolled her eyes. "It's only billed as just for seniors so the pretty juniors and sophomores will want to crash it."

"Well, I don't want to offend anyone by crashing." Lydia cast a sheepish look at Alexei. "I'm still new and—"

Aubrey's hand hit her hip. Her elbow stuck out in a perfect triangle. "I will be personally offended if you don't come. If you need a costume, I have one for you. I was deciding between two."

"Paris Hilton and Pamela Anderson." Alexei muttered. Joseph scowled at him.

Aubrey kept her attention on Lydia. "You can walk in with me."

"I don't know. Are you sure I should go?"

"Yes. Joey's friend Alistair is one of the seniors throwing the party, and he wants to meet you. He has a British accent. Very James Bond." Aubrey giggled.

Lydia smiled shyly. "Well, if he wants me to come."

"He absolutely does. Right, Joey?"

Joseph stretched his legs in the corner of the stage. He walked his hands back from the floor to his toes. "The more, the merrier."

Lydia brightened. "Okay. Sure."

Aubrey bounced on the pads of her toes. Nia didn't remember ever seeing her show such excitement. Bouncing was Lydia's thing.

"We'll all walk over together. I'll get you on our way, around eight. Cool?"

Nia wanted to answer for her. *No. Not a good idea.* But how could she? Lydia looked so relieved to be included.

"Sounds great," Lydia said.

The class began to disperse. Lydia walked toward her new friends, but Nia couldn't let her go skipping to a senior class party with Aubrey without some warning.

"Hey, Lydia. Would you stay for a moment? I need to go over something."

Aubrey hung back, waiting for her former rival.

"It's about the solo and could take a bit. You all should go on."

Lydia looked confused. "I'll catch up," she said.

"Don't be too long."

The door shut. Lydia nearly leapt into the center of the room, both excited and concerned. "Did Mr. Battle add something to the choreography?"

Nia lowered her voice, unsure whether or not Aubrey was listening outside the door. "Look, I'm not quite sure how to say this, so I'm just going to come out with it. Please be careful around Aubrey."

Lydia's brow knitted. She stroked her clavicle. "She's the first person to invite me to a party."

"I know, and I'm sure that seemed nice. But as her RA, I've seen some things and heard some things."

"Drinking?" Lydia asked.

And sneaking into clubs. And flirting with much older men. "She's a little wild."

Lydia shifted her weight from leg to leg. "I don't drink."

"So you won't go?"

Lydia's hand cupped her neck. She looked at her shoes. "I haven't been to any parties on campus. It's a chance to make friends, you know?"

Nia sighed. There was no way she would convince Lydia not to go to that party.

"Okay. But will you do me a favor? Please don't drink around her. It's easy to convince someone when they're a little buzzed that bad ideas are good ones."

"Don't worry. My father would kill me if I got caught with alcohol. I'll just go, say hi to Alistair, maybe dance a little. If it turns into a booze fest, I'm outta there. Promise."

Lydia executed a fouetté turn. "So passé, relevé, plié, en devant, and then keep my hip down to a la seconde."

"Um?"

"In case anyone's waiting for me," she whispered.

"Be careful."

"I will." Lydia strode toward the door. "Thanks for the tips." She said loudly. "I'll keep that hip down. See you Sunday."

The door swung open. Aubrey stood in the corridor, arms folded across her chest. She stared into the room, eyes like flames around a gas burner. They burned into Nia as if aware that she'd kept Lydia late to share Aubrey's bad behavior.

"Come on, Lydia," Aubrey said. "Let's go play dress-up."

33

Sickling [*sik-el-ENG*]

This term is used for a fault in which the dancer turns his or her foot in from the ankle, thereby breaking the straight line of the leg.

The weather woman's palms undulated from her waist to her shoulders, a green-screen hula showing the path of a cold front from the midwest to the northeast. The theatrical body movements seemed a bit excessive, even for a temperature drop of ten degrees. Nia guessed ratings increased when an attractive twentysomething gyrated in front of the Great Plains.

She snuggled into Peter's side. A woodsy, citrus scent saturated his neck. He smelled like a *GQ* lumberjack.

Music beat from the floorboards above: a poppy rhythm that drowned out all but the high notes in the singer's voice. Peter grabbed the remote and turned up the television volume. The weather woman shouted about a polar vortex.

Nia inhaled beneath Peter's ear. "Weren't we going to watch a movie?"

"Yeah. Just wanted to see the news. They said they had an update on Lauren's case."

The mention of the murder changed her mood. Nia sat up straighter. "How is Theo doing? Did you talk to him today?"

"He's a little better since people began buzzing about text spoofing. But he won't feel vindicated until the news reports that the text message was fraudulent."

The kettle whistled on Peter's stove. Nia rose to get it. "I feel so bad for him. I wish there was more we could do."

"I know. It's frustrating to wait for some Internet company to relinquish data."

Nia opened one of the kitchen cabinets. She grabbed two tea bags from a canister marked "Wild Orange Oolong." Peter's favorite. She slipped a bag into each of the two waiting mugs and poured the hot water inside. Delicious steam bathed her face.

"Is Theo eating? He looked so thin."

"I didn't want to bring it up with him. But I think he's still avoiding the dining halls."

Nia opened Peter's fridge and grabbed the soymilk she'd purchased earlier that day. A splash went into the plain white ceramic cup. She liked tea the British way. It tasted more like coffee.

Peter took his oolong straight. She returned the milk to the fridge and then carted over the cups to the couch. The outside of Peter's mug featured the words "Stay Drunk on Writing So Reality Cannot Destroy You." *The Ray Bradbury quote mug,* as he called it, was also one of Peter's favorite things. She'd learned a lot about his likes and dislikes after spending every day with him for nearly three weeks.

She settled in beside him again. The camera panned to the anchors. The male reporter had a youthful face that belied the thick, silver mane atop his head. He sat beside an attractive black woman with overtweezed eyebrows. The woman lowered her barely there brow in an exaggerated expression of seriousness while the man spoke.

"An update on the gruesome killing of Wallace Preparatory student Lauren Turek, after the break."

The screen faded to momentary black before a car zoomed onto the screen. Peter cursed under his breath and hit the mute button. The news always made viewers wait through the whole program before getting to the top story.

Without the television, the sounds of the party again became audible: a din of voices pierced by occasional laughter. Nia recognized the top-forty tune blasting in the background. She handed Peter the mug.

"Thanks." He took a long sip. "So what do you want to do this weekend?"

"I don't know. I have rehearsal Sunday pretty much all day. But tomorrow is free. It's supposed to rain, though."

"There's an outdoor sculpture garden about an hour north of here. It's a beautiful place to see all the changing leaves, and there's a nice bed and breakfast in the town. It's too late to book this weekend, but maybe we could go up next Friday after classes. We could spend the night, take in the scenery the next morning."

Guilt pulled at the corners of her smile. Nia lifted her mug and took a long swallow. "I actually have plans next Saturday. That friend of mine at the New York City Ballet landed a soloist part in *Agon* and asked that I come see the opening."

"Oh." Peter set his cup on the coffee table. He brushed his hair back. "So, how are you getting to Manhattan?"

"I was thinking I'd grab a bus to Claremont and then take the train."

"The buses don't run that late."

Nia had considered that problem. The last bus from Claremont back to Wallace ran at 10:00 p.m. Dimitri's show didn't even start until 8:00, and there was no way she'd make it to Claremont in time. But if she stayed in the city until the following morning, she could get a 5:00 a.m. train into Claremont and then grab an 8:00 a.m. bus to the school.

"My mom's in Queens, not too far from a station. I was thinking I could crash there and then get the first train out in the morning. I'd be back in time for rehearsal."

"You'll be exhausted." Peter relaxed into the couch. He put one leg on top of the other.

Nia tried to interpret his body language. She wouldn't have been happy if Peter had made Saturday night plans with an ex-girlfriend. But he seemed fine. Then again, he didn't know that Dimitri was anything other than a fellow dancer.

Nia kept her movements casual. She didn't want to alarm Peter by making it clear how much she wanted to see Dimitri dance. "I feel like I have to go. Landing a part in *Agon* is a kind of a big deal."

"Well, if it's helpful, I'll pick you up from the train Saturday night." Peter reclaimed his tea mug. "That way you don't have to wake up crazy early the next morning."

The last train from New York City to Claremont left at 10:00 p.m. *Agon* was only a half hour. But Dimitri wouldn't make it from backstage right away. She wanted to have a little time with him.

Peter sipped his tea. He stared at her, trying to read her expression, or waiting for an answer.

"I wouldn't want to put you out."

He brushed her hair behind her shoulder. His palm cupped her neck. "You could never put me out."

They kissed. When they broke apart, Nia saw a sad smile on his face.

"I love you," he said.

The three words stuck in her throat. She hadn't felt this strongly for anyone since Dimitri. But did she love Peter? She enjoyed being with him, she missed him when they were apart—which wasn't often. She found him funny and handsome. Her feelings for Peter didn't consume her the way her feelings had for Dimitri, but the lesser intensity didn't mean she wasn't in love. She'd fallen for Dimitri as a teenager. She was older now. She'd been hurt. And she knew that *I love you* didn't mean forever.

She kissed him, covering her pause with passion. Peter was a handsome, educated, kind, thoughtful man. He loved her. And part of her did love him—the part that wasn't reeling from Dimitri's latest change of heart.

Peter brushed her hair from her face. His steel-blue eyes demanded a reply.

"I love you, too," she whispered.

They fell onto the couch, intertwined. His mouth devoured her neck, her shoulders, her stomach. He pulled at her jeans. She lifted her butt up, pressing her pelvis against him. He yanked the pants past her behind.

A scream shot through the room like a stray bullet. Footsteps thundered above them, all in the same direction. Peter sprang backward.

"Damn it."

Nia grabbed his discarded shirt from the foot of the bed. She pulled it over her head.

The scream sounded again. "Oh, God!"

Marta's voice? No. Teenage girls just sounded alike. She shimmied the jeans over her butt as she followed her shirtless boyfriend out the door. Shouts ricocheted around the corner. They ran toward them. Several girls, each wearing a slutty version of some occupational uniform, peppered the stairwell. Their eyes pointed toward the floor.

A petite girl lay on her back at the base of the steps. Dark hair tumbled around her delicate shoulders. Lean, defined legs extended from a short, black minidress. A peep-toe pump dangled from one foot. The other appendage lay naked and twisted on the ground, as if in fifth position.

Nia pushed past Peter. She fell on the floor beside the body. "Lydia. Lydia. Wake up."

Nia pressed her fingers into the girl's neck. Something sticky coated them. A red smear ran down the girl's face. Blood? No. Too bright and shimmery for blood. Paint. Lydia's tan face was powdered white. She'd dressed as a zombie.

A pulse beat against the pads of Nia's index and pointer fingers. Lydia was alive. She was breathing. Why wasn't she waking up?

A large red bump swelled above Lydia's eye. Nia tapped her cheek. "Lydia. It's Nia."

Lydia moaned.

"You're going to be okay. You fell."

Peter knelt beside her. "Is she all right?"

Nia examined the length of the girl's legs. They appeared straight, unbroken—until the ankle. A red welt carved the leg, just above an askew foot. The joint was fractured, if not worse.

"I need ice. And an ambulance."

Nia slipped her palm behind Lydia's head, supporting it like a pillow.

"Is she going to be okay?" The slurred words fell from the steps above her. Marta leaned on the railing like a crutch.

A white tunic with buckles flopping from the sides hung around her body. A sexy straightjacket?

"What happened?"

"She had, like, a couple drinks, totally not much at all. The upstairs bathroom was occupied, so I went downstairs and I saw her lying there. Is she going to be okay?"

Tears welled in Nia's eyes. Dancers recovered from broken ankles, often with surgery, months of rest, and a lot of rehab. But damaged joints were never really the same.

Nia's fists flexed against her side. "Where is Aubrey?"

34

Battement [*bat-MAHN*]

Beating. A beating action of the extended or bent leg.

The IV bag hung from its metal hook, a strange hourglass ticking away the moments Nia spent at her student's bedside. Lydia slept sideways on rumpled sheets, matted brown hair pooled behind her head. Orangey-green spots freckled the corner of her pillowcase, remnants of vomit that hadn't made it into whatever container medical centers used for that kind of thing. The room's fluorescent lights jaundiced Lydia's tan skin, yellowing everything except the dark purple bruise on her forehead.

Lydia's foot rested atop the blanket, mummified in cotton and gauze. The swelling enlarged the appendage into an archless club, far larger than anything Lydia's thin leg should carry. Nia wished the hospital had put on a cast. Once on, it would hide the misshapen foot, allowing her to concentrate on Lydia's recovery rather than the career-damaging—possibly career-destroying—injury. Lydia needed to audition next year for companies. If the girl didn't land somewhere after high school, she would end up on the sidelines, struggling to recuperate while teaching younger replacements, praying for a triumphant return to form that would somehow erase her sabbatical.

Nia peeled back a clump of dark hair from her student's cheek. An acrid mix of sweat and sickness oozed from Lydia's skin, yet she looked parched. Dead skin and what was left of the Halloween face powder clumped into a thick white line atop the girl's cracked bottom lip.

Why hadn't Lydia listened? She couldn't have believed Aubrey wanted to be a real friend. When Lydia fell, Aubrey was nowhere to be found.

Lydia hadn't explained. She'd regained consciousness moments before the EMT's arrival, shaken awake by violent convulsions that expelled a green, foamy liquid from her stomach.

Footsteps clicked on the linoleum floor. Nia whirled around to see a woman, a few shades darker than herself, in navy scrubs.

"Is she going to be okay?"

The nurse unhooked the IV. "Springfield hospital wouldn't have sent her back to us if there were real problems."

"So they did a CT scan or something? She was unconscious when I found her."

The nurse examined her patient's face. She tilted her head, as if noticing the large bruise on Lydia's forehead for the first time.

"I'm sure Springfield hospital did a toxicology screen. But judging from that hematoma, my guess is she got fall down drunk and knocked herself out." The nurse pulled the plastic IV tube from the blue port protruding from Lydia's hand. "Don't worry. Faces bruise easy. If she had done real damage, that bump would be a lot bigger."

"What about her ankle?"

"She'll need an appointment with an orthopedist. There are some good ones in New Haven."

The woman pulled the tape from the back of Lydia's hand. She plucked out the IV and pressed a cotton ball to the spot it had occupied. "Such a nasty fall. Kids always end up here after drinking. They think they're just having fun, acting grown, but they don't know how to handle liquor at this age."

"She went to a party. She probably didn't realize how strong the drinks were."

The nurse shrugged. "Well, if all that vomiting didn't teach her not to drink, then I'm sure that injury will."

Profanities bubbled in Nia's throat. She didn't have an intelligent retort. Lydia had done something stupid. But people did stupid things all the time. It wasn't fair that Lydia's mistake had cost her the fall show and possibly her dancing career. Aubrey's underage drinking hadn't cost her anything.

Nia reached for Lydia's bandaged hand. Her student would need comfort when she saw her ankle, and there was no one else to give it. The campus medical center had undoubtedly alerted her parents, but the call wouldn't have gone out until Springfield had discharged her. Lydia's parents lived in Manhattan. Even if they'd jumped in a car while still on the phone, they might not arrive before their daughter woke.

Lydia's hand moved beneath Nia's own. The girl rolled to her back.

"Water?"

Nia scanned for a bottle. Damn it. She would have to call the nurse.

"Lydia. It's Nia. I'll get the nurse to bring you some."

Lydia's eyes opened like her lashes contained lead. She squeezed them shut almost as soon as her dark irises became visible. She turned back onto her side toward Nia, away from the overhead fluorescent lights.

"What happened?" The teen spoke with the raspy tenor of a chain smoker.

"I think you had some drinks at a party and then fell down the stairs."

Lydia fought her eyelids open. "How? I don't drink."

"You don't remember?"

The girl squeezed her eyes shut again. "I went to the party and there was beer, but I didn't have any. I had a Sprite or something. Maybe a Mountain Dew? It was, like, green."

"Marta said you had a couple drinks."

Lydia struggled to sit up. She pressed her hands into the bed and pushed back. Her swollen foot dragged the sheets as it slid upward. "No. Aubrey got a soda for me. It was just lime soda. I told her I wasn't drinking. It tasted just like soda."

Tears fell from beneath Lydia's closed eyes. She chewed the dead skin on her bottom lip. "My ankle. It's broken. I can't believe it's broken. I just . . ."

Lydia's shoulders shook. Nia patted her hand. "I'm so sorry."

"I just don't understand how this happened."

"It will be all right. You'll see a good orthopedist. The doctor will fix you good as new."

Tears dribbled down Lydia's cheeks and fell from her jaw. She nodded slowly, unconvinced. "I just don't get how this could happen. I had a soda and then . . ." She sniffed.

"Then I can't remember anything. How can I not remember anything at all?"

Nia lowered her voice to a near whisper. She didn't want to come across as judging. The last thing Lydia needed was to hear *I told you so.* "Sometimes, if you drink too much, you black out. Usually bits and pieces come back."

Tears trickled from Lydia's dark eyes. "But I don't drink. I wouldn't have. My dad . . ." Her face reddened. "He's going to be so disappointed in me. I just don't understand. I wouldn't do this."

"He'll be happy you're okay."

"No." Lydia's eyes fixed Nia. The pupils shivered in watery pools. "You don't understand. My mother was nearly killed by a drunk driver in Miami. She was in a coma for days, and now she's in rehab up here. That's why we moved. I would never, ever drink."

Lydia's determined expression shone through the redness in her face. It was the same look she'd had when she'd said she wanted the fall solo. She hadn't lied then. She wasn't lying now. That meant only one thing.

Anger roiled Nia's stomach. For a moment, she feared her rage would explode from her mouth, spewing bile and profanity. She pushed the feeling into her gut.

"You said Aubrey gave you the drink?"

35

Sur Les Pointes [*sewr lay pwent*]

On the points. The raising of the body on the tips of
the toes.

Nia stood on the stone steps outside the girls' dormitory. She blew into her hands to warm her fingers. The sun had yet to break above the eastern hillside. A hazy darkness cloaked the campus. The morning belonged in the dead of winter.

The temperature tightened Nia's muscles. She faced the dorm's arched entrance and planted her toes on the step edge. Her right heel dangled over the landing below. She pressed down on the right foot until she felt a dull ache in the back of her heel. She rose onto the pad of her standing foot and repeated the stretch.

Stress aggravated old injuries. She would warm up. Then, as soon as the sun officially announced a new day, she would confront Aubrey.

The door flew open in front of her. She nearly jumped at the sound. Five o'clock in the morning was a silent hour on campus. Most students didn't venture from their dorms until seven thirty, at the earliest, coaxed outside by the smell of breakfast wafting down from the cafeteria. She'd come straight from the medical center.

A hooded sweatshirt hid the advancing student's face. The girl watched the ground as she hustled down the steps. Near-opaque white tights hugged long legs that led up to a navy pea coat. Bright pink leg warmers bunched around her calves.

"Aubrey?"

The girl froze on the step above her. She pulled the hood back onto her neck, uncovering a neat blond bun. A sarcastic smile twinkled in her ice-blue eyes. She folded her arms across her flat chest.

"'Morning, Nia. I was just heading to the studio to get some extra practice in."

"I was looking for you last night."

The girl pulled her lips between her teeth. She raised her eyebrows as if to ask why.

"You took Lydia to that party. She fell down the stairs."

Aubrey's hand landed on her breast. "That's so horrible." She shook her head as though disappointed. "But don't worry about the solo. I'll do my best to make Lydia proud."

Nia stifled the urge to rip the blond bun off the teen's head. "I spoke to Lydia in the medical center. The last thing she remembers is you giving her a lime soda."

Aubrey sighed. "It's not surprising that she blacked out. I mean, she had so many drinks." She lowered her voice to a conspiratorial level. "To tell you the truth, it was embarrassing. It's a blessing she doesn't remember."

Nia crossed her arms in front of her, mimicking Aubrey's defiant stance. The girl might have Ms. V fooled with her doll eyes and feigned earnestness, but Nia wouldn't be taken in.

"Lydia doesn't drink alcohol. She has family reasons for not touching the stuff—"

"Oh, is her mom a drinker?" Aubrey's brow knitted with overacted concern. "Poor thing. That would explain a lot."

"Somebody spiking Lydia's drink would explain a lot."

Aubrey tilted her head, as though the suggestion were so outlandish that it had never occurred to her. "That's quite an accusation. It could land somebody in jail."

Nia's eyes narrowed. "It certainly could."

Aubrey descended to Nia's step. Mock concern still pinched the pouty face. "Well, of course, she'd need to prove it. If she doesn't remember anything, that seems pretty impossible."

"The hospital did a tox screen. If you put something in Lydia's drink, it will show up."

"Well, if her drink was spiked, I hardly see how the police would blame me. A bunch of senior guys threw the party and bought the beer." Aubrey shrugged. "I guess you can't put anything past horny seventeen-year-old boys."

"You may think you're going to get away with all the lies that you tell, but you're not."

Aubrey's oversized eyes widened. She put a hand to her cheek. "What do you mean?"

"Sneaking into adult clubs, giving Lydia spiked soda, telling the police that you didn't ask to meet Theo in Claremont—"

"I'd watch what you accuse me of." Aubrey's syrupy tone distilled into anger.

"It's all going to catch up to you, Aubrey."

The corner of Aubrey's mouth ticked up. "I better go. If I'm going to perfect the solo in the next week, I'll need to start right away."

The girl nearly skipped down the remaining steps. She strode across the courtyard and up the hill, a one-woman army in pink leg warmers, ready to dance.

36

Piétiner [*pyay-tee-NAY*]

To stamp the feet. A term of the French School
applied to accented movements sur les pointes.

"Marta, watch your fingers. Keep them together."
Marta corrected the claw hand without
acknowledging her instructor. She'd refused to
look at Nia since that day on the steps. The starved teenager hid between the T twins at the barre, staring at Talia's
back as Nia took the class through the well-worn cool-down
routine.

Aubrey refused to look at anyone but Nia. The teen's
giant blue eyes followed her every movement, singeing the
back of Nia's neck as she walked down the line at the barre.
They bored into her as she corrected Suzanne's hip position.
They pricked her arms as she pushed June's knee, urging her
to turn out.

Nia paid special attention to June. Aubrey's ill-gotten
ascendance to soloist had left Joseph without a partner,

and June would now dance the pas de deux. The girl's form was decent, but she lacked the finishing touches that separated the pros from the hobbyists. Her knees didn't turn out enough. Her feet didn't arch high enough. Her movements were as stiff as a starched collar, and she couldn't jump. Fortunately, her small stature meant Alexei would have little problem picking her up, whether she got the leaping height to make it easy or not.

Aubrey's stare needled into Nia's back. She couldn't take it anymore. She whirled to meet the gaze full on. Her hands flew to her hips. "Do you need help?"

Aubrey snickered and lowered into a plié.

Ms. V's bell rang out of the attached office. Monday's morning class was over. Nia would get a break from Aubrey until rehearsals later that afternoon. She retreated to the side of the room and worked her thumbs into her arch. Her rage—or maybe the stress of swallowing it—was making her foot ache for the first time in more than a week. Every muscle, tendon, and fiber of her being wanted to stand in the center of the room and point her index finger at Aubrey for orchestrating Lydia's fall. But she couldn't accuse her. She didn't have any proof. Not even Lydia's own father believed another student could be so evil.

Mr. Carreño had pulled Lydia from the school, citing a lack of official supervision at the party where his daughter had imbibed to oblivion. Ms. V had informed her after Sunday's class of the news and its impact on the fall show. She'd said he'd threatened a lawsuit.

Nia had already known about Mr. Carreño's fury thanks to an emergency Sunday meeting with Stirk. Surprisingly, the dean hadn't been upset by the belated RA rescue. When Stirk had recounted the conversation with Lydia's father to the RAs, she'd actually thanked Nia and Peter for responding in such a timely manner and reiterated that they were not required to supervise student activities after five o'clock in the afternoon on Friday, when school officially let out.

Nia missed Lydia. The two days without her made the class feel disjointed, less like a ballet school than an extracurricular activity. Her favored student had been a real preprofessional ballerina. Nia prayed the girl would have the same potential after surgery and rehabilitation. She wanted to check on her, but the dean had forbidden contact, given the lawsuit threat. Lydia had not been in touch.

Nia glanced in Alexei's direction. Was the rumor mill already churning about Aubrey's involvement?

As usual, Alexei gossiped with June on the way out the door. He whispered lower than usual, but he seemed to look at Aubrey sideways.

Once or twice, Nia caught June's eyes on her. An irrational voice said they were discussing her relationship with Peter, but she assured herself that her pairing with another RA was old news. More likely, June feared that Nia would overhear the latest secret. Whatever it was, it must have been juicy, because she couldn't make out any of the whispers. Alexei usually shared gossip at the top of his voice.

The class filed into the hallway. Ms. V's office door opened as the studio door shut. "Ms. Washington, a word."

Nia didn't like the woman's clipped tone. She stood extra straight as she walked into the office, prepared for another Aubrey accusation. She wouldn't let this one slide.

Ms. V's desk was the opposite of the Detective Kelly's. Not one paper sat on the tabletop. The office was clean, airy, filled with light from a large picture window overlooking the lake. Framed photos of prior students striking ballet poses were arranged on the walls. In the center was a black-and-white article from a Russian newspaper. Ms. V, thirty years younger, was pictured in the accompanying photo. She looked resplendent as "the Firebird," with the sharp, fanned tutu that Nia knew was red, even though the photo didn't show color.

The woman behind the desk contrasted starkly with the photograph. She wore a billowy black top and thick glasses that distorted her eyes like a fishbowl.

"Is something wrong?" Nia asked.

"I was hoping you could tell me." Ms. V's mouth set in a line. The skin tightened on her veined neck. "Your relationship with some of the students appears strained. Marta is avoiding eye contact and I've noticed Aubrey being rather curt with you."

Nia wanted to spill everything: Marta's secret, Aubrey's wild behavior. But she couldn't. She had no good reason to share Marta's problems with Ms. V, and the teacher was sure to interpret any disparaging remarks she made about Aubrey as spiteful retribution for Aubrey's complaints about her conduct.

Nia sighed. "Marta told me some things as her RA that I felt obliged to repeat to another involved party. That party told her parents, and I believe she's upset about that."

Ms. V looked at Nia over the top of her glasses. "Well, Marta is clearly having some issues. I'm sure it is good that the parents were notified. And Aubrey?"

Is a little psycho. She couldn't accuse the girl of orchestrating Lydia's fall without proof. "She's friends with Marta."

Ms. V removed her glasses. "Yes. I've noticed that they've become close. Do what you can to smooth out those relationships. You can't teach if you don't command the respect of your students."

"I'll work on it."

Nia's clenched her teeth. She didn't want Aubrey's respect; she wanted Ms. V to see that her favorite student wasn't worthy of admiration. Aubrey's little Ms. Perfect persona was an act. Nia would prove it.

Somebody had to have seen Aubrey add something to Lydia's drink.

37

Chassé [*sha-SAY*]

Chased. A step in which one foot literally chases the
other foot out of its position; done in a series.

N ia knocked on Marta's door: three steady beats. Firm
but not loud. She needed to start this conversation off
in the least confrontational manner possible.

The door swung back. Marta held it open with a large
smile that vanished as soon as she saw Nia.

"Oh, I thought you were Aubrey."

"May I talk to you for a minute?"

"I need to get ready for practice. Aubrey's meeting me
here in a second."

Marta started to shut the door. Nia stepped inside the
doorjamb, blocking it from closing.

"I just wanted to say that I'm sorry I had to tell."

A student brushed behind her. Academic classes had
ended for the day. Students walked the halls. Several doors
were propped open, advertising to fellow classmates that the

occupants were happy to talk to passing friends. Nia lowered her voice, both to ward off eavesdroppers and to make it clear to Marta that she respected confidentiality, to a point.

"Theo's freedom depended on it. I wouldn't have gone to the police if I thought there was any other way for the truth about his alibi to come out. And I know you wouldn't have wanted someone to spend their life in jail because of your secret."

Marta's eyes fell to her feet. She wore ballet flats with fuzzy gray legwarmers scrunched below her knee. The look reminded Nia of Aubrey. In fact, the whole outfit seemed Aubrey-inspired. Marta's gray sweater hung askew over a tank leotard, revealing a bony right shoulder from the neck hole. The leggings she wore underneath reminded Nia of something she'd seen Aubrey wear around the halls.

"Okay. Fine," Marta whispered. "I get why you told. I'm sorry I couldn't. I was too afraid of my folks."

"How is everything with your parents?"

"Okay, I guess." Marta sighed. "They say my ex took advantage because he was older and I was so far away from family. They kind of realized that they hadn't been spending much time with me, and they promise that's going to change."

"I'm really happy to hear that."

Marta attempted a smile. It pushed up the corners of her mouth but failed to make her look close to happy. The meek expression wasn't an invitation by any means, but Nia would have to take it.

"I also want to know what happened at that party Friday night."

Marta looked over Nia's shoulder down the hallway. "I don't know. Why don't you talk to Alistair and his friends? It was their party."

"They're all suspended indefinitely. An e-mail will go out later today."

Marta bit her bottom lip. Her gaze returned to the wooden floor.

"Mr. Andersen helped Alistair clean out his room on Sunday evening. Alistair said he didn't know anything about liquor or spiked sodas. They swore they only had some beers. But you said Friday that you saw Lydia have a few drinks."

"I saw her drinking something and getting tipsy."

"Was it lime soda?"

"Maybe."

"Did the boys lie? Or did Aubrey spike Lydia's drink?"

Marta's jaw pulsed as she swallowed.

"Marta, I saw Lydia in the hospital. Her ankle is broken, and she will have to have months of recovery and physical therapy before she can dance again. I know you would never have wanted her to get hurt like that. You're a good person. So who was it?"

Nia could see the struggle in Marta's face: protect a so-called friend or do the right thing?

Marta lowered her voice to an almost inaudible level. "Whoever did it probably didn't want Lydia to get hurt like that either. They probably just wanted to help her relax."

"Aubrey said she wanted to help Lydia relax?"

Marta shrugged and nodded at the same time, a non-committal yes.

"You need to tell the dean. Whatever Aubrey put in Lydia's drink wasn't just a little alcohol. It made Lydia forget everything. Aubrey didn't want her to relax. She wanted her to hurt herself."

Footsteps clacked down the hall. Marta looked up. Fear flashed in her eyes.

Nia turned to see Aubrey striding toward them. The girl broke into an easy jog.

Nia turned her attention back to Marta. She spoke quickly and beneath her breath. "Aubrey is not a nice person. What she did to Lydia is something you would never want to be a part of. You have to tell Dean Stirk."

Marta stepped around Nia, as if she'd been trying to leave the whole time but her teacher had blocked the exit.

"Oh. Am I interrupting something?" Aubrey flashed a beauty queen smile at the two of them. "I can come back."

"No," Marta said quickly. "Nia just wanted to talk about my parents' reaction to—"

"Careful, Marta. You know she'll repeat whatever you say."

"I won't—"

"Don't." Aubrey held up a hand beside her face, a perfect imitation of Ms. V's "stop" gesture. "We know you're not our friend. It's your job to blend in with the students and then report every violation you hear to the dean or our parents or, apparently, the police." Aubrey turned back toward Marta. "She's not allowed to keep secrets. The RAs are basically like undercover officers. That's why they choose the youngest teachers, so we'll trust them and lower our guard."

"I wasn't really talking." Marta mumbled. She grabbed a duffle bag with the school's crest on it and stepped out of the room, closing the door behind her.

Aubrey grabbed Marta's hand and brushed past Nia.

"Those tights look good on you." The compliment echoed in the hallway as Aubrey led Marta away from her would-be confessor. "I have another pair that might fit you too. We can go through my closet after rehearsal."

"Cool. Thanks, Aubrey."

"No problem."

Aubrey draped her arm over Marta's shoulder. The pair walked so close together that they could have run a three-legged race. Nia wouldn't be able to break them up. Marta didn't seem to have many friends and certainly none like Aubrey.

38

En Tournant [*ahn toor-NAHN*]

Turning. Indicates the body is to turn while executing a given step.

The curtain rose on four male dancers. Each wore black leggings and white short-sleeved shirts, practice gear in a modernist palette. They stood in a straight line, backs to the audience. Nia had read a review once arguing that Balanchine had intended for *Agon*'s dancers to be anonymous representations of piano keys—the men's wide chests denoting the white notes, their legs forming the sharps and flats—and she could've seen that vision, if it hadn't been for Dimitri. Even with his back turned, he would never be faceless to Nia. From her seat way back in the second ring, she could still recognize his wavy hair and bisque-colored arms.

The dancers turned toward the audience in unison, feet in a modified fourth position. They jerked to the music's broken rhythm and then stepped to their right. Backs bent and feet flexed to Stravinsky's offbeat march, as though the men warmed up for the show rather than performed in it. They stood erect and circled. Suddenly, they jumped with legs back in arabesque. Then they aligned and kicked their toes to their noses, one after the other, a cascade of feet and flexibility. They strutted. They showed off.

Despite the theatrical Greek name, *Agon* lacked a storyline. It epitomized dance as an art form, a Frank Stella painting set to music, all line and emotion. Still, whenever Nia watched the all-male opening, she thought of bucks playfighting for an unseen herd of does. The women appeared minutes later, driving the men off stage like a sudden rainstorm. Black leotards hugged their torsos. Nia studied the female principals, comparing her motions to their own. Was her grand battement that high? Did her split look that effortless?

It did when she was in top form. She wasn't there yet, but she would get there. Wearing the cushioned brace every night was stretching and supporting her damaged arch. The orthotics slipped into her heels also helped.

The men sneaked back onto the stage behind a loose gathering of female dancers. The girls split into two lines and the men took over, pushing the women back with a flurry of leaps, kicks, and pelvic thrusts. The dancers performed together for a minute before breaking into gender-specific groups again like teenagers at a high school dance. Finally, the men each chose a partner. They danced and then struck a sudden pose as the song abruptly ended.

Most of the dancers hurried into the wings. Three remained on stage: Dimitri and two women. They leaped around together before settling in the center. Dimitri stood between the ballerinas, turning each like a jeweler examining diamonds, checking for flaws. Then he burst forth with bravura, demonstrating the strength of his Achilles and his core, jumping, turning, falling backward only to pull himself up again with his abdominal muscles. The display was for the unseen ballerinas. He embodied everything a woman could want in a man: power, confidence, ability, and, above all, control.

He bowed after the solo. The audience clapped like they'd seen a particularly good golf shot. Her ex deserved better.

Dimitri hurried off stage. Another danseur performed with two women. Nia waited for Dimitri to return. When he did, it was in the company of one male and one female dancer. They performed together for a couple minutes, but three was a crowd. The ballerina left him to square off with the other rival for her attention. After a few minutes, she returned to dance with both men, as though still uncertain about which she wanted. The dance ended with her leaping into Dimitri's arms.

Dimitri reappeared for the final act, along with the other men. Each claimed a female partner, but it didn't stay that way. The other women returned. Again, the men battled a tyranny of choice. Again, Dimitri danced with two ballerinas. He reached for one, then the other, torn between partners.

The women flaunted long legs and fatless figures. Arms stretched outward to their male suitors, as if begging for approval. After a few agonizing minutes vying for attention, they abandoned the stage. The male dancers remained, paying for their indecision with loneliness. The curtain closed.

Nia applauded longer and louder than her fellow audience members, prompting several row mates to squeeze around her to the exits. After a few minutes, she followed the departing crowd into the Lincoln Center lobby. She stood by a wall of three-story-high arched windows, avoiding the river of people flowing out the main doors. The courtyard outside glowed golden. The famous Lincoln Center fountain shot forth shining white water, like liquid light.

Fingertips brushed her hand. Dimitri beamed at her. He wore relaxed blue jeans and a long-sleeved button-down. The casual attire announced that he'd performed. Most of the ballet audience donned business casual. Nia had shed the leggings and sweater ensemble she'd worn on the train for a knit dress. She'd changed in a Grand Central Station bathroom to keep Peter from seeing. She'd feared that wearing something so fitted to see a "friend" would bother him.

She kissed Dimitri's cheeks, a French hello. "You were amazing."

"You should've been up there with me."

Dimitri could never take a compliment without returning one. She smiled. "I wish."

His boyish face grew serious. The expression made him impossibly sexier. His palm engulfed her hand. "How are you feeling?"

"Good. Much better. Can't wait to get out of that school, though. It's crazy there."

"Yeah?"

She shook her head. No need to ruin their night. "I don't want to talk about it. I want to tell you how proud I am of you."

He embraced her like a lover. Strong arms supported her back. His defined chest pressed against her bosom. He smelled of basil and lavender. She'd always loved his cologne.

"Let's go to dinner," he said.

She wanted nothing more. She had so many questions: What was it like working with the principal dancers? What was the tone of rehearsals? How did his preparation differ from their time at SAB? Her interests weren't confined to the professional, either. Deep down, she wanted to claim his time. The idea of Dimitri celebrating his achievement with another woman made her anxious. Jealous.

But she had no right to feel that way. They weren't together. She had Peter.

Her new boyfriend had purchased her return ticket for exactly thirty minutes after the show's scheduled end—just enough time for a cab to drive the two miles from Lincoln Center to the train station, allowing for ten minutes or so of city traffic. She couldn't exactly argue for more time. As it was, she wouldn't arrive in Claremont, where Peter was picking her up, until 11:00.

"I have to catch a train."

The sparkle left Dimitri's eyes. He stared at her hand in his palm. His thumb brushed her knuckles. "I thought you would stay."

"I can't. I have rehearsal in the morning. The show is this Friday afternoon."

"I can drive you."

"I already have a ticket."

He squeezed her hand. "I'll take the taxi over with you."

They stepped into the cold night. Wind attacked her face and shot through her sweater-dress as they walked to the corner. She huddled into Dimitri's side for warmth. He wrapped his arm around her shoulders. Her head fit in the crook of his neck.

Headlights inched toward them. Vehicles crawled. Manhattan was notorious for Saturday-night traffic. She scanned for a lit taxi sign as Dimitri raised his free arm.

"Remember that night when we finished *Cortège Hongrois* and went out right after, still dressed in the costumes?"

Nia laughed. "Ms. Pavlik was not happy about that. What were we thinking?"

"We were excited. It was our last performance with SAB."

"I think I just didn't want to take off that white-and-gold tutu. I felt like a princess. It was like having an overdue sweet sixteen."

A taxi light shone from the far left lane. Dimitri extended his hand and waved. The cab's blinker flickered. A wall of cars refused to let the vehicle through. The taxi continued through the traffic light.

Dimitri shrugged. "Yeah. Like Cara did. That was an overtop party."

Her eyes rolled. "I saw the pictures."

He pulled her closer into his side and rubbed her arm. "You looked beautiful in that costume. I must have looked like a weirdo, though, because no cabs would stop for me in those white tights."

"I think they thought we were on a reality show or something." She laughed again at the memory. "Eventually one stopped."

"Well, he stopped at the light. Then I kind of just opened the door and he said . . ." Dimitri cleared his throat. His voice reemerged from his nose, an imitation of a thick Queens accent. "'I don't think so, Shakespeare, I am not headed out all the way to Roosevelt Island.'"

A yellow cab with a darkened sign pulled over. The man shouted out the cracked passenger window. "Where you go?"

It was illegal for drivers to ask. Either you were on duty or you weren't. But no one wanted to travel to the outer boroughs at the end of a shift.

"Grand Central," Dimitri shouted.

The locks clicked. He opened the door for her, always the perfect gentleman. She scooted over to the far side of the plastic bench. He slid in beside her, close enough for their thighs to touch. A chill ran down her spine. She wanted him to kiss her. What was she thinking? She looked out the window. A line of livery cabs and fancy cars crept beside them. The theater crowd had left the building.

Dimitri continued the story. "That guy must have thought we were in the circus."

"Then you started doing *Goodfellas*, but really badly." She mocked his fake New York City accent. "'Do I look like a clown? You think I'm here to amuse you.'"

"That did not help."

"I think we ended up walking to, what? The Olive Garden?"

"We did." He grinned. "I believe I convinced the waiter to serve us wine without carding."

"He figured anyone crazy enough to show up as a courtier at the Olive Garden had to already be drunk."

They laughed. The mirth in Dimitri's eyes morphed to desire. His hand brushed her thigh. She turned her attention toward the traffic beyond the window. The headlights blurred like a long exposure photograph. She should not feel this way. Peter was waiting for her. He would pick her up in a few hours. He loved her.

Dimitri touched her cheek, urging her to look at him. Brake lights illuminated his face.

He cupped the back of her head in his palm. She closed her eyes as their lips touched. The cab seat seemed to fall away. She felt displaced, suspended in water or time, weightless. She forced her eyes open. The cab turned onto Forty-Second.

She pulled away. "I can't. I'm sorry. I'm with someone."

"Who, that Peter guy? Just leave him."

"I can't do that."

"Why not? You've been together, what, a month? We were together for four years. You can't feel for him what you feel for me."

"I don't know."

She glanced at the time on the cab's dash. It read fifteen minutes until nine. She would barely make the train.

"What do you even really know about this Peter Andersen?"

The use of Peter's last name surprised her. She hadn't ever mentioned it. Dimitri avoided talking about him whenever he called. Had he searched the Wallace roster for Peter?

"I know that I care about him."

"Did you know that he was married before?"

The romantic sheen had disappeared from Dimitri's eyes. A vein in his neck throbbed.

"Yes, I did. And I didn't have to scour the web to find out. He told me. His wife left him after he decided he wanted to finish his novel instead of slave on Wall Street."

She added the last part to give Peter artistic cred. Dancers, like all artists, lauded their higher calling to compensate for the money they didn't make. Dimitri would have to respect the fact that her new boyfriend had abandoned the life of a banker for loftier pursuits.

Dimitri's chin tucked into his neck, as if surprised. The rest of his expression seemed satisfied. "She died."

"What?"

"It's in the fourth link after his name. She was killed."

"No. That's not right."

It couldn't be. Peter would have told her that his wife had been murdered—unless he'd feared it would be awkward with the talk of Lauren's killing. But after all this time, certainly he would have said something. And he wouldn't have made up that story about his ex-wife leaving him.

"It must be another Peter Andersen. The name is common."

"Their wedding photo was in the article. It was the same guy in Wallace's online faculty directory." Dimitri looked like a parent struggling not to say *I told you so*, simultaneously smug and concerned. "He never mentioned it?"

The cab stopped. Grand Central Station's red awnings spread out across the street. Shop windows glowed along with the street lamps and headlights, an electric sunset illuminating the night sky. The brightness added to Nia's disorientation. It didn't make sense. Dimitri wouldn't lie to her. But would Peter?

"This good?" The cab driver shouted from the front seat.

"Actually, we might not get out here." Dimitri responded. "You can keep the meter running."

Nia barely heard the exchange over the questions rattling in her brain. Why wouldn't Peter have told her? Why make up an elaborate story about his wife leaving?

"Did the article say how she died?"

"She was found in the East River."

Lauren's bloated body floated into Nia's mental vision. She forced her eyes shut, squeezing the image out of her mind. Had Peter's wife jumped off a bridge? Maybe she'd been depressed after the dissolution of their marriage. Was that why Peter hadn't said anything?

"So she committed suicide after their divorce." Nia said the words to herself, testing them aloud to see if the theory sounded sensible.

"No." Dimitri touched her arm. "The article said she was stabbed multiple times."

Her vision swam. She felt as though the car was moving, taking corners too fast. But the taxi hadn't budged from beneath the overpass that funneled traffic around Grand Central's second story. She could hear vehicles rumbling overhead.

"Stabbed?" The word didn't make sense. "But why?"

"Police aren't sure. Apparently, she was driving an expensive car in a bad neighborhood in Brooklyn. The police found it someplace in Miami a few months later with different license plates."

Peter's wife had been killed during a carjacking? And he'd never said? She had to talk to him. She reached into her purse for a twenty.

Dimitri placed his hand atop hers. "I got this. Are you really going back?"

Nia glanced at the time on the meter. She'd already stayed too long. "I have to ask Peter about this."

"Who cares what he says? He's lying to you. He told you his wife left and she didn't."

"You don't know that. There must be some mistake."

"I've never lied to you." Dimitri's eyes were deep pools, sucking her in. Again.

"You said you wanted to be together forever, remember? Before you changed your mind."

"Nia, come on. That's not the same."

A line of taxis crawled in the opposite direction in front of the station. People hurried from passenger doors into the massive building, running for their trains. She glanced again at the clock. It was 9:02 p.m. She'd already missed hers.

"Stay with me."

Dimitri's voice pleaded, but his face betrayed a satisfied confidence, as if he knew that he'd damaged her relationship.

She had to go. She couldn't trust herself with him, especially not after this revelation.

She freed her hand from Dimitri's grasp and handed the twenty to the driver. Dimitri grabbed for her fingertips.

"No. I can't."

She slammed the door behind her.

39

Fouetté [*fweh-TAY*]

Whipped. A term applied to a whipping movement.
The movement may be a short whipped movement
of the raised foot as it passes rapidly in front of or
behind the supporting foot or the sharp whipping
around of the body from one direction to another.

The BMW's lights cut through the darkness. They flashed
as she exited the train into the frigid air. It had grown
colder. The wind ripped through her tights and sliced
into her skin, penetrating her bones. Nia hurried down the
steps from the platform to the parking lot, desperate to get
into the warm vehicle, burning with questions.

She yanked the door handle. It didn't budge. She wrapped
her arms around her torso and hopped, generating heat any
way possible. The figure behind the tinted windows pressed a
button. The lock clicked. She jumped into the passenger seat
and shut the door, barring the cold outside.

The BMW's interior was only slightly warmer. She rubbed her legs as though trying to light them on fire with friction.

"Thanks for picking me up. I'm so sorry that I missed the earlier train. You wouldn't believe the traffic."

"You said on the phone."

"Would you turn on the heat?"

Peter's eyes rolled over her chest. His mouth set in a tight line. He didn't touch the dial. A sweatshirt hood bunched around his jacket collar. Maybe he was hot.

"Funny that it took so long. It should just be a ten-minute taxi ride. You can walk it in thirty."

Nia rubbed her arms, still trying to shake the chill from outside. "I couldn't walk in this cold."

He pinched the thin, knit fabric on her arm. Even in the dark, she could see the fire in his narrowed eyes. "Not really a cold weather dress."

With all her obsessing over Peter's ex, she'd forgotten to change back into her sweater and leggings. She could imagine what he must think.

Her lips parted, ready with an explanation. She shut her mouth. If he wanted to accuse her of lying, he could say so. She'd love to have a conversation about honesty given that he'd apparently lied about his ex's murder.

She reached over the gearbox for the heat dial. She turned it to maximum. Hot air blasted into the car, smothering all other sounds. She fiddled with the vent on her side, angling it so the air hit directly on her torso.

Peter's hand curled around the steering wheel. He grabbed the stick shift. Nia buckled her seat belt, prepared for him to peel out of the lot. She looked out the window into the black night. Claremont was such a small city that ambient light from buildings didn't illuminate the train station.

Peter's palm slammed into the edge of the steering wheel. The horn sounded. "Damn it. Did you fuck him?"

"What?" Her head snapped back toward Peter.

"Your 'friend,' who we both know isn't a woman and isn't just a friend."

Guilt at kissing Dimitri and her unspoken feelings for her ex heated her insides. She wanted to apologize. But she couldn't admit what had happened. She quenched the feeling with anger.

"No! How could you ask me that? And Dimitri," she said the name for the first time, confirming her friend's gender, "is *just* a friend."

"Guys don't want to be friends with girls that look like you. So unless he's gay—"

"He's not gay." Nia crossed her arms over her chest. "But I've *never* given you any reason to distrust me." She sounded like Dimitri. *I never lied to you.* Technically.

"Really? So you two never had sex?"

"We dated for a bit at SAB."

He slammed his palm into the steering wheel again. "I knew it."

She grabbed his arm. "It's been over for a long time. I went to see him perform because I love the New York City Ballet. It used to be my dream to dance with them, and I am still trying to keep up my contacts to get in with other companies. That's all."

His eyes burned into her. He looked like he wanted to hit her.

"I left right after the show. It took a bit to get a cab and then, with traffic, I didn't make the train. It was tight. You know it." She reached out to touch his shoulder.

He recoiled from her. "You lied to me."

"No. I said Dimitri is a friend. That's all he is. I just didn't want to make a big deal of the past."

"A lie by omission is still a lie." Peter growled the words under his breath. He palmed the stick shift and pushed it into drive, as if that would end the conversation. She couldn't let him act so high and mighty.

"Really? Then what about your wife?"

His head snapped around to face her as though rebounding from a hard smack. "What?"

"Dimitri looked you up online. He found an article about your wife's murder. You said she left you."

Peter's voice assumed an icy calm. "Why did he look me up?"

"He's protective."

"Of course he is."

She hardened her tone to match the man in the driver's seat. "Dimitri and I were together over a year ago. We are just friends now. I told you the truth. Now why did you tell me your wife divorced you?"

He raked his hands down his cheeks. Breath steamed in the air in front of his face.

"We were separated when she died. She'd moved back home with her family in Manhattan. I guess she was robbed coming back from seeing a friend somewhere in Brooklyn. The cops said her car was spotted on a traffic cam parked near Prospect Park."

He looked out the window. "She always just assumed that if there was a ritzy high rise, then the area had to be as safe as her parents' place on Park Avenue. She didn't realize that it was crazy to park a Bentley on some side street in Brooklyn."

He rubbed his temple, as if warding off a headache. "When you asked me why I was in the dorms, I didn't want to say, 'Oh, well, I got pretty depressed after my wife left me and was killed before we could patch things up, and I needed to be around people.' You would have run right back out into the rain."

The memory of their first romantic meeting intensified her guilt over kissing Dimitri. She lowered her head in contrition.

"I'm a writer. Sometimes I invent a little fiction for myself where she's happy in a new life in a fancy house to avoid the fact that I drove her away and she ended up dead."

Nia winced at the description. Of course he hadn't wanted to tell that story at their first meeting. Some people would never want to tell that story ever.

She met his gaze. His blue eyes still looked hard, but his mouth had softened. She leaned closer to him. "I am so sorry."

Peter looked up at the car's interior, rolling his eyes or blinking away tears. She couldn't tell. She touched his arm. "And I am very sorry about not telling you about Dimitri and my past. I should have. It was wrong."

"I don't want to be the guy always asking where you went and what you did. I'm not that possessive."

"I know. I wasn't upfront with you. I'm sorry I made you have to ask."

Peter settled back into the driver's seat and pressed the gas. "Let's just go home."

40

Variation [*va-rya-SYAWN*]

Variation. A solo dance in a classic ballet.

Nia peeked from behind the curtain shielding the dancers from the bright auditorium. More than a hundred tickets had sold, enough to fill the orchestra and pack the balcony. Moms, dads, and grandparents, most brandishing flower bouquets big enough to adorn a casket, filled the first three rows. Behind them sat Ms. V, Battle, and other faculty. The next two rows were reserved for school alumni, retired-looking couples wearing Wallace blazers over dress pants. Students filled the remaining seats.

Nia spied Peter in an aisle seat before a row of students, mostly girls. Her limbs tingled at the sight of her boyfriend in the audience, there just to support her. Dimitri had always been backstage, gearing up for his own performance.

Nia tried to identify her students' families. Two sets of parents that likely belonged to the T twins chatted with one another. She guessed June had brought the large Asian group in the front row. A statuesque couple resembled Alexei. Joseph's mother had the female version of her son's face.

Nia scanned for Aubrey's family. No one matched the mother in the old law firm photo. No one had a little boy. Nia reminded herself that the article listing Philip Byrne's survivors had been nearly a decade old. She searched again, looking for a twelve-year-old towhead and a woman with platinum or gray hair and piercing blue eyes.

She paused on a bottle blonde in the front. Nia realized a moment later that the woman belonged to Suzanne after seeing a middle school–aged girl beside her raise a "We love you, Suzie" poster board. A heavyset woman with Kim's broad shoulders stood next to the group.

Beside them sat a woman with Marta's big brown eyes and formerly heart-shaped face. Rapid weight loss had since cinched Marta's visage into a pointy oblong. Still, the woman was likely Marta's mother. A dark-haired man stood near along with an older boy. An elderly pair, each with Marta's deep brown eyes, flanked the boy.

Nia had accounted for everyone in the reserved rows. Aubrey's family hadn't come to the recital.

A tap pulled her attention from her game of parent match. Nia turned to see Battle standing behind her. The expression on his face advertised a problem. Nia braced herself for news about Lydia.

"Ms. Washington, I need to speak to you."

Had the toxicology report come back? Battle's stiff posture and taught face hinted that it might have. If he knew Lydia had been drugged, he might want to discuss her suspicions about Aubrey.

"Now?"

Battle glanced over her shoulder at the crowd. The show would go on in just a few minutes.

"No. Right after the show. Please meet me in my office."

"Of course."

He hurried away. His usual gliding walk appeared harried.

The overhead lights dimmed, cueing the stragglers in the audience to take their seats. The students in the balcony hollered, ready for a rock concert. Nia ducked backstage where the dancers stretched in golden skirts. She air-clapped and pointed to the wings. Showtime.

Battle's musical voice rang through the auditorium's speakers. He discussed the dance department and how fortunate the school was to have the dedication of parents and alums. The "wondrous work" the audience would soon enjoy would not be possible without "such continued, generous support." The appeal for money could only have become more transparent if Battle sent a basket through the rows.

The students sashayed to the wings. They assumed preparatory stances: left legs pointed, arms outstretched in fourth position. Nia glanced down the line. June appeared ashen.

"You'll be great," she whispered.

June brightened. Her posture lost some of the stiffness that made her more like a ballerina statue than an actual dancer.

Light piano drifted into the room. The dancers swirled onto the stage. Soft lights sparkled overhead, warm and yellow like sunlight slipping into a nighttime sky. The students performed in unison, bending and rising, turning and swaying. Aubrey and Suzanne took center stage. The girls tipped to their toes as the music assumed a triumphant march quality. They spun in beautiful, mirrored pirouettes that landed in arabesque. Aubrey kept her leg lower to match Suzanne's lesser flexibility. She would have gotten to show off if Lydia had danced. But it didn't matter. Aubrey would have plenty of opportunities to flaunt during the solo.

The singer's voice cried over the music, shredding the lullaby quality it held moments before. The students' movements sharpened on cue. Stage lights flickered red and gold, an explosion of sunshine breaking through clouds. The dancers performed a series of pique turns on a diagonal line with the boys leaping behind them like horses pulling twirling sunbeams across the sky. The students converged in the center of the stage as the music strode toward the finale. The girls dipped to the ground, revealing the two boys holding Aubrey and Suzanne at their heads in arabesque. The girls raised their arms high above their heads, ballet's version of a victory cheer. The sun had risen. The song ended.

The audience erupted in applause. Though she had not danced, Nia felt she owned some of the hooting, hollering, and clapping. She had demonstrated the dance, corrected form, aided with choreography, and helped the ensemble come together. The audience might not know it, but they applauded her efforts too.

Nia looked across the stage to Peter's aisle seat. One of the female students said something to him. He nodded as he clapped, agreeing with the girl's statement. He said something back. Nia imagined the words *My girlfriend is one of the instructors.*

The pas de deux followed the opening. Both pairs danced on stage at the same time. The boys demonstrated all the moves they would need to showcase in a company audition—lifting the girls in bent-legged arabesques, turning while holding their partner, rotating their girl in front of them while she posed on her toes. The dance provided visual confirmation for any informed parent that Wallace

Academy provided the same dance preparation as the famed Bolshoi Ballet Academy or SAB.

Nia found Suzanne and Alexei's pairing more beautiful than June and Joseph's combination. Alexei faked attraction to Suzanne as he danced. His lifts were tender. His movements showed care and gentleness, as if he were awed by her beauty. Joseph couldn't pretend. Though his performance was technically competent, his face betrayed annoyance whenever he turned from the audience. When Joseph pulled June from a bent knee position to his shoulder, he yanked too hard, nearly sending her flying over his arm. It was as though he wanted the audience to know he had an inferior, slightly off-balance partner.

If the audience detected the performance problems, they didn't show it with their applause. The final notes were barely audible through the clapping. June and Suzanne had brought the loudest cheering sections from home. Nia stole a glance beyond the curtain. A row of young men and women in the balcony held up a rainbow sign with Alexei's name on it. The school's LGBT community supported him. She was glad that they hollered for Alexei and not Joseph. Alexei deserved more recognition.

The couples hurried off opposite ends of the stage. The auditorium lights went out. The stage darkened. The clapping stopped, silenced by the change of mood.

A bony hip hit Nia's side.

"Break a leg," Nia whispered to Aubrey. She intended the encouragement to have hidden meaning. The phrase was part of the old performers' superstition that wishing someone bad luck on stage had the opposite effect. But dancers never said it. Instead, custom held that they wished each other "shit" in proper French. No one ever wished a dancer's legs ill will, even in jest.

"Lydia already did," Aubrey hissed.

Aubrey tiptoed to center stage and coiled on the ground, a spring set to explode with compressed energy. Nia didn't want to watch. But she didn't have a choice.

Nia stared at the faint outline of the figure in the center of the floor. Aubrey hid in the darkness, camouflaged by the black bodice wrapped around her torso like a second skin. Aubrey's dance would be the antithesis of the first piece. The company work celebrated sunrise. The solo reveled in shadow: the way it stretched, contorted, consumed the light. Battle intended the choreography to be intense and dark, fitting the apocalyptic soundtrack. But it had moments of comfort. Lydia's performance, though not lacking ferocity, had hinted at the softness in darkness, the repose brought by the night's stillness. Nia doubted Aubrey's version would contain such nuance.

The sound of a bow cutting across guitar strings screeched from the speakers. The spotlight hit Aubrey. She slithered from her position on the floor, rising like a hatched creature from the future—part human, part reptile. The beat pulsed. She attacked, executing a series of fouetté turns. Ms. V had apparently changed the choreography to suit her favored student. Aubrey finished the opening with her impressive standing split, made all the more startling by the shimmery black stockings encasing her legs.

Nia scrutinized the performance for mistakes. She failed to find one. Aubrey danced like the devil played fiddle. Every turn hit its mark. Every angle was spot on. When jumping, her legs never failed to part into a full split or perfect stag's leap. When en pointe, Aubrey's feet held an insane arch, as if they were naturally shaped like boning knives.

Nia had expected Aubrey's technical precision. What she hadn't anticipated was the emotion. Each move engendered a feeling: tortured, angry, aroused, triumphant. Aubrey didn't display vulnerability like Lydia, but Nia had to admit that her interpretation didn't require it. Aubrey's shadow was violent and voracious. It consumed everything like a giant funnel cloud, beautiful and terrifying, a force of nature.

When the music stopped and Aubrey stood in the center, holding a pointed foot to her head, the crowd sat in stunned silence, as if movement would startle the creature on stage. Tears burned behind Nia's eyes. It wasn't fair that someone so horrible could be so damn talented.

Ms. V started the ovation. The rest of the audience followed suit, rising in height and volume, like a passing sound wave. Even Peter took to his feet. Nia tried to tell herself that he was applauding the whole company's efforts. But it wasn't true. Peter applauded Aubrey.

Aubrey spun out of her position and curtsied. The auditorium lights rose on the standing crowd. The rest of the company joined Aubrey from the wings. The applause didn't increase in volume at the addition of the corps. It already thundered.

Lightning strikes followed the claps. Flashes ignited as parents put pricey cameras to work. Students rushed off the stage to accept flowers and hugs from family. Joseph's father and mother embraced him. Marta accepted a rose bouquet from her grandma. Aubrey wasn't with them.

Nia stepped onto the stage to better view the crowd. Battle and Ms. V chatted with alumni. Students filed out the doors. Parents drew closer to the stage, composing album shots with the performers. Aubrey didn't appear in either direction. The star performer had somehow slipped away.

Nia shrugged off her sympathy. If Aubrey weren't such a terrible person, maybe she would have friends to congratulate her instead of faceless applause.

She stepped off the stage toward Peter's seat. He wasn't there. He couldn't have gone far. Perhaps he was looking for her among the teachers. She needed to tell him that she'd meet up with him after talking to Battle.

Nia scanned for her boyfriend as she walked down the aisle.

"Ms. Washington." Anger seethed in Ms. V's tone. "You're wanted in the director's office."

Nia had expected Ms. V to be ecstatic after such a performance by her favorite pupil. Instead, she appeared red-faced. She must have known what Aubrey did—or she'd heard of Nia's accusations and was angry with her.

Nia held herself up straighter. She would stand by her claim that Aubrey spiked Lydia's drink, even if Ms. V didn't believe her.

"Follow me," Ms. V snapped.

Nia didn't dare argue. The woman wanted a fight and she would have to give her one. Someone had to stand up for Lydia.

41

Soubresaut [*sew-brah-soh*]

Sudden spring or bound. A springing jump from both feet usually performed traveling forward in either a croisé or efface direction and landing on both feet.

Battle's office was lit like a bunker. Navy curtains hid the large windows, blocking the view of the lake below. The heavy fabric absorbed the light emanating from the ceiling, darkening the room's cream walls to the color of decayed newspaper.

Ms. V joined Battle and Dean Stirk behind a walnut desk. A campus security officer stood by the curtains. His presence surprised Nia. Did a cop need to be involved because spiking a drink was a crime? Would he get Aubrey after she explained what the girl had done? Had he picked her up already?

Nia sat on the edge of an upholstered chair positioned opposite the trio. The faculty's expressions matched the room's grim mood. Nia welcomed their frowns. What Aubrey had done to Lydia couldn't be excused by a stellar performance.

Battle adjusted his tie. The group's formal clothing was more buttoned-up than Nia's black dress. She'd chosen a deep V neck, thinking she would spend the night with Peter after the performance. The cut wasn't appropriate for a meeting with the bosses. She pushed her hair over her shoulders, partially filling in the neckline.

"We called you here because of a substantial allegation that we must investigate thoroughly," Battle said.

Dean Stirk punctuated Battle's statement with a sharp nod. Ms. V hung her head. Maybe the Russian wouldn't fight Nia's allegations against Aubrey. Perhaps she felt horrible for failing to notice her favorite student's ruthlessness.

Nia fought the urge to launch into an anti-Aubrey tirade. She couldn't seem too eager to tell the teachers all the girl's horrible actions. They would wonder why she hadn't come forward earlier—when she'd picked Aubrey up from a nightclub, for example.

Stirk cupped her chin in her palm and stared. "You don't seem shocked?"

"I thought we might need to talk eventually about—"

"And you know these allegations are sexual in nature?"

Nia's back stiffened. "No. Lydia's ankle was broken. I didn't think anything—"

Battle pulled his chin into his neck, a theatrical demonstration of disgust that made him resemble a tortoise retreating into a shell. "We are not here to discuss a student falling down the stairs, Ms. Washington. We are here to discuss a teacher making advances toward a student."

"What?"

"You made clear sexual advances toward Aubrey." Ms. V spat the words. "We saw the texts."

The room spun. Nia gripped the edge of the chair. "I don't know what you're talking about."

Ms. V raised her hand like a policeman halting traffic. Battle cleared his throat.

"Aubrey came to us just before the fall show alleging that you propositioned her," Battle said. "She showed us several text messages sent from your phone in which you suggest performing lewd acts with her and another student."

Nia's chin dropped. No words emerged from her open mouth. Her face tingled as though regaining sensation after a hard strike. Tears stung her eyes. She fought them back. Crying could be misinterpreted as an admission of guilt rather than shock and stress.

"Lydia. Who I left in your care," Ms. V nearly shouted. "No wonder the girl took those sedatives. She probably had trouble sleeping knowing that a teacher—"

Battle patted Ms. V's hand, shutting her up. Nia struggled to process the new information. Lydia had taken sedatives? Had the toxicology report come back?

Dean Stirk shook her head. She folded her hands on top of the desk, assuming a lawyer's position. "The text messages we saw constitute a clear violation of the school's policies on student-teacher communication as well as state laws on corrupting minors and sexual assault."

"It's not true." The words finally tumbled out, falling over one another and rushing together. "I never sent Aubrey any text messages. I don't even know her number. I didn't—"

"There was a photo of her and Lydia in a suggestive position that was sent from your phone to Aubrey's cell," Battle said.

Nia racked her brain. Aubrey and Lydia were barely together, and never alone with one another. Could Aubrey have faked an image with photo editing software?

"Other students remember you taking the picture."

Aubrey's voice came back to her. *Let's get a pic of us in penchée position. It will make a cool shot for the yearbook.* She had taken that photo of Aubrey and Lydia during practice. But the picture was of a well-known dance position. It wasn't suggestive—to a dancer.

Battle continued. "Aubrey said that, soon after, you began sending text messages in which you made sexual comments about the photo and suggested meeting after class."

Anger finally melted through Nia's shock. She jumped from the chair as if scalded. "That is a complete fabrication. I never, ever texted her. I did take a photo of Aubrey and Lydia practicing, at their request. Aubrey said she wanted to submit it to the yearbook. Then she took my phone and sent it to herself. You can ask Lydia. I never even knew Aubrey's number."

Ms. V fixed her with a look that threatened to reach across the table and strangle the recipient. "So you admit that her number was in your phone. But, before, you said you didn't have it. And you admit to sending a photo to Aubrey, though, before, you claimed to have not sent her anything." The Russian's voice rose with each sentence. "I should have known when Marta and Aubrey avoided you—"

"Irina, please," Battle's voice matched Ms. V's volume. "Let me finish telling Ms. Washington the charges against her."

Charges? Did they plan to report Aubrey's lies to the police? Had they already called the cops?

The walls seemed to close in around her. How could she defend herself? Lydia would say that she never received any messages, but that didn't mean Aubrey hadn't. And she would never get Aubrey to admit the truth.

How many years behind bars did someone get for sexting a minor? Probably just enough to ruin her ballet career forever.

"Ms. Washington." Battle patted the air, motioning for her to return to her seat.

Nia fell into her chair. Her throat felt inflamed. She took a breath to compose herself. She needed to think. She'd sent the photo, but not any messages. How could Aubrey send texts from Nia's phone?

Detective Kelly's explanation came back to her. Aubrey knew how to spoof texts.

"Aubrey must have made the messages appear to come from my phone."

"And how would she do that?" Ms. V's French accent had disappeared. She sounded like a Russian.

"There's an app called SMStealer. It allows people to mask sender information with another number."

Battle chest rose and fell with a deep breath. "So you are saying that someone may have sent Aubrey the messages pretending to be you?"

Nia stared straight at Battle. "I did not send Aubrey any messages. I believe she faked those texts to get me fired."

Ms. V's smirk bent into a frown that carved deep crevices on both sides of her mouth. She looked all of her scowling, sixty years. "That's ridiculous. Why would our best student have it out for you? Jealousy?"

The world stopped swirling. For the first time, connections emerged. She could see Aubrey's motivations clearly now.

There was a reason Aubrey would go to such great lengths to ruin her reputation, but jealousy wasn't it. Neither was the fear that Nia would reveal the truth about Lydia. Aubrey had been after her long before that.

There was only one reason Aubrey would want Nia gone this badly: Lauren Turek.

Aubrey had killed Lauren and set up Theo for the murder as punishment for the sex tape. And Aubrey knew Nia could help prove it.

Ms. V's face was the picture of disdain. Nia angled her body to face Battle and Stirk. The dean's expression appeared disappointed and concerned but not repulsed. Perhaps she believed her. Maybe, over the years, RAs had reported Aubrey's bad behavior.

"I swear to you that I never sent any messages to Aubrey." Nia kept her voice steady, level. She spoke slowly, letting each word resonate. "I have never said anything to a student that could be construed in a sexual manner. If you have police look at these texts, I am sure they will tell you that my information was fabricated."

Nia wanted to add, *And that Aubrey did it.* But doing so would only encourage Ms. V to bring up Aubrey's prior lie about her behavior with her so-called male visitor. Nia needed evidence first.

She stood. Her legs shook beneath her.

"We will do our best to get to the bottom of this as soon as possible," Stirk said. "You are suspended, with pay, until we determine whether there is basis to these allegations. You must leave campus by tomorrow evening at six o'clock p.m."

Stirk motioned to the campus security officer. "We will need you to turn over your cell phone to police so that they may determine whether you committed any terminable offenses."

"You need my phone?"

Nia pictured the device in her purse. It was her main connection to the world outside of Wallace. She knew her mother's and Dimitri's numbers by heart, but no one else's. Without her cell, how would she even check the train schedule or call a cab to leave?

"When you took the job here, you agreed to abide by school policies, not just state laws. It is school policy to collect devices after an alleged breach of school or state rules governing digital communications for evaluation by proper authorities."

The last word triggered Nia's self-preservation instincts. She needed to talk to the *authorities*.

Nia leaned into her handbag and removed her cell. "May I please get a couple numbers off the phone? Just so I can tell my mother and boyfriend where I'll be?"

Dean Stirk nodded. Battle opened a drawer. He pushed a pad of paper and pen across the desk to her.

Nia retrieved Detective Kelly's number from her call log. She put the phone on the desk where her bosses could see that she hadn't deleted anything before copying the number on the piece of paper.

"Okay. That's enough." The campus officer appeared by her side. His gloved hands took the device from the desk and dropped it into a plastic ziplock bag, as though it were evidence in a real crime. Of course, propositioning a minor was a real crime. If found guilty, she could do real jail time.

"I am sure you'll see I didn't do anything," she said, before hurrying from the room. Tears burned behind her eyes. She wouldn't cry in front of her colleagues. She couldn't cry at all. There wasn't time.

She had to talk to Detective Kelly.

42

Couru [*koo-R EW*]

Running. As, for example, in pas de bourrée couru.
A term of the French School. Pas de bourrée couru
is a progression on the points or demi-pointes by a
series of small, even steps with the feet close together.
It may be done in all directions or in a circle.

Nia sprinted up the hill from the dance building to the boys' quad. Adrenaline, more than the past three weeks of therapy, kept her from feeling pain in her feet. She couldn't even sense the cold battering her chest. She needed to get to Peter. He had to take her to the state police station.

She reached the boys' quad. No one hovered outside the door. Lights shone into the dark courtyard from the slits in closed blinds. She approached the nearest lit window and rapped on the glass.

"Open the door, please?"

The blinds cracked open. Brown eyes stared at her. Nia could see from a nose to a forehead. The window slats hid the lower half of the student's face.

She pointed frantically to the building's entrance. "Please. I need to get in."

The blinds retracted. A young man with a book in his hand and a confused expression stood at the window. "Can't." He mouthed the word. "Sorry."

"Please?"

The boy again shook his head. He cracked the window so she could hear him. "Didn't you see the e-mail that went out? After that girl who hurt herself at Senior Samhain, the dean is threatening expulsion for letting girls into the dorm."

Nia's eyes welled. She was struggling to maintain composure. One more setback and she might lose it. "Can you get Mr. Andersen, please? Tell him it's Nia."

The boy's shoulders slumped. He placed the book on his desk, turned, and walked out his door.

Nia listened for some sign of Peter. She couldn't hear anything. A moment later, the lock to the front door clicked, and he burst through the entrance.

"Nia?"

The sound of his voice broke through the dam of adrenaline blocking her tears. They poured down her cheeks. Her hands fell to her knees. She thought she might be sick.

"Baby, what's wrong?" Peter's arms wrapped around her shoulders. "I went backstage after the show. I couldn't find you. What happened?"

She couldn't get the words out through the sobs. He led her through the building to his room. She cried into his side. He felt like a flannel shirt: warm, familiar, safe.

"Whatever it is, it'll be okay," he said.

Peter brought her to his couch. The room looked neater than she'd remembered from that morning. The laundry had been put away. A citrusy, sanitized scent lingered in the air.

Nia tried to concentrate on her surroundings and not the emotions tearing through her body. Her torso shook from crying. She struggled to catch her breath.

"Aubrey accused me of sexting her." The words bubbled out. "I just came back from a meeting with Dean Stirk, Battle, and Ms. V. They suspended me."

Peter's white skin turned a deep pink. His lowered brow shadowed his deep-set eyes. His lips pursed as though he didn't like the taste of his own saliva. "Don't worry." He grabbed both her shoulders. "She won't get away with this. I won't let her."

She'd seen Peter upset in the car last Saturday, but this was something else. This was rage.

Nia grasped his hand. Fury didn't do her any good right now. She had a plan and she needed him to help her execute it.

"Listen, I think I know why she's doing this to me." Nia took a deep breath. "Aubrey killed Lauren and framed Theo. She wants to discredit me because she knows that I can prove it."

The anger in Peter's face morphed into something akin to fear, and he slumped onto the couch beside her. His pupils expanded like the room had suddenly gone dark. "What do you mean? You think she's a m—"

Nia placed a hand on each of Peter's cheeks. She needed him to look straight at her, to believe her. He couldn't dismiss her theory as crazy talk from too much stress.

"Theo told us that he was meeting a girl off campus on the Saturday when Lauren was killed. He went to meet Aubrey. He made that tape with her."

"The sex tape was with Aubrey?"

Peter pulled away. He moved to his own cushion and stared at her, as if trying to gain perspective on her story.

"It's all over campus. And Aubrey confirmed as much to me a few weeks ago. My students were talking in class about Lauren's death and I let it slip that I found the body. Later, Aubrey pulled me aside to ask if I'd seen police take anything from the crime scene that might prove Theo had murdered Lauren. She'd acted upset by the possibility that she might've been in danger, too. Now I think she really wanted to know if I'd seen police take anything that could be traced to her."

Peter pushed his hair out of his face. "Nia, I know you hate this girl right now. But her asking what cops took from the crime scene doesn't prove anything. Maybe she did want know if Theo was a murderer. Maybe she was still seeing him."

"No. If it was just that, then why wouldn't she have confessed to police that she'd asked to meet him and stood him up? We know from Theo that she didn't back up his story."

Peter got up and walked in front of her. "Maybe she thought Theo did it and didn't want to give him a possible alibi."

From his standing position, Peter appeared to look down his nose at her. Nia rose from the couch to better meet his gaze. He still towered over her, but standing made her feel stronger. She had to convince him.

"Aubrey hates Theo. Since he sent out that tape, she's been teased by students. She can't eat in the cafeteria by herself. She wanted Theo to go to jail as punishment."

Peter's hands curled into fists by his sides. It must have made him furious to know that not only had Aubrey accused her, but she'd also plotted to destroy the life of his favorite student. He stretched out his fingers and took a deep breath.

"Okay. Fine. She wanted Theo punished. But why do you think she'd kill Lauren?"

"I don't think killing Lauren was about Lauren. The important thing is that she knew Theo would be blamed for Lauren's death if she got him off campus, where he wouldn't have an alibi, and then she faked a text from him to Lauren asking to meet."

Peter shook his head as though he couldn't connect the dots. But Nia knew she had the right picture. Aubrey was a murderer.

"Aubrey knew Theo wouldn't fight her denial because the press would have had a field day with the sex tape. They would have said it was evidence that Theo was the kind of guy who disrespected women and could kill his ex-girlfriend."

Peter walked into the kitchen and opened a cabinet. Nia saw bottle of Scotch. Peter removed the cork and put the bottle to his mouth. He took a long swig.

Peter winced as he swallowed. "I'm not sure I follow everything. But, assuming you're right, I still don't see why she's involving you in all this."

"Aubrey knows that I know she lied to the police."

"How?"

Nia walked into the kitchen, chasing Peter in his own apartment. He was always fidgeting. Of course he wouldn't be able to sit still through this conversation.

"When I confronted Aubrey about spiking Lydia's drink, I told her that all her lies would come out. I mentioned her denial of setting up the meeting with Theo." Nia took a deep breath. "She also knows that I told police about Marta seeing Theo in Claremont."

"So you're the reason Theo is free?"

"That's one reason Aubrey wants me as far away from campus and the authorities as possible. She knows that I'm the reason her plan didn't work. And she wants me fired for sexting so that when I tell the police about Lauren's real killer, they won't believe me. They'll think I'm a sex offender trying to blame the person pressing charges."

Peter's Adam's apple bobbed. He put the Scotch bottle back on the counter and pressed the glass cork into the top. "It's a lot to take in."

"But I'm right. The spoofed messages from me to her only prove it more."

She grasped Peter's free hands. He had to believe her. "I know it's difficult to imagine a sixteen-year-old could be so conniving, but she is. Look at what she did to Lydia. The toxicology report came back. Ms. V said that Lydia took sedatives. Lydia wouldn't have done that. Aubrey had to have put it in her drink, knowing it would make her loopy and have an accident that could cost her the fall show."

Peter looked longingly at the corked Scotch bottle.

"Aubrey is just the kind of person a doctor would prescribe sedatives for. She told me once that she doesn't sleep much. She's up and dressed by five o'clock a.m. most mornings, even after going out."

Air expelled from Peter's lungs like the contents of a popped balloon. His body deflated. Nia wasn't sure he bought her logic, but he'd given up arguing with her.

"So what do you want to do?"

"Aubrey can't have told the state police about the texts yet or they would have arrested me," Nia said. "I need to tell the police my theory before Aubrey gets to them."

43

Serré, serrée [*seh-RAY*]

Tight, close. As, for example, in petits battements serrés.

Peter sped down a curved road and blasted onto the highway. The three-lane interstate was as empty as the course in a car commercial. Claremont wasn't known for its nightlife, and most of the commuters had already gone home.

The car smelled of body odor and adrenaline. The metallic scent added to the nausea threatening to send the scant contents of Nia's stomach onto her lap. She cracked the window and filled her lungs with fresh air.

"What if Kelly doesn't believe you?"

Peter shouted over the wind barreling into the car. Nia could hear the doubt in his voice. She knew he asked because he wasn't convinced himself.

"He will."

She couldn't answer the question any other way. Detective Kelly had to believe her. Fortunately, given what happened with Marta, he already knew that she might have facts that the police didn't. Kelly wouldn't have agreed to meet on the promise of "more info about the Turek case" if he didn't think she could help.

Peter pulled into the police station just ten minutes later. They parked in one of the many empty spaces and headed up the steps. Nia gave her name at the front desk. A policewoman said Detective Kelly was expecting them.

They followed the officer past the area with the detectives' desks to a smaller room with stark, blank walls. Nia recognized the place from the background of too many prime-time police dramas: an interrogation room. Was that what was happening?

They each sat on aluminum chairs beside a large, blank desk. Peter grasped her hand. His palm felt moist—or hers did.

The door swung back. Detective Kelly and his partner marched inside. Detective Frank had a doughier physique than Kelly but a harder-looking face with heavy cheeks.

"So what do you have for us today, Ms. Washington?"

Kelly grabbed a metal chair from the opposite side of the desk. He placed a notepad in front of him. His partner stood nearby.

"I know that a student, Aubrey Byrne, is spoofing text messages."

"And how do you know this?" The question came from Frank. There was an edge to his tone. Nia wasn't sure if her nerves had made her imagine it.

"I was called into my bosses' office earlier this evening. Aubrey accused me of sending sexual text messages that I did not send. I believe that she sent them to herself and fabricated my information in order to get me fired."

Kelly's bottom lip stuck out and curled. "You didn't see her spoof the messages?"

"No. But she had to have. I didn't send them."

"Maybe someone else knows how to do it. You knew that messages could be spoofed . . ." Frank trailed off.

Nia understood the implication. Maybe she had committed the act, knowing she could blame it on someone else. She wondered whether the Wallace cops had already informed the state police of the allegations against her. Maybe Detective Kelly had planned to interrogate her all along.

The air felt humid. Sticky. She pulled at the sweater draped over her dress, but didn't dare remove it. As hot as she felt, the extra layer served as armor, protecting her from Detective Frank's accusing glare.

"She didn't do anything." Peter squeezed her hand. He sounded firm, angry. His tone quelled Nia's rising panic. At least one person in the room was on her side.

"The campus officer took my phone and is giving it to Wallace police, who I'm sure will give everything to you guys. When you look at it, you'll see my phone didn't send those texts. Or you can get my phone records from my carrier and verify it."

Kelly tapped a finger against his chin stubble. "Okay, then. Why do you think this Aubrey sent the messages?"

"Because she has motive." Nia looked only at Kelly. He was more likely to trust her than Frank. After all, he'd believed her before and she'd been right. "Aubrey wants to get me fired because I know she murdered Lauren Turek."

Kelly blinked rapidly. "Whoa. That's a big allegation."

"She did it."

"How would you know that?"

Nia took them through the same argument she'd made to Peter an hour before, adding the information about Lydia's accident to show how Aubrey treated people who got in her way. She also explained about the photo as evidence of how carefully Aubrey planned her actions. The girl was intelligent, ruthless, calculating—and she had a motive.

"But she's not violent," Kelly said. "Even if she spiked this Lydia's drink—rather than the girl, say, forgetting that she shouldn't mix sleeping pills with alcohol—that only shows that Aubrey tried to get her to black out, maybe embarrass her. She didn't push her down the stairs."

Nia could imagine Aubrey doing just that. Thanks to the drugs, Lydia wouldn't have remembered if Aubrey had led her to the staircase, perhaps under the guise of showing her the nearest bathroom, and given her a shove. But Nia could tell that neither Frank nor Kelly would buy a teen doing such a thing just to get a better part in a high school show. If they did any research on Aubrey, they would be even less likely to believe her. After paging through Aubrey's accolades, Nia would be the one to look guilty.

"I know it's difficult to imagine that a sixteen-year-old would kill someone just to get revenge against an ex. I know how farfetched it sounds." Nia looked straight at Kelly. She wanted him to see the truth in her eyes. "But I also know that I did not send those text messages. And no one else has any reason to make it seem as though I did."

Kelly and Frank exchanged a look. Nia couldn't read it.

"Can we get a cheek swab?" Kelly asked.

"What? Why?"

"Turns out the lake didn't destroy all the evidence," Frank said. "There were some particles under Lauren's nails."

"It's just to rule you out," Kelly said.

The hairs stood up on the back of Nia's neck. If police procedurals were any indication, the people detectives wanted to "rule out" were often their biggest targets. Had she made herself a suspect by bringing them information? By finding the body?

"I was moving in all day the Saturday Lauren went missing. I spoke to some parents. I said hello to the kids."

"Just to rule you out," Kelly said.

Maybe it was just a test? If she didn't say yes, the police would think she had something to hide. But if she agreed, they'd believe her. Why not agree? There was no way Aubrey could have planted her DNA under Lauren's fingernails. She hadn't been out to get her then.

Nia nodded. An officer with a black plastic suitcase appeared, as if on cue. She opened her mouth and let him swab the inside of her cheek with a long Q-tip.

"How about you, buddy?" Frank looked at Peter.

Her boyfriend's brow furrowed. "I'm sorry, but no. Nothing against you guys. I just don't do anything police say without consulting an attorney."

Frank chuckled. "One of those."

Nia swallowed the chalky taste of the cotton swab. She zeroed back in on Kelly. "I have nothing to hide, and I was right about Marta and Theo's alibi. If I hadn't come forward, the state attorney would still be prosecuting an innocent kid."

She leaned over the desk, bringing her face closer to Kelly's askew nose. "Please. You have to at least check my theory out. Aubrey must be using the same program to spoof the messages from me that she used to send that message to Lauren. If you look at the SMStealer data, you should be able to find Aubrey's IP address. Something."

Kelly dragged his hand over his mouth. The gesture seemed defeated. Nia braced for bad news.

"Damn company is based in Russia." Frank spoke from the side. "They swear they don't keep any information on a central database, and they won't give us their logs. But they insist that the SMStealer app stores message information that we can use—if we ever find the device that sent the text in the first place."

Her hand fell. Peter had dropped it.

More defeated body language? Why was everyone so eager to give up? A girl was dead and Nia's own career, maybe even her freedom, was on the line. Ballet companies constantly worked with teenagers. Children often danced small parts. They'd never hire a sex offender.

"If the info is on the device, then you have to check Aubrey's phone. That's how she got my number: when she sent the picture from my phone to hers. The app must be there."

Frank's arms folded across his barrel chest. His eyes narrowed. "If it was that easy to check a student's phone, don't you think we would have taken everyone's phone at the school and checked it? We can't just confiscate personal electronics without cause. Remember the Fourth Amendment?"

"But Aubrey sent those messages."

"You don't have any proof," Frank growled.

Kelly rose from his seat. "Here's what I can do. I'll call over to Wallace police for your phone and make sure to have our digital forensic department take a look at it first thing Monday. We'll inform the school right away of what we find or don't find."

Kelly stood and extended his hand for a shake. Nia couldn't let things end like this.

"The school took my phone for *suspicion* of sending those texts. They didn't have a warrant. They just had the word of a student. Can't you do the same? Isn't my word worth anything?"

Kelly's hand cupped his mouth and then fell to his chin. His eyes opened wider as if trying to shine more light onto an idea in his head.

"Your word is worth something." A finger tapped against the side of his mouth. "You told your bosses that you think Aubrey faked the text messages, right?"

"Yes. They didn't want to hear it. But I did."

"Well, then you made an allegation against her: fraud. And you just repeated that allegation to us," Kelly said.

He looked at his partner. They both smiled. Kelly pointed a finger at her.

"That might be enough to get the school to give us her phone."

44

Taqueté [*tak-TAY*]

Pegged. A term used to indicate a dance sur les pointes consisting of quick, little steps in which the points strike the floor sharply in a staccato manner.

Nia dragged a half-full suitcase from her living room to her bathroom door. She hadn't brought much stuff to Wallace, but she'd acquired a surprising amount in the past month: coffee cups, an umbrella, toiletries, a sweatshirt with the Wallace monogram on the breast. Everything that didn't fit in her carry-on or the nearly full duffle in the corner was destined for the garbage. She wanted everything except the sweatshirt.

After talking to Detective Kelly, Nia felt certain that she would be cleared of Aubrey's allegations. Once the police examined her call records, they'd realize that she'd only sent the photo, and Lydia could verify that Aubrey had asked her to take the picture for the yearbook.

Unfortunately, the investigation would take time. She still needed to be off Wallace's campus by six o'clock in the afternoon.

"Is this stuff going?"

Peter's voice echoed inside an open kitchen cabinet. Nia looked up from her bag to see his face framed by the oak interior. His skin looked sallow. He hadn't slept well last night.

The conversation with Detective Kelly had put her more at ease, but it had made Peter jittery. He'd tossed and turned in his bed beside her, mumbling about murder.

"Why don't you rest? I'll clear that out."

"It's all right," he said. "I got it."

Nia thought it romantic that he worried about her so much. He honestly feared for her career and that Aubrey would get away with it. It was comforting to know that someone else cared as much as she did.

She had pored over the school handbook until past two o'clock in the morning, looking for more ways that she could help the detectives demand Aubrey's phone. The allegation she'd already made was her best bet. An accusation that a student or teacher had committed a cybercrime—such as sending sexual texts to a minor, spreading inappropriate content, or impersonating someone else—was sufficient reason to confiscate any electronic device that tapped into the school network. However, the complaint would have to be judged nonmalicious. In other words, Dean Stirk had to believe that she hadn't made up the whole story about Aubrey in retaliation for the girl's accusations.

Nia had faith that the dean would follow through. Above all else, Stirk cared about Wallace's reputation. She would want to prove, without question, that she had not hired a pedophile. Though Nia's phone records would make it clear that the messages hadn't come from her cell and thus protect her against legal charges, only finding the source of the texts would erase all doubt. Otherwise, Aubrey could always argue that Nia had spoofed her own messages in order to cover her tracks.

Nia squeezed the contents of her medicine chest into the front pocket of the black bag at her feet. She zipped it and then walked over to Peter in the kitchen.

"Don't worry. They'll see that I didn't send those texts." She hugged his back. "It will all come out."

He turned around in her arms. "That's what I'm afraid of."

"What do you mean?"

He coughed. "You know that Aubrey will make more accusations once they arrest her, right? She'll say things about you. She might even say things about me."

"What could she say?"

"I don't know. But if police find that she did fake those texts from you, her back will be against the wall. She'll say anything she can against us."

Nia could picture Aubrey inventing a new lie about her, but she couldn't see why the girl would target Peter. Aubrey didn't even know him. She wasn't in any of his classes. She probably hadn't seen him all year, except for outside Nia's apartment—and at the casino.

The casino! Nia finally understood.

"Are you worried because we didn't tell the dean about taking her home that night?"

"Yeah." His chin went up and down, a hammer hitting a nail. "I'm concerned that she'll accuse you or me of sexual assault. She could claim that she was trying to get you because we had previously molested her after taking her home, drunk, from a nightclub."

Nia's mouth went dry. She forced herself to swallow the new fear. "Once the police see she sent the texts from my number, they'll also see that she sent that message to Lauren. No one will believe anything a murderer says."

Peter's shoulders sank. "I hope you're right."

She patted his arm and then returned to her suitcase. There was nothing else to say. She pulled the bag back into the living room and scanned the apartment. Nearly everything had been packed. Now she just had to figure out where she would bring it all.

Nia sighed. She had to call her mother.

Instinctively, she reached into her sweater pocket for her cell phone. She would say that she planned to come for a visit. The details could wait until she arrived in Queens.

Her fingers found lint. Of course her pocket was empty—the campus police had confiscated her phone.

Nia called over to Peter. "Hey, can I borrow your cell to call my mom and let her know I'm coming?"

Peter looked over his shoulder. "Uh. Sure. The password is oh-three-two-four. March twenty-fourth. My birthday."

"Thanks."

Nia spied the phone on the kitchen counter, beside her still-unpacked coffee maker. She would have to remember to take that.

She crossed the room into the kitchen. Before she could pick up the device, Peter grabbed her arm and pulled her toward him. His nose pressed against the top of her head.

"Move in with me?"

Nia took a step back. "What?"

"Move in with me. We can get an apartment off campus while you fight this." He forced a smile. His eyes didn't share in it.

Nia felt a pang of guilt. Did he want to live with her because he thought she had nowhere to go?

"That's really nice of you, but I won't be homeless after I leave here. I can stay with my mom in Queens while the police investigate. It will be okay."

Blond strands fell into Peter's face. He pushed them back. "It's not just about the case. Even if the police clear you Monday and you get your job back, we should still move in together."

He rested his butt on the edge of her counter. His skin looked dry. Fine lines etched across his forehead. The stress made him own all of his thirty-two years.

"I'm too old to live on campus. It seemed like a good idea after my wife died, but I realize that I need a broader boundary between the students and myself. And if we lived together, Aubrey's allegations—whatever they turn out to be—will carry less weight."

Nia didn't know how to answer. Part of her felt so battered that she just wanted to say yes. Yes to anything. Yes to the path of least resistance. Still, it seemed wrong moving in with someone just to undercut Aubrey's lies. What about love or wanting to share a life?

"So you want us to get a place together so fewer people will believe Aubrey if she says we did anything to her?"

He exhaled. "No. Look. I'm stressed and I'm worried about you, so nothing I say is coming out right." He grabbed her hand. His palm felt clammy. "I want to move in with you."

"I won't be at Wallace next year." Technically, her contract ended in June. But after everything that had happened, Nia wasn't sure that she would stay past January—if, of course, Battle even kept her on after the police cleared her phone. Her worker's comp claim would cover continued therapy on her foot for the next several months. After that, she could start auditioning.

"We can worry about that later. There's plenty on our plate right now."

Nia thought of Dimitri. "Maybe we shouldn't make any big—"

"I love you." His throat bobbed. His eyes looked glassy. "Move in with me."

She couldn't say no. At least not now. Regardless of what he said, he wanted to protect her. She couldn't repay that kindness with a refusal. Besides, she'd said she loved him. If you loved someone, why wouldn't you move in with him?

"Okay."

He pulled her to his chest. She buried her face in his T-shirt, and he ran his fingers through her hair. The gesture felt comforting. Normal. She could almost pretend that she'd just woken up from a bad dream.

But she hadn't freed herself from this nightmare. She was still on Wallace's campus and accused of sexting a minor. The police hadn't yet cleared her phone.

And Aubrey still lived next door.

45

Enlèvement [*ahn-lev-M AHN*]

Carrying off. The male dancer lifts his partner in the air in a step or pose.

A cold, gray fog had descended on the campus, hiding the afternoon light. Nia followed Peter down the steps and onto the walkway, suitcase thumping behind her. The carry-on's wheels were designed for linoleum floors or fresh asphalt, not cobblestones. Peter appeared to have an easier time carrying the large duffle propped atop his shoulder, even though it was far heavier.

Light rain fell. The drops dotted the walkway with dark spots the size of dimes. Nia wouldn't miss running between the dance building and her dorm in bad weather. She would, however, miss teaching. Sadness weighed on her body, dragging her steps. She'd been a good instructor. Lydia had learned something in just a few weeks with her. What a shame to leave this way.

They walked around to the girls' parking lot. As she turned the corner, a familiar voice shouted behind her.

"Aw, are you leaving?"

Nia turned to see Aubrey standing on the grass. Her long blond hair and tight, cropped sweater made her look like a Barbie doll. But the smirk was all sociopath.

Rage trembled through Nia's extremities. She wanted to confront her, but it would be a mistake. Aubrey would just use the encounter as more ammunition for her lies.

"Bye, Ms. Washington. It's been real." Aubrey giggled. "Peter, I'll see you in the dorms."

Peter whirled to face the girl. "You won't see either of us in the dorms, Aubrey. We're getting an apartment together."

The smile remained on Aubrey's face, but the mirth drained from it. Nia guessed she was pissed to hear that her accusations hadn't driven Nia all the way back to Manhattan.

"Oh, are you?"

"Yes, and no lie is going to change that," he said. "Now leave us alone."

Aubrey's hands hit her hips. She stared at Peter, a predator sizing up prey.

"Just go." Peter's voice commanded.

Aubrey opened her mouth as if she planned to say something else. It closed in a scowl. She stormed off.

"I know you're trying to defend me, but you didn't have to do that," Nia said. "You're making yourself a bigger target for her."

He kissed her head. "She should know that I'm going to protect you."

Peter had parked in the handicap spot, closest to the entrance. The car beeped as the trunk popped open. He tried to push the duffle inside, pressing on its sides, squeezing it into a more compact package. None of his efforts could force it into the sports car–sized compartment.

He yanked the bag back out. "Toss the carry-on in there. I'll put this in the backseat."

Nia hoisted the suitcase to her waist. Fatigue weighed on her arms. The plastic wheels hit the edge of the trunk as she pushed it into the car.

Two beams of light pierced the air. Nia turned to see a blue-and-white police beacon flashing from the dash of an unmarked car heading up the road. A campus cop car followed behind.

The vehicles pulled into the lot. Nia saw Detectives Kelly and Frank in the front seat of the unmarked sedan. They made eye contact as they exited the car. She caught a smile at the edge of Kelly's mouth. It erased any fear that the detectives had come for her.

She shut the trunk and walked over.

Dean Stirk exited the campus vehicle with an officer in tow. Stirk appeared unkempt in a bulky Wallace sweatshirt and dress pants. For once, she'd really just thrown something on.

"Ms. Washington." Nia's name buzzed between the dean's teeth. "The detectives informed me of your formal allegation against our student Aubrey Byrne. We treat all allegations with the utmost seriousness." Stirk stared at Nia like a professor about to send someone to detention.

"Is it that building?" Kelly pointed to the dorm. The gray stone blended into the cement-colored sky, turning the building into a hazy mirage.

Instead of answering him, Stirk continued looking at Nia, as if waiting for her to suddenly confess. *Yes, I made the whole thing up. I propositioned Aubrey.*

Nia maintained eye contact. She had nothing to feel guilty about.

Frank cleared his throat. "It would be best if you returned to your room. We would like to speak to Ms. Byrne in private, and we may need to bring her back here."

Nia looked over at the BMW. Peter sat in the driver's seat, hand on the steering wheel. He wasn't getting out of the car.

She held up a finger in his direction and mouthed "one minute" before turning back to the cops and Stirk. "Fine."

"Well, go on," Stirk snapped.

Nia ran back around the building and up the stairs. The wet soles of her shoes slipped against the hallway tile as she hurried into her room. She doubted either Stirk or the officers realized that she lived beside Aubrey. She wanted to be in her room before it dawned on them.

Peter's concern repeated in her head as she slipped into her emptied apartment. She needed to hear whatever new accusations Aubrey made against her—or him.

The grief-counseling book lay abandoned on the empty kitchen counter. Nia shoved it beneath the door, propping open the entrance like the students did when they wanted to receive visitors. The book would finally be good for something.

Door secure, she hurried over to the window and looked down into the courtyard. The officers walked up the stairs and then waited, puzzled, by the door. The dean ran up and pressed a wallet to the keypad on the side.

Footsteps sounded in the hall. Nia didn't move from the window. She couldn't let the detectives or the dean realize who lived in the neighboring unit.

Four steady knocks reverberated outside. A door creaked open.

"Hello?" Aubrey sounded puzzled but not afraid. Maybe she thought the police had come to ask her additional questions about her RA's misconduct.

Nia moved into her doorway. She saw the group fanned out in profile in front of Aubrey's room: Stirk, Detectives Kelly and Frank, and a campus cop.

"Aubrey," Dean Stirk said. "There has been an allegation that you falsified text messages. These men are here to confiscate your cell phone for investigation."

"I don't understand." Aubrey stepped into the hallway and closed her door behind her. "Why are there so many of you?"

More doors opened. Students peered at the scene in the hallway.

Dean Stirk stood up straighter. "Ms. Washington claims that you falsified the text messages, which would be a violation of the school's electronic communications policy. We need your phone."

"She's just saying that to cover up what she did." Aubrey crossed her arms over her chest and leaned back against her door. "You can't take my phone if someone clearly makes up a story to get back at me."

Detective Kelly stepped forward. "As we informed Dean Stirk, we believe an investigation is warranted."

Aubrey pressed herself against the door. She grabbed the handle. "I didn't realize that the police dictated school policy."

"They don't, Ms. Byrne." Dean Stirk's voice rose. Other students looked on. She would want to clarify school policy to her audience, not to mention put Aubrey in her place. "But we can't selectively apply the rules. We must examine all electronic devices alleged to have used school resources to violate the rules governing this campus or this state."

"Martha, it's me." Aubrey's voice sounded hurt. Childlike. "You can't honestly believe her after what she wrote to me." The girl shuddered, as though she would cry. "She said such horrible things. I . . . I thought you would protect me."

It took all Nia's willpower not to run into the hallway and scream, *She's lying!* Aubrey wasn't just a great dancer. She was a powerful actress. Nia prayed her performance wouldn't deter the dean or the detectives.

Dean Stirk stepped back. Her posture softened. In the sweatshirt, she almost looked like someone's sweet grandmother, the kind that doled out cookies, despite bad behavior.

"Aubrey, I'm sorry. We—"

Detective Kelly stepped forward. "We believe Ms. Washington's allegations could have merit and, in light of the recent murder on school grounds, your dean is doing everything in her power to enforce school rules and create a safe environment for all students and faculty. She has already given us permission to confiscate the property."

Whispers slipped from the open doors. The dean whirled around, trying to find the source of the unseen chatter. Nia ducked inside.

"Students, I expect doors to close and for everyone to pay attention to their work."

A few doors shut. Nia heard more open. She stepped back into her doorway and peered toward Aubrey's room.

"I didn't do anything," Aubrey said again.

"I'm sure that if you just let these men take your phone, we can clear everything up."

Aubrey turned to face the door. "Sure. I'll get it for you."

Detective Frank stepped forward. "No, Miss Byrne. That's not gonna fly. We want to make sure everything that was on your phone stays on your phone."

Aubrey opened the door. "No, really, I'll get it."

She disappeared into the room. Frank grabbed the door before she could slam it in his face.

"Hey!" she yelled. "What gives you the right—"

"Aubrey. Please don't create a scene. Just let these men do their jobs," Stirk said. "Perhaps it is all just a misunderstanding."

Aubrey stepped into the hallway as the men disappeared into her room. She paced back and forth in front of Stirk, who tried to calm her down.

"They'll just check your phone and, if you didn't do anything, you'll get everything back. Probably as soon as Tuesday. In the meantime, you can use the landline in the dorm if you need to call anyone."

Aubrey buried her head in her hands. "How could you let them do this? After all I've been through?"

She pulled her hair back as if yanking it into a ponytail only to let it drop. She paced faster, a trapped lion hunting for a way out of the circus tent. Her body language screamed guilty.

Nia fought the smile threatening her face. The victim routine would not work for Aubrey this time. A mix of nerves and relief fizzed in her gut. A nervous chuckle slipped from her lips.

Aubrey whirled around at the sound. Blue eyes targeted her like electricity in a bug zapper.

"You bitch," Aubrey hissed.

Dean Stirk's body went rigid, as though the curse was directed at her.

Aubrey strode toward Nia's door. "You think you've got me, don't you? You think you can just get rid of me? Is that it? You think that you'll go skipping off into the sunset with your boyfriend?" Aubrey's voice rose with each sentence until she was shouting. "That is not going to happen."

Nia kicked the grief-counseling book, trying to dislodge it from beneath the door before Aubrey reached her.

Aubrey flung herself forward. The impact of the girl's body sent Nia off balance. She fell backward into her room. Her butt hit the wooden floor. A sharp pain traveled from her tailbone up her spine.

Fists hit her sides. Nia's arms went to her head, like a boxer. She rolled to her side with Aubrey on top of her, trying to protect her face from the blows. From the corner of her eye, she could see Aubrey's arms waling her body.

"Restrain her. Somebody!"

Nia could just hear the dean yelling above the profanities spewing from Aubrey's mouth.

Hands wrapped around the side of her neck. Fingernails scratched beneath her ears.

"That's enough."

The weight lifted from on top of her. A detective held each one of Aubrey's arms. Kelly and Frank raised the girl into the air, hands around her biceps, like male partners in a pas de trois. Aubrey's legs flailed, trying to run without touching the ground.

Nia rolled away to the breakfast bar and stood, using the counter for balance. Her side hurt. The skin on her neck felt raw. Fortunately, Aubrey had not landed many blows to her head.

"We are taking you in for assault." Detective Frank pulled Aubrey's hands behind her back as he rattled off her Miranda rights. "You have the right to remain silent. You have the right . . ."

Cuffs clicked around Aubrey's wrists. The sound of the metal seemed to subdue her. She stopped thrashing and stood up straighter. She stared at Nia. An odd smile, equal parts sad and amused, wrenched the bottom half of her face.

"I sent you something, you know. A little good-bye present." Aubrey looked at the ceiling. For a moment, it seemed as though the girl might actually cry.

Detective Kelly turned to Nia. "We got her phone. It's going straight to our digital forensics department, along with your device. You should know by Monday."

Dean Stirk stood in the doorway. A mix of horror and confusion wrinkled her face. "Ms. Washington, you still need to leave until we get this sorted out."

"I know." The words burned in her squeezed throat. "I'm all packed."

Stirk's heels clacked down the hallway, following the officer's heavy footsteps. The downstairs door shut with a thud.

Nia wished for her phone. She wanted to open Aubrey's "gift."

46

Échappé [*ay-sha-PAY*]

Escaping or slipping movement. A level opening of both feet from a closed to an open position.

Nia patted a wet towel to her inflamed neck. She examined the damage in Peter's bathroom mirror. Four raised, red welts marred the skin beneath her ear where Aubrey's nails had drawn blood.

The sight of the scratches sent tremors through her body. She'd never been in a fight before, much less one with a murderer. The attack had erased whatever doubts she'd had about Aubrey's guilt. The girl had gone for her jugular, just like with Lauren.

She couldn't look at the injury anymore. She went into Peter's living room and slumped onto his couch, wishing he were sitting beside her. He'd gone to get some bacitracin from the school store to soothe the marks on her neck. Once she applied it, they'd get out of here. Peter thought that bed and breakfast would take them for a few nights until they got an apartment and sorted out his RA replacement.

A clock ticked on his nightstand. Air hissed in the radiator. Aubrey's face, contorted in a mask of rage, blared in her mind. *A little good-bye present.* What had she meant?

Whatever Aubrey had sent was electronic. Another text? But Aubrey knew that Wallace had confiscated her phone. An e-mail?

Nia opened a laptop on Peter's desk. A screen with a blank space for a password appeared. He'd never told her his computer login. But he had provided the code to unlock his phone.

Nia typed in 0324. The computer's home screen appeared. A captioned photo of author Vladimir Nabokov was his background.

She opened a web browser and navigated to the campus mail server. Another login page appeared. She entered her username and password. A hollow sensation overtook her gut as the page loaded. What had Aubrey sent?

An unread message from AByrne@wallace.edu topped a column of undeleted e-mails. The subject line read, "Your New Roommate." Nia double-clicked.

A video was pasted into the message. Nia could tell from the JPEG frozen behind the play button that it featured a Wallace student. Long, brown hair cascaded over the shoulder of a navy blazer. The image reminded Nia of someone, but she didn't know whom. The play arrow lay over the girl's face.

Aubrey had captioned the video with a poem:

> *Peter, Peter, lying cheater,*
> *Had a girl but tried to leave her.*
> *She did what she does so well*
> *And now her ex will go to hell.*

Nia didn't understand. Aubrey had killed the girl and then tried to send her ex-lover to "hell" by framing him for the murder. But hadn't that ex-lover been Theo? Why was the poem about Peter?

"Aubrey is a liar." Nia said the words aloud, wanting to hear them stick in the air. "A crazy liar."

She braced herself and clicked on the video.

Lauren smiled at the screen, a resurrected ghost. Her head tilted to her slight shoulder. Pale lips pressed together. She looked sweet. Shy. Fifteen. She sat on a brown leather couch. The video was cropped too closely for Nia to see any more of the background. Something seemed familiar.

"Are you recording?" Lauren sounded young. Nervous.

"Yeah. I wish you could see yourself. You look so pretty."

A man's voice. Peter's voice.

Nia pushed away the thought. No. No. No. It couldn't be. Theo, maybe? He'd made a sex tape before.

"Show me what's underneath that blazer."

The teen glanced away from the camera. She bit her lip. "I don't know. I shouldn't."

"Come on. You're already here."

Lauren's arms drew into her body, covering her chest. She twisted the blazer's top button.

"Don't be a tease. That's not nice." The man scolded. The voice just sounded like Peter. "Let me see. It's just me."

Nia's stomach churned as she watched Lauren undo the top buttons. She saw a flash of skin between the lapels where a shirt should have been. She didn't need to see the blazer open to know that the girl wasn't wearing anything beneath.

Heavy breathing overwhelmed the speaker. The image jostled as the filmmaker placed the camera on the coffee table. Nia saw a flash of wood. Books. A thick hand dipped in front of the image, trying to prop what must have been a cell phone against something upright.

The camera focused again on Lauren. "Could we, I don't know, maybe just talk? Like before?"

"There's nothing to be afraid of."

The man's lower body came into view as he rounded the coffee table to join the girl on the couch. He was tall. All Nia could see were khaki pants and the bottom edge of a blue button-down.

"I know what I'm doing."

The man sat and reached into the teen's blazer. Nia couldn't deny it anymore. It was Peter.

She recoiled from the screen. Her hands flew to her face, blocking her view of whatever else the video contained. She'd been wrong about everything.

Aubrey was the "girl" in the poem, the one that Peter hadn't kept. She hadn't killed Lauren because of Theo. She'd killed Lauren because of Peter. And Aubrey hadn't hated Nia because she was worried her teacher would put the pieces together. Nia had stolen Aubrey's boyfriend.

Fury shook her extremities. Nia hit the forward button on the message. She typed Dean Stirk's e-mail address and hit send.

"What are you doing?"

She spun to her right. Peter stood in the doorway, a plastic bag dangling from his fingers. She hadn't heard the door open.

The gray light stealing inside from the window blurred his expression. Still, she could tell he wasn't happy. How long had he watched her?

Part of her wanted to scream what she'd seen, but some instinct forced her to remain calm. Peter was capable of acts that she'd never imagined. She didn't know what role he'd played in Lauren's death. She had no idea what he would do if he knew she'd seen that video.

She closed the message and stood, blocking his view of the screen. "I was trying to e-mail my mother, to let her know that I don't have a phone in case she's calling."

Her voice sounded lifeless. She forced a smile. "Were you able to find anything for my neck?"

Peter pulled an ointment tube from the plastic bag. "Yeah, got it right here." He threw it.

She flinched as the object hurtled toward her face. Her hand reflexively batted it away before it could hit her between the eyes.

Peter strode toward her. "So you figured out my password. I leave and you're going through my computer."

"You gave me your phone code. I . . . I just checked my e-mail."

He shoved her out of the way of the screen. She fell to the side. Her hand caught the edge of the desk, saving her from hitting the ground.

He leaned over the laptop and clicked. His head snapped up. Fury burned in his eyes.

Nia ran to the exit.

"What are you doing?" Peter caught her hair in his fist. He pulled her back toward him and wrapped an arm around her chest. She screamed, an enraged, blood-curdling sound.

Peter shoved his free hand over her mouth. "Let me explain."

She brought her teeth down on the soft skin between his thumb and forefinger. He yelped and raised his hand beside his ear, prepared to strike her.

His bicep wrapped around her neck. She felt his forearm beside her head. The plastic bag crumpled beneath her ear.

"Just listen. I didn't hurt Lauren. Aubrey found that video and flipped out."

She struggled in his arms. He embraced her like a python. Every movement tightened his grip.

"Calm down." His voice lowered. "Aubrey killed Lauren. Not me. She got jealous. We'd had a thing for a bit, but Aubrey wanted me to leave my wife. When I refused, she showed up at my house . . ."

Nia scratched at his arm. "Let go of me."

"Not until I know you understand. My ex-wife. She just didn't understand."

Her body went cold. The way Peter sneered made her doubt that his wife had died in a carjacking.

"I . . . I understand." The pressure on her throat made her gasp the words.

"I knew you would."

Nia's heels scraped the floor as Peter dragged her backward. He released her neck and shoved her onto the bed.

Coughing shook her body. She forced herself into a sitting position. She needed to run.

Before she could leap from the mattress, he fell on top of her. He held her arms down and straddled her pelvis, pinning her with his two-hundred-pound body.

"Lauren, she was just . . . You would have liked her. A sad, sweet girl who was so brokenhearted when Theo broke up with her." He shook his head, as though disappointed. "Fucking Aubrey. She just couldn't handle that, even with my wife out of the picture, I couldn't be *with* her."

Nia again tried to rise. Peter put the full weight of his arms onto her wrists. She felt the plastic bag against her forearm.

She couldn't break free. There had to be another way.

"Please, Peter." She softened her tone, trying to sound the way she would have just a few hours earlier, trying to remind him that he loved her. "You're hurting me."

"I never wanted to hurt you." The anger on his face flickered. "I thought you were the answer to my problem: twenty-two years old with a pretty face and a teenager's tiny, sexy body. The first time I saw you, I thought you were a student. Then we met and I realized, I could love you, legally."

His face contorted. Blood vessels pulsated in his forehead.

"Please, just let me go. I won't tell anyone."

"I know you won't."

He lifted a hand off of her wrist. She swatted at him, but one hand was not enough to fight Peter. He was nearly double her weight and nine inches taller.

The plastic bag spread across her face. She choked as he shoved it into her mouth. She thrashed on the bed. She couldn't breathe. He was going to kill her.

She stopped moving and focused all her strength into her legs. She pressed her heels against the edge of the bed for leverage and then pushed off, bringing both knees up into her body. The bony joints slammed between his thighs.

His hand flew from her face to his privates. He rolled off of her, balling himself up in pain.

She spit out the plastic as she ran. Her throat burned. She couldn't swallow. She could barely breathe. But she couldn't think about that now. She had to move through the pain.

She pulled open the door. Peter nearly caught her hair again as she escaped into the hallway. Strands ripped from her scalp as she made for the exit. Footsteps pounded behind her.

"Help!" The sound barely emerged from her swollen throat. Again, she croaked the word.

Campus police officers burst through the double doors. They hurried toward her. Dean Stirk ran behind them.

Nia threw herself onto a security guard. "Please. Help me."

Peter ran in the opposite direction. The campus police pursued. One spoke into a handheld speaker. "This is Wallace Academy security. Need backup at the boys' quad. Block all exits."

Sirens sounded in the distance. Only the real police had sirens.

"Nia. How—"

Stirk couldn't finish her question. The door behind her flung open. A mix of security guards and real police officers flooded the hallway.

"Aubrey sent me the video." Sobs stifled the words. "Peter slept with students."

Shouts echoed in the hallway. A series of thuds reverberated off the walls, like someone had stumbled down the stairs. An officer shouted, "Raise your hands!"

"Okay," Peter yelled. "They're up. They're up."

"You have the right to remain silent. Anything you say can and will be used against you in a court of law. You have . . ."

Tears streamed down Nia's cheeks. She couldn't pinpoint the emotion that drove them: fear, relief, sadness, disappointment. A mix of all of them, maybe.

"Are you okay?" Dean Stirk's face hovered above the guard's shoulder. Nia stood back from the officer. She wiped her eyes with the back of her hand. She needed to get control of herself and assess the damage.

"Did he hurt you?" The guard stepped back to make a determination.

Her wrists burned with finger impressions. Her throat felt raw. Her knee pulsed from slamming against Peter's body. But nothing was permanently damaged. Bruises would fade. Her body would recover.

Still, Nia knew there were other ways to leave scars. She only had to think of what Peter had done to Aubrey.

47

Terminé, terminée [*tehr-mee-NAY*]

Ended. Example: pirouette sur le cou-de-pied terminée en attitude.

"Nia? I'm looking for Nia Washington."

She heard Dimitri's voice over the din in the police station. The sound of it brought fresh tears to her eyes, washing away the last of the adrenaline that had kept her answering Detective Kelly's questions for the past two hours. Dimitri had come to take her home.

Nia stood from her chair beside Detective Kelly's desk. She could just make out Dimitri's face, darting between two uniformed cops at the entrance to the room. She tried to wave to him, let him know she was okay. He couldn't see her.

Her throat was still too sore to yell, and he wouldn't hear anything less.

Someone, probably a student, had tipped off the media about all the police activity on the Wallace campus. Phones screamed from desks, and the station was full. Nia guessed that catching Lauren's killer and the pedophile that had driven the girl to it had brought all hands on deck.

She turned to her host. Detective Kelly spoke into a phone. "I said, we have made an arrest. That's it. No comment. You'll know when charges are filed."

He rubbed his forehead. Bags hung beneath his eyes. He needed sleep almost as much as she did.

"What part of 'no comment' don't you understand?"

Nia guessed that the folds beneath Kelly's eyes would only become more pronounced in the coming weeks. The media would have a lot of questions, and if the nightly news shows liked putting Lauren's face on the news, they would love showing Aubrey.

"Excuse me. I'm looking for Nia Washington."

"Wait here, we'll ask. No one gets past this line."

"Is she here?"

Dimitri sounded panicked. It was her fault. She'd asked him to pick her up at the state police station. He'd answered from somewhere outside. Wind had rattled through the speaker, making it hard for her to hear. She'd caught pieces of his questions: What had happened? Was she okay? She hadn't had the energy to put it elegantly. She'd said, "Peter tried to kill me. I can't be here anymore. Please come soon." Then she'd hung up.

Eventually, he would want the full story. The detailed explanation would be worse.

Kelly slammed the receiver into the holder. He looked up to the ceiling. Praying for the night to end?

"My friend is here to pick me up," she said.

Kelly nodded. He opened up his desk drawer and pulled out a plastic bag. He pushed it across the desk to her.

Nia recognized her phone. "I'm good?"

"It's all clear. We found the SMStealer app on Aubrey's phone. Those texts sent from your number were included in the app's logs. The digital forensics team came in and verified it. The message to Lauren from Theo's phone was there too."

"So I'm free to go?"

"Yes." He stood and extended his hand. "Thanks for all your help. I am sorry about the way things turned out for you."

Nia shook. She was done feeling sorry for herself. It could have been worse. She did, however, feel sorry for Aubrey. Peter had taken an apparently beautiful, brilliant, vulnerable girl and unhinged her.

"My clothing and all the rest of my stuff is in Peter's car. Do you know when I can get that?"

Detective Kelly rubbed the back of his neck. "I know it seems crazy, but we have to get a warrant to go through Peter's trunk and get your bags back. It's going to take some time."

"I understand," she said. "When will he be charged?"

"Monday," Kelly said. "We're seeking attempted murder charges for what he did to you and first-degree sexual assault charges for Aubrey and Lauren, since they were both fifteen at the time. And now that they have a good theory for his motive, my guess is that Brooklyn PD will be taking a long, hard look at their evidence to see if they can tie Peter to his ex-wife's murder."

So many crimes, each with long sentences. If convicted of them, Peter could go away for the rest of his life. Nia couldn't see how he wouldn't be. The police had the video of him assaulting Lauren, and they would have her testimony and whatever Aubrey said.

"What about Aubrey?"

Nia had to ask. As much as she disliked the girl for what she'd done to Lauren and Lydia, she blamed Peter for destabilizing her. Maybe Peter's abuse coupled with her father's violent death had flipped an awful switch.

"She's sixteen, but I know the district attorney will want to try her as an adult."

"What about the abuse?"

"It's up to her lawyers to argue that was a factor, and I'm sure they will. The mom came up to get her with an army, shouting about suits against Wallace."

"Excuse me. I'm looking for Nia Washington."

She couldn't make Dimitri wait any longer. She shook Kelly's hand. He promised he would be in touch.

She waved as she walked to the exit. When he saw her, Dimitri pushed through the officers in front of him. His arms wrapped around her.

"Are you okay?"

"I'm . . ." Nia forced a weak smile. Her sore throat tightened. "I will be."

She leaned into him. He brushed his palm against her hair. "I'm so sorry."

He supported her weight as they walked out of the station. She could see the questions in his dark eyes, but they didn't talk. He knew she needed time.

He opened his car door. She sat in the passenger seat.

"Where do you want to go?"

Nia didn't have a destination in mind. She only knew that she needed to get away from Wallace. The farther, the better.

"I don't know. I didn't have a chance to speak with my mom. I just," Her eyes welled with tears. The stress of everything had broken her family rule about crying. "I just need to get out of here."

"Then let's go."

Dimitri backed out of the station and turned down the road leading to the interstate. He entered the ramp to I-95 South. New York City.

Nia closed her eyes. She let the rumble of the car lull her to sleep. She was safe here, in this car, with Dimitri.

She woke a few hours later to the glare of sunbeams reflecting off of skyscrapers. They danced on the metal facades like ballerinas in amber tutus. The Hudson River shone golden below.

They'd passed Queens and were traveling down the West Side Highway. Nia could guess their destination. Dimitri was taking her to the Upper West Side. His place. Their old place.

She looked over the river and smiled at the warm light. She was headed home.

48

Coda [*COH-dah*]

The finale of a classical ballet in which all the principal dancers appear separately or with their partners. The final dance of the classic pas de deux, pas de trois or pas de quatre.

Four Months Later

The floor was fast. Nia's pointe shoes traveled across the black vinyl like a pebble skipping across water. She was supposed to hate the slippery feeling beneath her toes— it was the mark of a temporary floor placed in less-than-ideal humidity conditions. But she liked how it made her just a little out of control.

She spun and then froze, hands behind her, head tilted to the golden lights in the ceiling. The classical guitarist increased the speed of his fingerpicking. She kicked her leg toward her head, held it for a moment in the air, and then shook it down to the ground. She pivoted and then, just for kicks, performed another grand battement.

The director liked the little touches she added. Melanie Wyles bragged that BalletProchaine maintained the discipline of more renowned companies but took the perfectionist edge off of its dancers, enabling them to really feel and move. The live music helped with the emotion. Nia fed off the energy of the varied guest musicians, picking up on the idiosyncrasies of the players, the way one stressed the last note in an arpeggiated chord while another always emphasized the downbeat. Unlike an orchestra, the visiting musicians never played the same way twice. As a result, performances were never rote. There was room for improvisation. For fun.

Nia loved the freedom. As much as she'd dreamed of dancing at the New York City Ballet, she'd never been a good fit for the company. Here, in this small group of eight dancers, it was different.

She felt stronger than ever before. For first time in eighteen months, she could trust her body. Three months of therapy with a New York orthopedist, at Wallace's expense, had made her feet feel solid. Once again, she had the confidence to jump and turn, let loose, without worrying about aggravating old injuries or damaging fine ligaments and tendons.

She performed a series of pique turns across the floor and then jumped as the guitarist switched to a faster rhythm. Her legs parted in a split, as rehearsed. She landed on her toes and then traveled backward, arms moving wildly as though she were buffeted by an invisible wind.

An alarm rang from somewhere in the audience. The guitarist stopped.

"Okay." Wyles stood up from her seat in the front. "I like it. Even more motion with the wind, though. Really let it take you. You can pick up there tomorrow."

The show was in a week. It had taken some getting used to the schedule: learn a dance in four days, perform in six. But after three weeks of dancing with the company, Nia was getting into a groove.

She thanked the director and then descended the stage steps. Dimitri was waiting for her in the aisle. He held open a puffy black coat that would cover her dance gear until she got home to change. The coat was relatively new, like most of her clothing. Her suitcases hadn't arrived until the first week of December.

"You looked good out there."

Dimitri's lips landed on her own, a familiar peck between two people at ease with one another. It had surprised Nia how quickly they'd fallen into their past rhythm. It was as though their relationship had muscle memory.

They held hands as they left the performance space and stepped out into the freezing January night. Heavy white clouds hung in the sky, illuminated by lit antennas atop skyscrapers. The smell of roasting nuts and powdered sugar wafted from carts on the corner—leftovers from Christmas.

She huddled into Dimitri's side for warmth. "Snow again?"

"Looks like," he rubbed her arms through her coat.

"What a miserable winter we're having."

He kissed her neck. "Best winter in a long time."

They'd spent the season together. She'd never returned to Wallace after leaving the police station. All involved parties seemed to prefer that her leave become permanent. Though Battle and Ms. V hadn't ultimately blamed her for anything, they also hadn't wanted her presence to become a "distraction." Battle had broken the news. Nia was fine with it. Wallace had continued paying her, as though she were on a medical leave. Battle had even put in a good word at BalletProchaine.

Dimitri raised his arm, hailing a cab. A yellow taxi pulled over to the side of the street. Her boyfriend let her in first and told the driver their address.

They leaned into one another as they traveled uptown on Eighth Avenue, both tired from a full day of dancing, comfortable with the silence. Nia's days were longer than Dimitri's, mostly because her season was shorter. BalletProchaine packed more performances into a tighter amount of time.

She looked forward to a night cuddled beneath blankets, watching television. Maybe they'd order a movie.

"I read something about the case today," Dimitri said.

His words interrupted her reverie. He always referred to it as "the case." Lauren was "the victim." Aubrey was "the murderer" or "the blonde." Peter was "the devil." Dimitri said he didn't want the names to bring back bad memories. The monikers suited her fine. It made the whole experience seem surreal, as though September had happened to the heroine in that film she'd seen.

"What did you read?"

"The *New York Times* said that the blonde struck some deal by claiming the devil's abuse made her do it. She said he tricked her into getting rid of the victim because it looked like the victim might tell her family."

Nia sighed. She didn't buy that defense. Aubrey was ruthless when it came to competition. If she could maim a dance rival, she could murder a romantic one, unaided. But then again, Nia did believe Peter had sent the girl overboard. If he hadn't led Aubrey on and then pushed her to keep silent about the whole affair, maybe she wouldn't have become so crazy.

"I don't know. I hope she gets help. In an institution. With locked doors."

When she blinked, she saw Aubrey going for her neck. The image often came back to her, accompanied by a phantom soreness in her throat. She pushed away the picture with thoughts of the inside of her refrigerator. What would she cook for dinner tonight? They had a whole chicken and an onion. She could put it in the oven, though it would take a bit.

Nia had taken up cooking again during the holidays. Dimitri's mother had seemed particularly happy about her cranberry sauce, or maybe it was just her presence. A couple of Bordeaux glasses in, the woman had pulled her aside and said she was happy they'd gotten back together. "I guess, sometimes people do just know," she'd said.

Nia relished the memory. She knew. She had a gut feeling about Dimitri—the same way that, deep down, she'd had a worrying sense about Peter. That day in the hallway, when she'd surprised Peter walking with another student, she'd known something was odd. But she hadn't wanted to think badly of him.

Now Nia knew better. She would trust her instincts.

The taxi pulled up to their apartment. Nia paid the driver as Dimitri held open the door. They hurried up the stairs to their first-floor unit. Once inside, they slipped off their coats. Nia walked toward the bedroom, ready to change into something more comfortable.

Dimitri grasped her hand, stopping her forward momentum. He stepped toward her and wrapped his arms around her waist. His full lips landed on hers, soft and familiar.

Sometimes, you did just know.

Acknowledgments

S omeone, maybe Einstein, defined insanity as doing the same thing over and over again and expecting different results. Yet that's what first-time authors do. We write and rewrite the same tortured tale and then send it out to agents and publishers hoping that, this time, someone will be crazy enough to believe in us.

Thank you to all the people who had faith in me over the years. I owe an immeasurable debt to my agent Paula Munier of Talcott Notch. Paula helped me understand the mechanics of a good thriller and how to tinker with my novel so my story could run. She encouraged me to keep writing when my first book stalled and also gave my ego the jumps necessary to restart my engine.

I am overwhelmingly grateful to Matt Martz and Dan Weiss, who saw how my story could look cleaned up and on its meds. I am fortunate to have Matt as my editor. In addition to launching a publishing company, he helped me re-envision my novel and craft a much-improved book. I don't know how he has the energy. Nike Power, his assistant, is a force. She not only pinpointed plot problems but also somehow knew when I'd used the same adjective twice within fifty pages. An author could not ask for a better team than the folks at Crooked Lane.

ACKNOWLEDGMENTS

Big thanks to my mom, Angela Holahan. Some moms encourage their kids by patting them on the back. My mom mailed my first fiction story—written and illustrated by me at age seven—to a large children's publishing house for consideration. She also saved the very nice rejection letter telling me to keep writing, and she never gave up emotionally supporting my dreams.

Thank you to my dad, Jay Holahan, for believing that I could be a thriller writer and encouraging me, even if he couldn't understand why on earth I would want to be one. Gratitude to my grandfather, Jim Holahan, for showing me that wordsmiths, storytellers, and dreamers can do great things. You'll always be an inspiration.

I am immensely blessed to have my daughters, Elleanor and Olivia. My ferocious love for them inspires the fear that I channel into thriller plots. More importantly, they are each joyful, smart, caring human beings who force me to be a better person on a daily basis.

Thanks to the first readers of my story or earlier works: My brother, James Holahan, for your honest and considered criticism. My sister, Tara Williams, for your gentle critiques and encouragement. Linda Honneus for not just reading it but getting excited about it. Saundra Ayala for the long lunches and letting me voice ideas. Margot Rayhill, for telling me that I was destined to be a writer and using examples from our childhoods to back it up and also being a great cheerleader and friend. Denize de Aquino for letting me talk through plot points for hours, asking random questions, and keeping me sane.

Thanks to my writing buddies Sue Homola and Daniel Davis. You each have a wonderful way with words. Your criticism and conversation were immensely helpful. Sue, you tell beautiful stories and you are just a great gal. Dan, you write poetry capable of scaring people's pants off. A rare talent. Thanks to Michael Neff and the Algonkian Pitch Conference for introducing me to Paula, Sue, and Dan.

Thanks to the dear friends and family members that read my story or earlier work before I could claim anything close to a publishing deal. Lisa Hsu, you've read the good, the bad, and the worse and still told me to keep at it. Karin Kin, my sounding board for decades with the patience of a saint. Where would I be without you? Shana Travis, the kind of girl who is so amazing that her willingness to count you as a friend makes you believe in your own worth. My grandparents Gloria Fidee and Madeline Holahan, for reading scenes that were in no way their *cup of tea* and still insisting that I'm a good writer. Paul Holahan for not only reading it but also wanting to help sell it and for providing sound career advice. Megan Holahan, Julie Holahan, and Gabrielle Ayala for being the kind of folks that offer to read and critique and mean it. Signian McGeary for reading the story and your love of ideas. Michelle Shuey, a fun-loving new friend. You made me feel legit instead of like an ex-journalist who might just have made the biggest mistake of her career. Thank you.

High-five to John Melloy for congratulating me when I left my job to write full time. Other bosses would not have been so understanding.

Thanks to the friends and family who encouraged me along the way: Erika Van Natta, Ken Monahan, April Campos, Tamiko Zetrenne, Jen Ferriss-Hill, Soroya Campbell, Madeline Banks, Dyandra Canty, Dennis Lin, Garth Naar, Cheryl Naar, Sydney "Nino" Mullings, and Stacy Esser. Thanks to my dog, Westley Honneus, cuddler extraordinaire and woman's best friend.

Big thanks to Tom Szaniawski for driving your motorcycle in the middle of the night after talking me through contract law for hours. Much gratitude as well to Jeremy McCurdy for explaining how guys handle things.

Thanks to Myung Sook Chun for teaching ballet to a thirty-two-year-old woman with no dance experience for two years so she could write a better novel.

I've had some wonderful writing teachers over the years that improved my craft and inspired a lifelong love of words. Kathryn Watterson and Barton Gellman, who taught writing at Princeton: thank you. Also a big thanks to Teaneck High School English teachers Alice Jacobs Twombly and Rhetta Maide.

Above all, thanks to my wonderful husband, Brett Honneus. The fact that you are not an avid reader makes your unwavering willingness to support me all the more incredible. You've encouraged, listened to, and believed in me. You've fallen asleep to a keyboard clicking beside your head and insisted we get help so I could work even when my "work" didn't involve monetary compensation. You've listened to me read aloud entire pages. I'd break into a Bette Midler song if this paragraph were recorded and not just notes on a page. I love you. I am blessed to have you. You are my better half and, for the record, are not and could never be the inspiration for any male villain.

Last but not least, thanks to God. I know some people equate believing in a higher power to a kid having faith in Santa Claus, but all the aforementioned people are the only proof I need. And if that makes me crazy, so be it.